WHITE GINGER

THATCHER ROBINSON

WHITE GINGER

SEVENTH STREET BOOKS™

AN IMPRINT OF PROMETHEUS BOOKS

59 JOHN GLENN DRIVE • AMHERST, NY 14228
www.seventhstreetbooks.com

Published 2013 by Seventh Street Books™, an imprint of Prometheus Books

Cover image © 2013 Maciej Toporowicz/Arcangel Images
Cover design by Nicole Sommer-Lecht

Inquiries should be addressed to
Seventh Street Books
59 John Glenn Drive
Amherst, New York 14228–2119
VOICE: 716–691–0133
FAX: 716–691–0137
www.seventhstreetbooks.com

17 16 15 14 13   5 4 3 2 1

Library of Congress Cataloging-in-Publication Data

Robinson, Thatcher, 1952-
    White Ginger / by Thatcher Robinson.
        pages cm
    ISBN 978-1-61614-817-1 (pbk.)
    ISBN 978-1-61614-818-8 (ebook)
    1. Buddhist women—Fiction. 2. Missing persons—Fiction. 3. Chinatown (San Francisco, Calif.)—Fiction. 4. Mystery fiction. I. Title.

PS3618.O33376W48 2013
813'.6—dc23

2013022057

Printed in the United States of America

Dedicated to my wife and editor,
Susan Noguchi,
who never ceases to amaze me.

chapter 1

He who is drowned isn't troubled by the rain

The knife arced. Light danced off the blade as it slowly rotated three hundred sixty degrees before dropping, hilt first, into the palm of her hand. A flick of her wrist sent the dagger sailing into the air again to pirouette gracefully. Her other hand held a Chinese cup made of fine, white porcelain. She lifted the vessel to her lips and breathed in deeply, the fragrance reminiscent of fresh mowed grass. As she sipped, hot green tea filled her mouth and ran down her throat. She sighed, the first caffeine of the day.

Outside, raindrops beat against the glass panes of the window to produce a lulling sound, like leaves fluttering in the wind. The knife continued to flip, a repetitive, mindless exercise in which the rhythm never wavered, a silent chant.

"You're going to cut yourself."

Lee's warning was delivered with a frown. He sat on the sofa, dressed impeccably in tan slacks and a blue blazer, looking like a magazine model with high cheekbones, full lips, and an aquiline nose. Taller than most Chinese men, he stood six-two with broad shoulders and a small waist. Lee was her partner, her friend, and her protector. Mostly from herself.

She lifted her cup to acknowledge his admonishment. "I find it relaxing. Some people do crossword puzzles. I toss a knife. If I were doing a crossword puzzle you might have reason for concern. I'm not nearly as good with words." A sad smile set her features as she looked up to meet his gaze. "And words, I've found, can wound more deeply than a blade."

Her name was Bai Jiang, pronounced "by chang" with long vowels, a suitable moniker for a tall, willowy Chinese woman with a penchant for black leather and black jeans. Short, spiky hair, high cheekbones, and a surly attitude only served to enhance her tough image.

Her feet rested on her desk next to her computer. A screensaver flashed pictures of her daughter. At twelve, Dan had her father's features, only softened. The girl was pretty, perhaps even prettier than her mother. Bai hoped she'd be smarter. Smart enough, at least, to avoid men like her father.

Lee interrupted her thoughts. "There was a message on the phone from Tommy. He wants to see you."

"I know. I'm avoiding him."

One eyebrow lifted as he leaned forward to study her. "Triad business?"

"Unfinished business," she quickly replied, providing a smile to set him at ease. "Not to worry. Tommy and I are playing nice these days. He seems to be mellowing with age."

"Maybe it seems that way because he's your godfather," he asserted.

He seemed unconvinced of Tommy's benign nature. Tommy was *Shan Chu*, the head of the dragon, overlord of a local triad. Lee had good reason to be skeptical.

Her response was jaded. "Tommy's everybody's godfather."

She'd been only four when a car bomb had vaporized her parents. At the time, her late grandfather Ho Chan Jiang had headed *Sun Yee On*, a Hong Kong triad expanding into U.S. markets. Tommy had been *Fu Shan Chu*, second in command. After the death of her parents, Tommy had treated Bai as if she were his daughter. That was to say, unlike a son, she was expendable.

The bell in the lobby dinged to let them know someone had entered their outer office. She snapped the knife out of the air as she came upright in her chair. Her feet met the floor while her other hand placed the fragile cup carefully on her desk. The knife was tucked into a sheath sewn into the cuff of her jacket where it would remain out of sight.

Her office was situated in the heart of San Francisco's Chinatown, a second-story walkup. There wasn't a sign on the door to indicate her occupation. Clients typically made an appointment. Their eyes met as

Lee stood to walk across the polished hardwood floor toward the lobby.

"Are you expecting anyone?" she asked.

"No. You?"

She shook her head. "It's probably a lost tourist."

He opened a door and passed through to the lobby. A moment later, he returned to usher in a caller, a young, very wet Chinese girl. She stood just inside the doorway and dripped water on the shiny floor. Her head hung down to look sheepishly at the mess.

Bai's brow furrowed in contemplation as she studied the young woman in silence. Black hair in sopping strands ran down the girl's back. A too big, black leather jacket with metal studs hung from her shoulders to render her shapeless. Worn, soggy jeans, which had been strategically ripped, revealed brown goose flesh.

"'He who is drowned isn't troubled by the rain.'" Bai muttered.

The girl lifted her head and in a timid voice replied, "I don't understand."

"It's just something my grandfather used to say."

"What does it mean?"

"It means sometimes being wet is the least of your problems."

The girl looked like a drowned puppy. Bai fought an impulse to jump up and hug her. She had to remind herself strays were always trouble, regardless of the species. Her eyes narrowed at the thought.

"Are you the *souxun*?" the girl asked.

Souxun is pronounced "so-SOON" and translates to "people finder." Bai found lost people whether they wanted to be found or not. A natural doggedness made her good at her job.

"I am. Who might you be?"

"I'm Yu."

"Do you have a last name, Yu?"

"Yu Ma," the girl mumbled.

"Jade horse," Bai mused, voicing the English interpretation, "a pretty name. What can I do for you, Yu?"

Yu's arms hung limply at her sides, like they were new and she hadn't yet learned how to use them. Her words, when she spoke, came out in a rush. "Jia told me about you. She thinks you're really cool. She talked about you like she knew you. She said that when someone goes missing in Chinatown, White Ginger was the woman to talk to."

The girl looked up slowly, her eyes rounded in anticipation. Lips, painted dark purple, formed a tentative smile. Black mascara ran in tracks down the side of her face. Beneath all the makeup, she might have been pretty.

Her testimonial rendered Bai momentarily speechless. She wasn't used to praise, let alone that much enthusiasm, so early in the morning. "I had no idea I was cool." She glanced over at Lee to see if he appreciated how cool she was. "Why didn't you tell me I was cool?"

He grinned and shook his head. "You hide it so well. Who would know?"

She raised her eyebrows and turned back to Yu while nodding in Lee's direction. "You can see how being really cool can instill jealousy in those less fortunate. I prefer to be called Bai Jiang, by the way, not White Ginger. The translation of my name is dependent upon the dialect of Chinese being spoken, which, of course, you could care less about. All that aside," she continued, "Jia who?"

"Jia Yan. Her mother owns the Far East Café."

"Ahhh . . . I see."

Mrs. Yan was a formidable woman with a reputation for being spiteful, the type of person who would spit in your coffee if she didn't like you. She didn't like a lot of people, Bai included. It seemed best not to take her malice personally since the woman showed contempt for pretty much everyone. Still, it's difficult not to take offense when someone spits in your coffee.

A good Buddhist would have forgiven the slight. Bai considered herself, at best, a mediocre Buddhist. Plagued by anger issues and an inclination for what she liked to think of as "aggressive assertiveness," her objective of achieving enlightenment had shown itself to be as elusive as the perfect weight for her height. Unprecedented growth seemed her only hope of reaching either goal.

As she contemplated her own many shortcomings, Bai remembered that Mrs. Yan had several children. She wasn't familiar with any of them. "And how do you know Jia?"

"We're best friends. Then, two days ago, she just disappeared." The girl's voice cracked and her eyes filled.

Yu's distress managed to soften Bai's initial reluctance. The only thing more heartbreaking than a stray was a weepy stray. She gestured toward the couch. "Why don't you have a seat, Yu, and tell me your story from the beginning."

Bai's office was austere, the only furniture being her desk and the leather couch situated in front of it, both styled in blond wood and tan leather. The girl's sneakers squished as she walked across the room to gingerly take a seat on the edge of the sofa.

When Yu spoke, her voice was just above a whisper. "There's not a whole lot to tell. I saw Jia at school on Wednesday. We texted that night. When she didn't show up for school, I tried calling her and texting, but she didn't answer. I went to see her mother." She hesitated again before her gaze drifted up to look at Bai. "But Mrs. Yan wasn't home. Jia's brother told me to mind my own business. Something's wrong. I can feel it. Please. You have to help me."

Bai leaned slowly back into her chair. "How old are you, Yu?"

"Fifteen."

"And how old is Jia?"

"She's fifteen. She's a sophomore, like me."

Bai turned to Lee, who rested with his back against the wall next to the door. "What do you think, Lee?"

He turned his head to look at Bai and shrugged. "It seems a small favor to ask. The Far East Café is only a few blocks away. What's the harm in looking?"

Bai closed her eyes and inhaled deeply. The thought of dealing with Mrs. Yan made her stomach churn. The woman spit out karmic poison like a PEZ dispenser. But then, if Bai didn't take the time to find the girl, and it turned out something had really happened to her, Bai'd have only herself to blame.

Opening her eyes and turning reluctantly back to Yu, she said, "Fine. You win. Do you have a dollar?"

Yu looked from Bai to Lee and back again, obviously confused. "I think so."

Bai's hand snaked its way across the top of her desk palm up. "Give me the dollar. Please."

The girl's manner was uncertain. She slowly worked a bill loose from the pocket of her wet jeans and laid the soggy dollar on Bai's outstretched palm.

Bai's fist closed around the bill. "The dollar is payment for my services," she stated with as much grace as she could muster. "We now have a contract. I'll find Jia for you."

Yu bit down on her lower lip but couldn't hide her pleasure.

Bai noted the girl's reaction and frowned. She couldn't help feeling she'd been steered, roped, and trussed, the bill in her fist binding her more tightly than any knot. Her word had been given to a stray. And strays, she remembered, were always trouble.

chapter 2

Don't open a shop unless you like to smile

A call to San Francisco's Police Department didn't yield any clues to Jia Yan's whereabouts. No one had reported her missing. After a moment's hesitation, Bai picked up the phone to call her contact in Child Protective Services. The call was a long shot, but if there'd been trouble in the Yan household, Jia might have been put into juvenile detention, which would explain her inability to communicate with the outside world.

When John Fong answered, Bai again went through the events leading to the girl's disappearance.

"There's nothing in the system on a Jia Yan," John informed her.

"Do you have any incident reports on the Yan household, anything that might indicate a problem?"

"Nothing, Bai, but that's not unusual. The Chinese community is pretty tight-lipped."

She thanked John and ended the call to lean back in her chair and brood.

Lee walked into the office to perch on the edge of her desk. "I got Yu's contact information and told her we'd call when we have news."

Bai nodded in acknowledgment. "Jia hasn't been reported missing, and she's not in the juvenile system. It seems I don't have any choice but to go to see Mrs. Yan."

"You'd better be careful. She won't like your interfering in her affairs."

Bai snorted. "For reasons that remain a mystery to me, the woman has failed to embrace my every attempt to befriend her. Nonetheless, I'm going to ask nicely. I'm going to use my uncanny guile to ferret the truth out of her. As you well know, I'm a ferreting fool. She won't stand a chance against my awesome interrogation techniques."

He stood and turned to face her. "I think I'll go with you."

"Do you think I'll need assistance dealing with one matronly woman?"

"No, but I suspect it might turn into a brawl, and I don't want to miss out."

The corner of Bai's mouth twitched up. She wasn't entirely sure having him along was necessary, but the determined look on his face told her she didn't have much choice. "I don't suppose it would hurt to have you tag along. Just don't start anything."

His eyebrows shot up. "I don't think I'm the one you have to worry about."

She stood to brush past him and into the lobby where she grabbed an umbrella from the stand next to the door. Lee stopped to lock the office behind her as she stepped down the stairs from the second-story landing. Pushing past the heavy glass door at the entry, Bai walked into the pouring rain and chaos of Chinatown.

The pavement beneath her feet shed water in tiny rivulets while vendors unloaded goods from double-parked vans. Hand-trucks, loaded with boxes, forced their way through the crowd like barroom bruisers. Voices trumpeted as people yelled over the din of rain and traffic. To the uninitiated it might seem like bedlam. To Bai it was home.

Despite the foul weather, people crowded the sidewalk. She was jostled as she struggled to open her umbrella. An elbow nudged her from behind to send her careening into a man wearing a garbage bag like a Mexican serape. She bounced off wet, black plastic and turned, angrily. A tug at her elbow caused her to turn again. Lee gently took the umbrella from her hand to open it as he steered her into the crowd.

They walked north on Grant as far as Sacramento Street before stopping at a red light. They stood behind a swarm of pedestrians as umbrellas bumped each other and jockeyed for position. Waiting at the edge of the crowd, next to the Hoshun Deli, Bai spied Cantonese roasted ducks hanging in the window, a gallows row of greasy delicacies.

She made a beeline over to press her face and hands against the glass.

"What now?" asked Lee.

She detected a note of impatience in his voice and turned her head to stare at him. "The ducks, they're talking to me."

He shook his head and looked away. "I know I'm going be sorry I asked." A lengthy pause revealed his inner struggle. "All right, I give up. What're they saying?"

"They're saying, 'Forget that salad you were planning to have for lunch. Bite into my crisp, spicy skin. Taste my sweet, tender flesh while succulent fat rolls down your chin. And don't worry about it. You look good carrying a few extra pounds.'"

When Bai turned to gaze at Lee, his expression seemed doubtful. He peered at her with his lips canted to the side. "Those are some long-winded ducks."

"Ducks are charmers. There's no doubt about it. And, sure, maybe they're a little chatty, but that's part of their charm. It certainly doesn't detract from their allure. Just look at them. Aren't they gorgeous?"

He pointed to a rack of barbecued pork. "I suppose the *cha shiu* ribs've got something to say, too."

She turned to stare at the ribs, their surface a bright red but burned black around the edges. They glistened enticingly. She could almost smell the caramelized sugar through the glass. When she spoke, her voice was wistful. "Pigs are aggressive and very direct. The ribs just say, 'Eat me. You know you want me.'"

Food had always conversed with her; since she'd turned thirty the conversations had become more intense, more confrontational. She craved fat and sugar.

Lee dismissed her comments with a wave of his hand. "Your spare-ribs sound a lot like a man I know."

She glared at him.

"Pigs and men do seem to have a lot in common," she said with disdain. "You certainly know how to ruin a girl's appetite."

He took her hand in his. She smiled, convinced he'd seen the error of his ways.

"It's for your own good," he said as he pulled her forcefully away from the window. "You'll thank me later."

She balked. "I might thank you later," she said as she turned to face him, "but I want you to know I'm not feeling it right now."

"Think of this as an intervention."

He linked arms to walk with her. They made their way nearly to Washington Street before stopping again. The Far East Café was located one door down from the corner. Large gold letters frayed with age displayed the café's name on dark glass. Peeling paint on the door served as an omen of neglect.

Lee closed their umbrella. The rain had slowed to a drizzle. He opened the door and ushered her through the entrance. Stopping just inside the doorway, Bai let her eyes adjust to the subdued lighting. She took her time to visually inventory her surroundings.

The café had changed. What had once been a meeting place for the geriatric set now catered to a much younger clientele. About a half dozen *Wah Ching*, young thugs, sat at tables in the far corner near the window. Their girlfriends sat with them. The crowd stared at them with disaffected interest.

Wah Ching is a boy gang, teenagers mostly, though older members might reach into their thirties. They're triad wannabes with a reputation for being vicious. Their eventual goal is membership in a triad, though few have the aptitude or discipline to make it that far.

The boys sitting at the small tables looked like a mixed crew—short, tall, fat, and skinny. They dressed in leather jackets and dirty jeans with knee-length swag chains clipped to their belt loops. Heavy, industrial-type boots covered their feet. Tee-shirts, featuring heavy metal rock bands, rounded out the look. They'd apparently developed allergies to soap.

Bai's reputation in Chinatown was that of a well-connected, if somewhat meddlesome, woman. Her business was getting into other people's business. Lee's reputation was somewhat less affable. In his youth, he'd developed a reputation as a street fighter. But that had been years ago. He'd mellowed with age, for the most part.

The *Wah Ching* gave no indication they recognized either of them. Bai nodded and smiled a greeting to the crowd who silently eyed them. Lee just stared at the bangers then turned away—a dismissal. They strolled over to take seats at the counter on round stools covered in pea-green Naugahyde. A green Formica counter, faded with age and chipped along the edges, provided a place to rest their elbows. The café smelled of old grease and burned coffee.

No one stood behind the counter. Bai couldn't see anyone through the service window to the kitchen. The place was quiet, too quiet. She stole another glance at the kids in the corner. They stared back with deadpan faces. Coffee mugs and soda glasses crowded the small tables in front of them. Half-eaten burgers congealed on plates.

As she reached over and grabbed a couple of menus off the back of the counter, a young Chinese woman shuffled out of the door leading to the kitchen. A drab girl with a flat face and wary eyes, she appeared to be in her late teens.

Bai smiled, hoping to set the girl at ease. "Hi, my name's Bai Jiang. What's your name?"

The girl didn't respond at first. When she did reply, her voice was sullen. "Ling. What do you want?"

Bai squared her shoulders. The girl's attitude bordered on disrespect. "Have you ever heard the saying, 'Don't open a shop unless you like to smile'?"

Ling held a pencil poised over an order pad. She glared at Bai, her bottom lip thrust out in defiance. "You ever hear the saying, 'Bite me—I could care less'?"

Bai's jaw tightened, and her fists clenched. She started to rise off her stool, but something about the girl gave her pause. Bai could see fear in her eyes. The girl tried to hide the fright behind a brittle veneer of indifference, but Bai could feel it in the stale air of the café, like a wool blanket on a hot night.

Reining in her anger, Bai settled back onto her stool and replied mildly. "Two cups of coffee to start. Is Mrs. Yan here? I was hoping to speak with her."

Ling looked surprised. The girl turned abruptly to face the *Wah Ching* and gestured curtly before scuttling back into the kitchen.

Chair legs scraped against linoleum to catch Bai's attention as the gang members stood. They sauntered in her direction as she and Lee swiveled around on their stools to face the young thugs.

A heavyset kid in front addressed Bai. "My name's Jimmy Yan. What do you want with my mother?"

Jimmy stood about six feet tall with a round belly that appeared to be soft with fat. Long, greasy hair framed an oval face dotted with pimples. He loomed over her with a subtle threat in his pose. Bai suspected that's exactly what it was—a pose.

She turned up the wattage on her smile, determined to charm him. "I'd like to speak with her. It's a private matter."

Bai liked to delude herself into thinking she could unravel any mystery with a kind word and a gracious smile. Jimmy looked around to make eye contact with his boys. He smirked at them knowingly.

When he turned back to Bai, his voice was flippant. "My mother's gone back to China. You got somethin' to say, you need to say it to me."

Bai glanced at Lee, who pursed his lips in a sign things weren't going well. She didn't need him to tell her that. She'd managed to "ferret" it out on her own. But she wouldn't be deterred.

"When did your mother leave for China?"

"That's none of your business. You're kind of a nosy fuckin' bitch."

Jimmy grinned as he appended the insult. The *Wah Ching* chuckled at the disrespect. Their girls tittered from the other side of the room.

She refused to let her smile falter. "You're not the first person to mention that."

"Nor the last, no doubt," interjected Lee as he turned on his stool to speak to her.

His expression was amused. He seemed to be enjoying himself.

"Whothefuck are you?" Jimmy demanded.

Lee spun around on his stool to face Jimmy. His tone was pleasant when he spoke. "My name's Lee. Lee Li. As you might have guessed, my parents weren't terribly imaginative. My therapist says that's why I'm so prone to acting out. I have a deep need to prove I'm nothing like my parents, though, in retrospect, it seems that we're all destined to inherit some of their traits as a matter of genetic predisposition. From what I've heard, you, for instance, are much like your mother."

Jimmy looked confused. His words sounded uncertain. "Whaddaya mean I'm like my mother?"

Lee leaned toward him as if to speak in confidence. "From what I hear, she's kind of an asshole." The room went silent. "You seem to be following in her footsteps, but it's not too late to change. As a matter of fact, I'd suggest now would be a good time to start."

Jimmy froze. The muscles in his jaw twitched; his eyes narrowed. "I'll take care of you next," he announced as he pointed his finger in Lee's face. "But first, I want you to watch while we show your old lady a good time." He looked aside at his companions. "Who wants to be first?"

He threw the question out as he turned back to leer at Bai.

The smile dropped from her face. "You're big, and you're stupid, Jimmy. And you're about to make a huge mistake."

Her words went unheeded as Jimmy lunged at her awkwardly with his arms open wide. Bai's foot arced swiftly up to catch him squarely in the crotch. His mouth made a silent "O" when her foot connected.

Everyone watched as Bai's foot lifted Jimmy off the floor. She shot off the stool as his head came down in response to having his balls kicked up between his ears. Her knee caught his nose and snapped his head back. He stumbled into a skinny kid behind him, knees buckling as he crumpled to the floor.

Immediately, a fist flew her way—a wild swing, off-balance and wide. Bai stepped in and jabbed the skinny kid in the eye. The fight went out of him as he staggered around holding a hand to his weeping socket.

The human body has a number of weak spots—eyes, ears, nose, throat, and groin, each being easily accessible. The eyes are sympathetic organs. Poke one and they both tear up. The ears are attached by a thin membrane that's easily detached and remarkably sensitive to pain. The throat is tricky. Too much force inflicted will result in death.

The sound of smacking flesh caused Bai to turn around. She saw Lee swing his foot over his head in a move called "whipping the dragon's tail" to kick a kid in the jaw and slap him to the ground. Another gangster was already lying on the floor. The only *Wah Ching* left standing was a short kid with a ponytail. He looked at them hesitantly before backing away a step with his hands held up in front of him, palms out.

It had taken five seconds to subdue the *Wah Ching*. Bai thought it might have been a new record.

Lee pulled his thirty-five caliber Tomcat from his jacket and swung it around to cover the girls seated across the room. Bangers would be used to getting rousted. They would let their girlfriends carry their guns rather than take the rap for carrying a concealed weapon.

It wasn't likely one of the girls would open fire, but there didn't seem to be any point in taking chances. Lee walked over to relieve the girls of the hardware before herding the bad boys to the side of the room where their girlfriends waited to console them.

Bai walked to the front door and locked it before turning the sign around to let people know the café was closed. Jimmy huddled on the ground holding his bloody nose and nursing his aching balls.

She turned to yell into the back room. "Ling! Up front, pretty please."

It was never too late to be polite.

The girl with the wary eyes shuffled out of the back. She looked at Bai and then over the counter at Jimmy. She smiled when she saw he was hurt.

Bai spoke to the girl bluntly while nodding down at Jimmy. "Are you his sister?"

A note of sadness entered the girl's voice. "'Fraid so."

"Where's your mother?"

"She gave up and went back to China. She said she was done with us. Left Jimmy in charge of the family. Oldest son, you know the story."

"How long ago was this?"

"Day before yesterday."

"Where are your siblings?"

"They're in school. They don't get out 'til three."

"Where is Jia?"

The question caught Ling by surprise. She averted her eyes and looked nervous. "You should ask Jimmy."

Bai reached over the counter and placed a hand on Ling's shoulder to keep her from turning away. "I'm asking you, Ling. Where's your sister?"

Ling took a deep breath and visibly trembled. When she spoke, she sounded frightened. "Jimmy wanted into the gang. He traded her to the *Wah Ching*."

chapter 3

Vicious as a tigress can be,
she never eats her own cubs

Bai turned, leaving Jimmy where he sprawled on the floor, to walk over and speak to his associates. Lee followed with his gun pointed at the ground. The *Wah Ching* seemed sufficiently cowed, but it didn't hurt to have Lee at her back. She'd learned early in life that stupid people did stupid things.

The boys hung their heads to avoid her gaze. Their feet shuffled nervously. The four young girls stared at her as if mesmerized with their eyes big and their mouths hanging slightly open, like guppies.

The young women were dressed alike in anti-school uniforms: tight jeans, tight tee-shirts, and over-sized leather jackets. Their eyes were smeared with black eye shadow and their lashes clumped with mascara. They probably thought they looked more grown-up that way. They didn't. They looked like little girls who lived on the fringe of society, seeking acceptance with little to look forward to other than a revolving door in the legal system.

Bai couldn't help thinking of her own daughter, Dan, and wondered if any of the aimless young women who stood before her had mothers who worried about them. The thought saddened her. With a weary voice, she asked, "Who's in charge here?" She wanted to speak with the leader. Like all packs, the *Wah Ching* would have an alpha male. "This is me asking nicely." She stopped to look around and see if anyone cared to volunteer an answer. "If we can't talk like civilized adults, you'll soon get acquainted with the not-so-nice me."

When she still didn't get an answer, she stepped forward and grabbed the skinny kid by his ear and pulled down. He dropped to his knees and screeched.

"Answer my question," she ordered, "or I'll pull off your ear." She looked up to glare at the skinny kid's friends. "If that doesn't work, I'll pull off the other ear."

The boys looked away. A couple of the young women put their hands over their ears protectively. Bai had to bite her tongue to keep from smiling.

The short kid with the ponytail mumbled, "What do ya want?"

She maintained a hold on the skinny kid's ear while she turned to Ponytail. "I want Jia Yan back."

He mumbled again with his head down. His words were lost to the checkered tiles on the floor.

Bai tried again. "Could you look at me when you talk? And try moving your lips when you speak. It isn't that hard—really."

The young man looked away. He seemed incapable of meeting her gaze. His words were barely above a whisper. "*Ngaw din nei la.*"

He'd told her to fuck off. She let go of the skinny kid's ear to confront the smartass. "*Dai jek gwan,*" she said, calling him a big talker. His head dropped lower. "What's your name?"

"Jan."

"Jan what?"

"Just Jan."

"OK, just Jan, tell me where the girl is," she demanded.

He remained silent.

She leaned over to whisper in his ear. "*Da sei nei.*"

She told him she'd kill him. His head jerked up to see if she was serious. She locked eyes with him. From the shock on his face, he apparently believed her.

"Oaklin," he whispered.

"*Sao jee!*" hissed the skinny kid. Squealer.

Bai whirled around to slap the skinny kid hard across the mouth with the back of her hand. The sound of the blow was like the crack of a whip. His head snapped back from the force of the cuff. He stumbled before catching his balance.

She'd wanted to make a point. The slap had a sobering effect. Nobody else, it seemed, was in a hurry to get bitch slapped by a girl.

She turned back to Jan. "Where in Oakland?"

He shook his head and looked at the floor before whispering, "*Gai dao.*" Brothel. The young thug looked up and smiled. "*Ka si nai* make good *cheen.*" He told Bai the young girl would make good money.

The little pimp spoke the words as if he were discussing an object, a thing, and not a young woman. For a brief moment, Bai lost it. Her hand shot out like it belonged to a stranger. She felt the cartilage in Jan's nose break beneath her knuckles; the entire room heard the crunch. Jan staggered back into the girls, who caught him and kept him from falling.

He held his hands cupped to his face and wheezed, "Ou bro' muh nose."

"That's just the beginning unless you tell me where to find Jia Yan. If you don't tell me, I'll make sure you crawl out of here—blind, deaf, mute, and crippled. They'll prop you up with a bowl in front of the transit station where you'll earn lots of *cheen*, you little shit."

Lee chuckled. He enjoyed seeing her get wound up, and she was thoroughly pissed. High school girls weren't supposed to be sold into the sex trade. The more she thought about it, the angrier she became.

"*Nei se yan chee seen ge,*" squealed Jan, holding his nose.

He screamed that Bai was crazy. She didn't feel any obligation to dispel the notion. She glared at him and hissed, her voice seething with anger. "*Gwai gung?*" Who's the pimp?

Jan stared at her and yelled defiantly. "Sammy Tu . . . *tai lo . . . jai sei ma.*"

He spit blood that had dripped into his mouth onto the linoleum floor at her feet. His face was twisted with rage and pain. He'd told her that Sammy Tu was the pimp, she'd better be careful, and she'd better be ready for a fight. Jan had finally found his courage.

She got in his face, standing toe to toe with him, her voice soft but filled with threat. "*Puk gai baan chat*. Get Real."

She'd called him a stupid prick and told him to drop dead in gang slang. "Get Real" is universal gang speak for "prepare for war." Bai had declared war on the *Wah Ching*.

Only after he'd dropped his gaze was she willing to turn away to sit on a stool at the counter. She needed time to think—time to let her temper cool. Ling stood behind the counter as a silent observer.

Bai turned to the girl. "Any chance I can get a cup of coffee nobody's spit in?"

Ling smiled and turned around to pick up a pot that had been resting on a warming station. She poured the steaming liquid into a brown mug and handed it to Bai. "You take cream or sugar?"

Bai's tone softened at the courtesy. "No. Thanks."

"You really wanna thank me, you can kick Jimmy in the balls again."

The request was delivered in a soft voice, but Bai could see from the look in her eyes that Ling was serious. She looked down at Jimmy as she sipped. The coffee had been sitting too long on the warmer and was bitterly strong. He gazed up at her, having heard the appeal. She took a guilty pleasure in witnessing his fear. She hadn't forgotten he'd called her "old."

With her back to Lee, she heard him addressing the *Wah Ching*. "Why don't you all sit down again until we decide what to do with you? And no phone calls," he warned. "I'd feel really bad if you compelled me to shoot one of you."

His tone implied he wouldn't feel bad at all.

The scrape of chairs and angry grumbling informed Bai the *Wah Ching* were complying with Lee's request. He came to sit next to her while keeping an eye on the gangsters. "I told you it would be fun."

He turned briefly to smile at her in encouragement. She stared at him, unamused.

Her face scrunched up as she took another gulp of acidic coffee. "Great. I'm glad you're having a good time. Jia Yan is being held in Oakland, and we've got a pack of juvenile delinquents on our hands. Now what do we do?"

He swiveled his stool around to watch the *Wah Ching* while showing Bai his profile. "Have you thought about calling Jason?"

Jason, her ex, was *Hung Kwan*, Red Pole of the *Sun Yee On* triad. He led their strike teams, which meant he commanded a small army of triad enforcers. In the hierarchy of the brotherhood, he held the number three position. Jason epitomized what the *Wah Ching* strived to become—a stone-cold killer. They probably wouldn't know Jason, but they'd surely know of him. And, they would fear him.

Bai spoke softly. "Shit! Shit! Shit!"

"So eloquent." Lee put his hand on hers. "I couldn't have put it better myself."

She dug into her pocket to pull out her cell phone. She had a number for Jason but was reluctant to use it. If she called him, she'd be admitting she'd run into a situation she couldn't handle on her own. If she didn't call him, she'd have to deal with the *Wah Ching* herself, which would entail beating the little thugs into submission. Although tempted, she dialed.

Jason's voice surprised her. She usually got his voice mail. "It's been a while, Bai. How are you? How is Dan?"

"I'm good. Dan's good." She hesitated. "Jason, I've got a bit of a situation."

There was silence. She thought maybe she'd lost the connection.

"Am I going to be sorry I answered this call?" he replied with caution in his voice.

She gritted her teeth. "I've got a mess on my hands. I could really use your help."

"Last time I helped you it cost me. This time I think there should be compensation."

She swallowed an angry reply. His comment was only a tease, but she wasn't in the mood to play. Her hand hurt from smacking the *Wah Ching* around, and she was hungry. She could ignore the throbbing hand, but her empty stomach put her in a foul mood.

"I'll make it worth your while."

She put meaning behind the words but couldn't filter out the resentment in her voice.

He must have sensed her mood. His voice changed, becoming more serious. "Where are you?"

"I'm at the Far East Café. And Jason, come alone."

Jason disconnected before she could add anything more. She turned to look at Lee. He raised his eyebrows.

"You are such a slut," he said with a sly grin on his face.

"Yeah, I'm working on that."

Bai thought she might have made a mistake in calling Jason. His Chinese name was *Hu Lum*, forest tiger. There was a saying ... something about letting sleeping tigers lie.

Jason was a violent man. She'd grown up around violent men and understood them well. Her grandfather had been legendary, perhaps the only *Shan Chu* in history to die of old age. In an organization where assassination was the ladder to success, his longevity spoke volumes about his survival skills. Her grandfather had raised her, and the brotherhood had become her family. It was, she mused, probably the most dysfunctional family in existence.

Jason pounded on the café door to disrupt Bai's reflections. He must have been close when she'd called. She stood to unlock the door. As he stepped into the room, the *Wah Ching* muttered then grew silent.

He looked at Bai and nodded a curt greeting. He wasn't smiling. His stolid appearance didn't make him any less handsome. He wore a black silk suit that showed off his lean, muscular body. Black hair, worn slicked back, gangster-style, accentuated his sharp features. He looked like the ultimate bad boy. Her stomach drew taut at the sight of him.

Jason turned to look at Lee, who remained sitting on a stool at the counter, and voiced a curt greeting. "Pickle licker."

"Psychopath," Lee replied while raising his eyebrows in salutation. The *Wah Ching* flinched at the exchange. They didn't realize they were nicknames, crude endearments between old friends.

"What's going on, Bai?" Jason sounded tired. Dark circles showed under his eyes.

She nodded down at Jimmy, still sprawled on the floor and apparently content to stay there. "Two days ago, Jimmy Yan here, traded his little sister to the *Wah Ching* as payment for admittance into the gang. She's a fifteen-year-old high school student who's been sold into the sex trade. I want her back."

Jason looked at Jimmy and frowned. He then turned aside to look at the rest of the *Wah Ching* and their girls before his eyes came back to rest on Bai. He spoke in a low voice. "I can't ask for her back. You'll have to go get her. I can provide you with information that might help you find her."

She thought about his proposal and wasn't at all happy with the restrained offer. She'd hoped he would be able to scare the *Wah Ching* into giving up Jia Yan. "It'll have to do. I realize there are limitations to what you can do on my behalf. I'm a woman, after all. I stand outside the brotherhood. There are rules."

"And I'm breaking most of those rules just by being here," he said brusquely, taking her arm and leaning into her. "And I'm very familiar with the fact you're a woman. I don't need to be reminded."

She bit down on her lip and swallowed the sharp reply she wanted to spout. Instead, she smiled sweetly. 'You're grumpy when you're tired."

"And you're shrill when you're hungry."

She glared at him. He knew her too well. "You might try feeding me."

"Sorry," he replied. "I don't have the time. I'm a very busy man these days. I'm sure you understand."

She moved closer and dropped her voice. "I understand that you're being an ass, but since you're doing me a favor I'll just suck it up."

He stared at her long enough to make her uncomfortable then looked off into the distance. Bai assumed he was either gathering his thoughts or searching for a scathing reply. She was surprised when he quickly turned around and walked over to speak with the *Wah Ching*. The punks actually stood up to bow respectfully.

She walked over to take a seat next to Lee.

Jason addressed the boy gangsters in a dispassionate voice. "The *Wah Ching* are in Chinatown without my permission." Jason's face remained expressionless. His arms were relaxed at his sides and his back ramrod straight. He'd gone deadly cold. "You're trying the patience of *Sun Yee On*."

The *Wah Ching* remained silent with eyes cast down. He held their lives in his hand. It was within his rights to kill them for encroaching on his territory.

"But, 'vicious as a tigress can be, she never eats her own cubs.'" He lectured them with a proverb. "You're free to go. You'll speak of this to no one. And don't let me catch you in Chinatown again without my consent."

The skinny kid hesitated. He pointed to the pile of guns on the counter and spoke softly to Jason. Bai heard the words "*cheung gai,*" firearms. Jason tilted his head and stared at the thug in disbelief before his hand whipped out to grab the skinny kid's offending digit. Before the kid could protest, Jason had forced the finger back.

The crack of the breaking finger shocked Bai. She started to get off her stool. Lee's hand came down on her shoulder to hold her in place with an iron grip.

Jason snatched up a wad of napkins with lightning-fast hands and stuffed the paper into the boy's mouth to stifle the emergent scream. He pushed the boy roughly away. His eyes flashed angrily. "MY PATIENCE GROWS THIN!"

The *Wah Ching* and their girls disappeared like smoke.

Jason strolled over to speak with Jimmy, his voice harsh. "Go back to China. If I see you again, I'll kill you myself."

Jason turned to Bai. "I'll see what I can find out about the girl and be in touch." He started to turn away then turned back. He reached up to stroke her cheek with his fingers, his touch gentle. "I'll let you know when I'm ready to collect."

An amused, almost playful, smile crossed his lips.

"Collect for what?" she asked, her tone tinged with disbelief. "I could have let them go myself. All you managed to do was piss them off before turning them loose. I thought you might reason with them and get the girl back or, at least, make some kind of deal with them. All you've managed to do is make things worse. You're unbelievable!"

He stared at her, his lips drawing taut. His hand came up to point an index finger in her face, but he couldn't bring himself to say anything. She stared at him and shook her head. He offered one final wave of his finger before storming out of the café, the glass rattling as the door slammed at his back.

"I love you, too," she whispered under her breath.

chapter 4

Great souls have wills;
feeble ones have only wishes

Bai took a seat at the counter to let the angry heat dissipate from her face. She turned to find Lee staring at her.

"What?!"

"You're an embarrassment," he said, shaking his head. "You can't be in the same room with Jason for five minutes without either tearing off his head or tearing off his pants. You need to make up your mind. You either love him or you don't."

Embarrassed by her reaction to Jason, she turned away. Jason confused her. On the one hand, her rational mind told her it was over between them. Yet, she still loved him, which made her angry . . . which was completely irrational.

"It's not that simple," she blurted.

Swiveling around on her stool, Bai found Ling staring at her with a pokerfaced expression. "Where do you find guys like these?"

"They're pretty," Bai said, looking aside at Lee, "but, believe me, they're more trouble than they're worth."

"That's easy for you to say," Ling replied. "You're beautiful. You have choices."

"You're young. When you get older, you'll realize nothing's that simple. Everything comes with a price." She could see that Ling had stopped listening at "when you get older." She decided to change the subject. "What do we do about you, Ling?"

Ling looked confused. "What do you mean?"

"You've been left with three children and no visible means of support. Do you want to try to find homes for you and your siblings? Do you want to go back to China and find your mother? What is it you want to do?"

"This is our home. My mother ran out on us. Why would I want anything to do with her?"

Bai looked around at the small café. It was dingy, dirty, and run-down.

"I know what you're thinking," said Ling, defensively. "The place is a dump. I know that. But it doesn't have to be. I know how to cook. I've been cooking here since my mother took me out of school when I was twelve. I can make it work. I can make a home for my little brother and my sisters. It's not their fault we have a crappy mother. I just need a chance."

The girl seemed sincere, but Bai still had doubts. "How old are you, Ling?"

"Eighteen."

From the hesitation in her voice, Bai surmised that Ling wasn't really eighteen.

"I've always wanted to own a café," interjected Lee. "Would you be interested in a silent partner, Ling? I could help you fix this place up and maybe lend a hand with the décor."

Bai turned to look at him. Her face questioned his interference. He ignored her.

Ling looked at Lee warily then turned to Bai. "Can he be trusted?"

Bai shook her head in despair. "Lee's a man of his word. I trust him with my life. That doesn't mean he won't drive you nuts picking out the perfect colors for this place. You have to understand he's a perfectionist. It's the only thing keeping him from being perfect."

"In my own defense," Lee offered, "you won't recognize this place when I'm through with it."

He grinned, a captivating smile with perfect white teeth.

Ling studied him. She looked worried. Her mouth forged into a hard line. With her hands clenched together in front of her, she asked, "You're *tongzhi*, aren't you?"

She'd asked if Lee was homosexual.

The smile slowly drifted from his face. "Why do you ask?"

"The other man, the one who scared away the *Wah Ching*, he called you 'pickle licker.' You didn't get angry. I've seen you fight. You could have made him eat his words."

Lee took a deep breath before answering. "Does it matter?"

Ling stood silent in thought. "I don't think so." She took a small step toward him. "Are you sure you couldn't like girls—even a little bit?"

Ling's voice was wistful. Bai had seen the symptoms before. Women were constantly falling for Lee. His charm was like an airborne virus.

"It isn't that I don't like women," he replied. "I love women. I just don't like having sex with them."

"We're a lot alike in that regard," Bai confided, hoping to change the subject.

He looked aside at her and scowled. She shrugged off the silent reprimand and turned to Ling. "To answer your question, Ling, you have a better chance of scoring Brad Pitt than you have of seducing Lee. Putting all that nonsense aside, do you want him as a business partner? I've warned you. He can be a pain in the ass."

Ling's brow furrowed, and her hand came up to press against her lips. "It'll take a lot of money to fix this dump up. What do you want in return?"

"I'd like to be your business partner," he replied. "I believe in investing in people. You appear to be willing to work hard to succeed. And, to tell the truth, I'm not good at running the day-to-day affairs of a business. I have a short attention span. Partnerships work for me."

"Fifty-fifty partners?" Ling asked.

He put out his hand. "I'll have the partnership papers drawn up so you can look them over. My name's Lee Li, by the way. I don't believe we've been formally introduced."

She took his hand timidly. "It's nice to meet you, Mr. Li."

"Well, that's settled then," Bai said. "Now we just have to find Jia and bring her home."

Ling dropped Lee's hand reluctantly to turn to Bai. "I didn't know what Jimmy was up to." Her voice was full of regret. "Him and his friends came in the middle of the night and just took her. I couldn't stop them. I should've at least tried. Jimmy's so stupid; he couldn't see the *Wah Ching* were just using him."

Bai fished a business card out of her pocket and handed it to Ling. "If they bother you again, call me."

Ling looked at Bai's card. Her mouth moved as she silently sounded out the words. "So you're the *souxun*. I've heard of you." She looked up to study Bai. "You're not at all like I imagined."

The statement surprised Bai. "What did you imagine I'd be like?"

"More Nancy Drew and less Kelly Hu."

Bai's eyebrows flicked up. "I'll take that as a compliment though I'm not entirely sure it is one."

"What do we do with Jimmy?" Lee asked, diverting Bai's attention.

"You can't trust him," Ling insisted. "He's like my mom—mean and stupid."

Hate glinting off his eyes, Jimmy stared up at Bai. His expression reinforced his sister's opinion of him. He was a rat.

"I wanna go to China." Jimmy made the statement with a hint of authority. "I know where my mother is. The guy told me to go."

Apparently, Jimmy was recovered enough to start backing his way out of the mess he found himself in. But Bai couldn't trust him to leave town, and she couldn't have him interfering with her search for his sister. Jimmy would have to go on ice for a few days. She just had to figure out where to stash him until she could find Jia.

Bai grabbed a handful of Jimmy's hair to pull his head up. She wanted to see his face. "'Great souls have wills; feeble ones have only wishes.'" She spoke to him as if he were a child. "I think it's time I introduced you to Uncle Tommy."

Jimmy looked disappointed. He should have been terrified.

Lee got up from his stool. He nodded to Bai and Ling before turning to walk out the door.

As *Shan Chu*, Tommy couldn't be seen with Lee because Lee was *tongzhi*. The brotherhood had strict prohibitions against its members' associating with homosexuals.

After the door had closed behind Lee, Ling turned to Bai. "Where's he going?"

"He can't accompany me on my next stop." Her words were a sad commentary. She turned around to see the look of confusion on Ling's face. "It's a long story." She dismissed Ling's unasked questions with a wave of her hand. "Do you happen to have a picture of Jia?"

"Sure. I have a school picture upstairs. I'll get it for you."

While Ling ran to get the photo, Bai tugged the cell phone out of her pocket. As she dialed, Jimmy decided he'd been sitting on the floor long enough and started to get up. Bai swiveled around on her stool and slapped him on the top of his head. "Stay down until I tell you to get up."

The slap did the trick. He complied while the phone rang. The woman who answered had a pleasant voice. When Bai identified herself, the receptionist put her through to Tommy.

"Bai. It's good to hear from you!" Tommy sounded jovial. "I've been meaning to call. We have some business to discuss. When can we get together?"

"Actually, Tommy, I'm thinking now would be a good time. Could you send a car and driver? I'm at the Far East Café on Grant near Washington. I have an unmanageable package that needs transport."

The line went silent. Her words were code. Tommy would send soldiers to escort her back to *Sun Yee On's* offices.

"I'll send someone right over. I look forward to hearing about this." His voice was full of amusement.

"Thanks, Tommy. See you soon."

She looked down at Jimmy. "You're about to find out karma's a bitch. *Tai lo.*" Be careful.

Jimmy glared at her but said nothing, too stupid to be scared.

chapter 5

Once on a tiger's back, it is hard to alight

A black limousine double-parked in front of the café. The driver, a burly Chinese man in a black suit, took Jimmy by the arm and roughly escorted him to the waiting car. Bai followed a few steps behind, shadowed by another triad enforcer who bowed her into the limo with deference.

Although not a member of the triad, she was the granddaughter of Ho Chan Jiang, the man who'd ushered *Sun Yee On* into the twenty-first century by legitimizing many of their operations. He'd funneled money from illicit gambling, prostitution, smuggling, and drugs into fast-food chains, luxury resorts, pharmaceutical companies, and oil. The triad had prospered, and nothing, it seemed, engendered loyalty like money.

The trip to the Businessmen's Association Building, which served as triad headquarters, took only a few minutes. As the car pulled into the underground garage, Bai asked that Jimmy be kept in seclusion while she spoke with Tommy. The last she saw of him, he was being led away by a couple of triad enforcers.

She rode the elevator up to the penthouse offices on the top floor and stepped out of the lift into a bright and airy atrium. Cow lilies, their fragrance filling the room, grew in a massive planter that rested against the wall next to the lift. Across the room was a receptionist's kiosk, a round, elevated desk, where a very pretty Chinese woman in a tailored black blazer answered the phone via a wireless headset while gesturing for Bai to have a seat in one of the overstuffed leather chairs.

As Bai settled into an armchair to wait, another receptionist appeared to offer tea. Bai declined. The stale coffee from the café had already torched her stomach.

Tommy stepped out to personally usher her into his office. He offered her a seat in a guest chair before walking around to the other side of his desk. He sat facing her and leaned forward to rest his elbows on the desktop. "It's good to see you. You look beautiful as always. How is Dan?"

"Dan's fine. You're looking well."

He smiled. "Thank you. Now that we have the pleasantries out of the way, what can I do for you?"

A slight, fit man in his late fifties, Tommy personified the direct and forceful executive. He continued to smile affably as he waited for her reply.

"Your men are holding someone for me downstairs. It's a long story. But to sum it up, I have a contract to retrieve a fifteen-year-old girl who's been sold to the *Wah Ching*. I understand she's being held in Oakland. The young man downstairs is her brother, also a *Wah Ching*. I need him held until I can find his sister."

He sat back in his chair to reflect a moment. The smile disappeared. "It would be easier to kill him—less messy. If we turn him loose, he could cause trouble."

"I don't see any justification for killing him. Besides, being an accessory to murder would wreak havoc on my karma. When it's all over, I'll put him on a plane headed for China and we'll never hear from him again."

Tommy's fingers pressed together before his face to form a steeple. He closed his eyes and spoke in a measured voice. "We'll keep him here for you . . . but not without a price."

He opened his eyes to smile at her. She was familiar with his Cheshire grin. It didn't bode well.

"What is it you want, Tommy?"

"Ho Chan's estate has lingered now for two years. I want you to come to a decision regarding his remaining holdings. I want resolution on the Hong Kong property."

She wasn't too surprised that he pushed for closure on her grandfather's estate. She'd been stalling on instructions from her lawyers. The

Hong Kong real estate market was still booming, while the market in California was in the toilet. Her overseas properties served as a hedge against her domestic holdings. But from Tommy's perspective, the Hong Kong estate, a five-acre oceanfront compound, held significance beyond money. It had served as the palatial home of her grandfather, the seat of power.

She assumed the serious demeanor of a businesswoman. "I won't sell you the Hong Kong estate." She made the statement flatly. The reaction on his face wasn't angry, but he appeared to be disappointed. "But I will do a swap. I just can't afford to recapture the depreciation since the property is held in a stateside corporation."

He nodded solemnly as he mulled over her suggestion. A small smile played across his lips. "Do you have any properties in mind?"

She was familiar with the triad's holdings. Her grandfather had managed them for decades. In reply, she held up her hands, palms out, and surveyed his office.

He barked a laugh. "You want this building?"

"I believe you'll find that with the decline in the California market, the property in Hong Kong will be on parity with the current value of this building. And . . . you've been holding this building far too long. You could do better with a higher rate of depreciation."

He stared at her while he thought about her offer. "I suppose you've already worked this out and have the appraisals in order."

His wasn't so much a question as a statement. She nodded in reply. "The lawyers at Hung and Chin have all the paperwork. If you'd care to have your people vet the deal, I'll have the files sent over. I've also worked out a long-term lease option on this building. I wouldn't want to lose you as a tenant."

"I should've known you'd be one step ahead of me. You truly are Ho Chan's prodigy. I'm only sorry you couldn't follow in his footsteps."

Tommy raised his hands, an apology of sorts for running an all-boys club. She wasn't sorry. She'd escaped life in *Sun Yee On*. Besides, she didn't need the money, and the power was just an illusion. Life can't be controlled with a gun.

He beamed at her and seemed to take pride in her shrewd business acumen. "Is there anything more I can do for you?"

She hesitated before asking the next question. It was a sensitive topic. "Can you tell me how heavily the *Wah Ching* are involved in slaving?"

He shrugged to communicate either he didn't know or saw no reason to tell her what he knew. She stood outside the brotherhood. There were limits to what he could, or would, do on her behalf.

She smiled and spoke with a dramatic flair. "I certainly hope nothing happens to me. My estate would go into probate . . . for years."

She grinned at him and waited for a response.

Bai's relationship with Tommy was complicated. He'd acted as a surrogate father when her parents had been killed. He'd been part of her life since she'd been a child. He'd also taken from her one of the things she loved most: Jason. Tommy had made Jason his heir apparent. They struggled over the heart and soul of a man neither could relinquish.

He looked at her sourly. He'd thought he could twist her arm and force a sale on her. Now it was her turn to do a little arm twisting. He needed her alive until the sale of the Hong Kong properties closed. She had him right where she wanted him.

He leaned forward, one eyebrow raised in anticipation. "What exactly is it you want?"

"I need you to loan me Jason." She kept her face neutral to play down the request.

As *Hung Kwan*, Jason had a small army of seasoned soldiers at his disposal. Not that she needed them. It was Jason she wanted, though she could no longer rationally explain why.

Tommy eyed her knowingly. "You and Jason have some issues to work out. 'Once on a tiger's back, it is hard to alight.'" He let the truth of his words sink in while she sat quietly under his scrutiny. Punching a speed dial on his office phone, he put the call on speaker. Jason's voice answered. "Jason, could you step into my office, please. There's something we need to discuss."

Like guarded opponents, they eyed each other until a knock

sounded at the door. Jason walked in without waiting for a response. He gave no indication he was surprised to see Bai.

He bowed slightly and addressed Tommy. "You wanted to see me?"

"Yes. Bai has requested that she 'borrow' you for a short while. How do you feel about that?"

Jason looked at her briefly before returning his attention to Tommy. "I'll do as you think best."

Tommy let out a long sigh and gazed at her. His facial expression didn't tell her anything. "Very well," he uttered, as if in defeat. "It's in the best interest of *Sun Yee On* for Bai to stay alive until we can conclude certain business transactions. You are charged with seeing she remains so, even if that means going against her explicit wishes."

Tommy stared at her with a crooked grin, an expression that let her know she might have overplayed her hand. She'd been looking for an obedient helper. What she'd gotten was a nanny with a gun.

chapter 6

Wealth is but dung, useful only when spread

Jason walked with Bai out of Tommy's office and into the lobby. He glanced at her then looked away with features that appeared to be set in stone. The elevator doors opened, and they stepped in to take the lift to the underground garage.

"Where are we going?" Bai asked.

"We're going to get the girl. I thought that's what you wanted."

His voice implied he wasn't happy.

"Are you angry with me? Do you know where the *Wah Ching* are holding her? You could've said no if you hadn't wanted to help me."

He took a deep breath and let it out slowly before answering. "No, I'm not angry with you. And no, I don't know where the girl is. But I do know where Sammy Tu bases his operations. If we can find him, there's a good chance the girl won't be too far away. As for my saying no to you, that's always been a problem. All I ask is that you follow my lead and try not to get in the way."

She turned to him, doubt written across her features. "Are you thinking about going after him now? Why don't we try to sneak the girl out in the middle of the night?"

"Now is the best time to catch Sammy Tu. The sex trade runs late and sleeps late. I'm hoping we can catch the lazy pimp before word gets out you're looking for him. To do that, we need to get to him before he wakes up."

The elevator doors dinged as they opened. Jason walked quickly out of the lift with Bai trailing behind. He stopped to open the passenger door of a black BMW, allowing her to enter, before walking around the car to the driver's side.

"Do you want to stop and pick up Lee?" he asked as he backed the car out of the parking stall.

The offer took Bai by surprise. She peered at his face, trying to figure out whether he was serious. As usual, his expression told her nothing. "What will your associates think?"

His face tightened. It wasn't until they'd exited the parking garage that he spoke. "It was never personal with Lee. You don't seem to be able to understand."

His excuses didn't make her any less offended. "I think you fail to understand there's no way not to take it personally. You made the decision that Lee wasn't good enough to be your friend because he's gay. That was your choice."

Jason threaded his way through traffic. He gripped the steering wheel until his knuckles blanched. His lips narrowed to a thin line.

"The decision's been made," he stated harshly. "I sometimes wonder if I made the right choice—taking the oaths. But it's done. We both know there's no turning back."

She turned to look at him. For an instant, their gazes met before she quickly averted her eyes. She understood what he was saying. He'd made his choice to join the brotherhood. In doing so, he'd given up his old life, his old friends . . . and her.

Reluctant to look at him, she fumbled around in her jacket pocket for her cell phone. When Lee answered, she asked him to wait on the street. He didn't ask any questions.

Lee stood on the sidewalk as the big beamer pulled up to the curb. He jumped into the back and slammed the door shut as Jason eased the car back into traffic.

Jason drove aggressively, weaving in and out of the choked thoroughfares to avoid double-parked vehicles and pedestrians, who demonstrated an inexplicable aversion to crosswalks. They flew down The Embarcadero and past the old Ferry Building before crossing the Bay Bridge to pick up Interstate 580 to Oakland.

Jason spoke loudly enough for Lee to hear in the backseat. "Sammy Tu is headquartered in an old Victorian in Oakland. It's near downtown. I understand he keeps an apartment on the third floor and leaves the bottom two floors for paying customers."

"How do we get inside?" asked Lee.

Jason flashed a smile and glanced back at Lee. "You ring the bell."

"And then what?" Bai asked.

He stared straight ahead at the road. "Then we run up the stairs and shoot anybody that gets in our way."

Lee popped his head between the seats to look at Bai. He mouthed a silent "no" in protest of Jason's plan.

"We'll be fast—in and out," Jason added, ignoring Lee's antics. "The less noise we make, the fewer people we'll have to shoot. We'll wear ski masks, but Sammy Tu will eventually realize you're responsible, Bai. Word will get around if you're successful in retrieving the girl. You're going to have an enemy if we leave him alive."

"There's no need to kill anybody!" she snapped. "What is it with you and killing people? Let's just grab the girl and run. I'll deal with Sammy Tu, if and when the time comes."

Jason grunted a reply.

The car exited off the interstate and onto Main Street in Oakland.

If you have money, you live in The Oakland Hills, an enclave of trees and gently rolling knolls. On the Bay side, the mean streets of Oakland are inhabited by the poor and the lawless. Downtown, gangs are endemic. Urban blight can be seen on every corner. Parts of the city look like a war zone, complete with barred windows and blast-shield doors.

Sammy Tu didn't live in the hills of Oakland.

Jason stopped the car on a side street populated by older homes—dilapidated Victorians. Clad in a patchwork of once-vibrant colors, the painted ladies looked tired and worn, remnants of a grander era. The street appeared deserted.

Jason pushed a button to pop open the trunk lid before exiting the car. Bai and Lee followed him to the back of the car where he entered a four-digit code to unlock a gun case bolted to the floor of the open compartment. Guns and mysterious green canisters filled the metal box.

Jason handed Lee a 7.62-caliber Nagant revolver equipped with a silencer. "It won't make any more noise than a cough."

He then turned to Bai with an identical gun.

"I won't need it," she said.

He stared at her, his eyes tight with frustration. He kept the gun and handed her a ski mask. "Once we're inside, put on the mask."

Bai felt exposed while standing on the street with two armed men and a ski mask clasped in her hand. The avenue remained empty. If the local inhabitants noticed the strange activities, they showed remarkably good sense in minding their own business.

Jason stuffed one of the green canisters into the front pocket of his jacket where it made a large lump, ruining the lines in his tailored suit. He then closed the trunk and turned to walk across the street. Lee and Bai followed, still unsure of where they were going.

Wooden steps led to the veranda of an old Victorian. The porch wrapped around the house like a tattered shawl on an aged dowager. Columns, painted a faded pink, supported a frog-green overhang. Paint peeled and cracked to expose a patchwork of faded colors underneath.

Lee pushed a button next to a red door while Jason and Bai stepped back to remain out of sight. When nothing happened, he rang the bell again and pounded his fists against unyielding wood. Finally, a sleepy-eyed girl cracked the door. A heavy security chain kept the door from opening farther.

The girl was small, just over five feet, and Asian. She was pretty, despite the annoyed look on her face. She stared at Lee petulantly.

"I'm here for my date," he claimed.

The girl looked him up and down, bleary-eyed, before replying in broken English. "You too early. Come back later—four."

As she started to close the door, Lee put his foot in the opening and drew a money clip out of his pocket.

"I don't want to wait."

He held up the bankroll so she could see the hundred-dollar bills clearly. "I'll make it worth your while. After all, 'Wealth is but dung, useful only when spread.'"

The girl looked at him, then at the fat bankroll. He waved the money in front of her face. She seemed to waver.

Lee pressed her. "Show me a good time, and I'll let you have it all."

She shrugged nonchalantly, giving in to temptation, and closed the door far enough to release the chain. When she opened the door, Jason and Bai rushed in behind Lee, who already had his hand over the girl's mouth. She resisted for a moment then went still. Jason and Bai pulled on ski masks while Lee held the girl firmly in his grasp.

Stepping around the girl, Jason thrust the barrel of his pistol between her eyes and made a shushing gesture with his other hand. He jerked his head at Lee, who slowly removed his hand from the girl's mouth. When she didn't scream, Lee stepped away to pull on his own mask.

Jason pressed the silencer roughly against the girl's forehead. "Where is Sammy Tu?"

Tears rolled down the girl's cheeks "Not here."

Bai could see she was telling the truth. The girl was too scared to lie. She barked at her. "Do you know where he is?"

The girl jerked around at the sound of Bai's voice. Their hostage seemed to realize, for the first time, there was a woman behind the mask. She stared at Bai blankly before replying. "No, he tell me nothing."

Bai took the picture of Jia out of her pocket and showed it to the girl. "Have you seen her?"

The girl nodded her head frantically. "Yes, upstair, but Sammy take. Dunno where."

Bai looked at Lee, who then bolted up the stairs to check out the girl's story.

Jason grabbed the girl's jaw roughly and turned her head to look at him. "Is there someone else here who will know where he is?"

The girl's eyes drifted to the right. She was hiding something. Jason cocked the hammer on the revolver.

"Your choice," he whispered.

"No, wait," the girl pleaded. "Chan and Shen in basement—they maybe know where Sammy go."

Jason eased the hammer down on the revolver as he stared at the girl. "What are they doing in the basement?"

"Dunno. Off-limits."

Lee returned, taking the stairs two at a time. "The girl's telling the truth. The top floor's empty. But someone's been there recently. I found this."

It was a pink cell phone with the initials J and Y. Jia Yan's phone.

Jason spoke to the girl as he grabbed her roughly by the arm. "Take us to the basement."

The girl's head bounced up and down in agreement.

"Don't make a sound, and maybe you'll live," he added.

They passed through a dining room and a round table cluttered with dirty dishes and empty beer bottles. The room smelled of cheap perfume, rancid food, and cigarettes. On the far wall was a door leading to the back of the house. As they walked through the door to the kitchen, the girl nodded toward another door across the room, positioned next to an old, white enameled stove the size of a Buick. "Basement. Don' tell I rat."

Lee spoke to her comfortingly. "Don't worry. When we leave, you're going to go back to bed and forget we were ever here. You can tell them you slept through the whole thing."

The girl nodded enthusiastically.

"Stay with her," Jason said to Lee.

Jason turned and nodded to Bai before cautiously opening the door to the basement. He slipped swiftly and silently through the entry. She followed, dogging his footsteps as he moved rapidly down crude wooden steps.

Reaching the foot of the stairs, Bai stepped off onto soft soil. Light filtered down through cracks in the porch decking overhead. As she looked around, Bai realized the girl had been wrong in calling it a basement. It was a tall crawl space. The house was supported by thick brick columns eight feet high and spaced roughly ten feet apart.

Cautiously slipping around the stairwell with Jason, she spied a light at the far end of the crawl space near the back of the house. Two men, framed by the glow of an electric torch, held a conversation. One leaned against a brick column and talked, as the other man, standing knee-deep in the ground with a shovel in his hand, listened.

Jason motioned for her to stay behind him as he crept in the direction of the diggers. The ground rolled and swelled gently like waves on open water. The single bulb of the electric torch cast deep shadows, creating the impression the ground reached up to meet her. She concentrated on her footing while, at the same time, trying to keep an eye on the men under the light.

The man standing in the hole and leaning on a shovel saw them first. He picked the shovel up to point it at them and yelled, "Who are you?"

Jason ran forward to stab the barrel of his gun against the other man's head before the dazed gangster could figure out what was going on. Bai stood between the digger and the stairwell. She slipped the knife from the sheath on her arm. The digger froze. His eyes darted around furtively while his mouth hung slack.

Bai realized immediately the hole was a grave. Next to the grave lay a black plastic garment bag stuffed to the point of bursting. Her heart sank. She motioned for the grave digger to put down his shovel. When he'd tossed the potential weapon aside, she walked over to kneel down next to the garment bag and slit it open with her knife.

The stench of voided bowels made her head jerk back. The person stuffed in the bag was familiar. Standing up in shock, she took a step back and put a hand over the opening in her stocking cap to cover her mouth.

Bai motioned to the grave digger with her knife and took her hand from her mouth. "Sit down! And keep your hands in the air where I can see them."

Jason shoved his hostage toward the grave. He gestured with the barrel of his gun for the man to take a seat next to his friend. "Sit."

The gangsters did as they were told. Deep frowns etched their faces. Bai could empathize. She wasn't enamored of the situation either.

"Who's in the bag?" asked Jason.

"Mrs. Yan."

"I thought she went back to China."

"In spirit only, it would seem."

Bai's mind whirled with questions. She knew a mother's instincts to protect her young were strong and wondered what Mrs. Yan had gotten herself into. Did Jimmy Yan know his mother was dead? What had happened to Jia? The woman's death posed more questions than answers.

She caught Jason's eye and motioned in the direction of the men sitting in the partially dug grave. "Keep an eye on them for a minute. I need some time with Mrs. Yan."

He acknowledged her request with a nod then turned back to watch their prisoners. Bai returned to the garment bag with the sleeve of her leather jacket pressed against her nose. She sliced the bag wide open with her knife then tried to move Mrs. Yan's arm to the side. She wanted to see what kind of wounds, if any, the woman had suffered.

When she touched Mrs. Yan's clammy skin, she gagged. She had to hold down her bile as she pulled on the arm. The woman was stiff. Rigor had already advanced, which meant the woman had been killed more than three hours, but less than three days, ago. Bai's eyes were tearing as she tugged Mrs. Yan's arm away from the body.

The limb straightened but remained raised in the air in a final salute.

"Shit . . ." The word just escaped her lips.

Jason had ears like a bat. "What is it?"

It took her a moment to answer. "Mrs. Yan looks like a pincushion. Defensive wounds are on the insides of her arms as well as her hands. The wounds look shallow."

She forced herself to count the wounds that ranged from the area around the woman's upper thighs to her chest. She quit counting at thirty. Mrs. Yan had obviously fought her attacker. Somebody either really hated the woman, a reaction Bai found understandable, or was just a horribly incompetent killer.

She turned again to the two men sitting in the grave. "She must have fought like a demon. Who did this?"

Bai stood to walk over and confront the men. The grave diggers looked at one another and shook their heads, refusing to talk. She thought one of the men had coughed. The grave digger sitting in front grabbed his shoulder. Blood seeped from a small bullet hole. She turned to Jason, stunned.

He shrugged. "The lady asked a question. Answer her."

The wounded man's eyes were bright, tearing with pain. He cried, "We don't kill 'em. We just bury 'em."

Then it registered. Bai's eyes darted around the dark confines of the crawl space. Her voice sounded shrill in her ears. "It's a graveyard!"

Jason's stare caught her eye. He willed her to breathe, something she'd somehow forgotten to do. She put her hand up to acknowledge the unvoiced directive and took a deep breath.

Jason looked around at the rolling ground with a smile showing through his mask. "Sammy's been a busy, busy boy." He turned back to the grave diggers. "So, where is he?"

The wounded man glared at Jason and spit on the ground. Another cough. A small hole appeared in the man's forehead. He toppled face-down in the dirt.

Jason addressed the remaining prisoner. "You're going to have to dig that hole a little deeper." He pointed the gun at the man's head. "That is, unless you want to join your friend. If I were you, I'd start telling me everything you know about Sammy Tu."

Bai looked at Jason with her jaw agape. He'd just casually killed a man. She found herself uncharacteristically speechless.

The man, either Chan or Shen—not that it mattered—blurted out a confession: "Sammy drove a girl to Vancouver. He's going to auction her overseas. He left last night. He'll be back the day after tomorrow."

The man's eyes were like saucers, his face ashen. He trembled with fear.

Jason's voice was calm. He seemed almost disinterested. "Where in Vancouver?"

"I don't know. I really don't. I'd tell you if I knew."

Bai blurted out, "Who killed Mrs. Yan?"

The grave digger's head jerked around to look at her. "I don't know, lady. I got a call from Sammy this morning. He told me there was a body down here to bury. That's all I know."

"You don't know much," Jason said coldly.

The man turned to Jason and shrugged. Jason's gun coughed again. The grave digger toppled forward to lean against the back of his dead companion.

Jason and Bai were alone with the dead. She could feel their ghosts surrounding her. Clammy perspiration formed beneath her mask while a roaring in her ears left her deaf. Cold fear wrapped her in a coiled embrace then swallowed her whole.

chapter 7

Failure is not falling down
but refusing to get up

Bai panicked and ran. She stumbled in the loose dirt and went down on one knee as her fingers plunged into moist soil. Tears blurred her vision. She realized crying didn't make any sense. Then again, the death she'd witnessed didn't make any sense.

Jason was suddenly beside her. His hand gripped her arm, like a steel band, to lift and steer her as she blindly stumbled across the crawl space. She glanced back once as she careened toward the stairs. Under the electric torch, Mrs. Yan's arm stood aloft as if beckoning. The two dead gangsters slumped in the shallow grave in a lovers' embrace.

When she reached the stairwell, Bai angrily brushed off Jason's hand to bolt up the stairs. She scrambled to the top and lurched through the door. Lee looked up, startled. She ignored him as she ran to the sink and shoved aside a pile of dirty dishes. She held onto the edge of the counter with one hand while she pulled up her mask with the other to retch. Her body trembled.

When she finally looked up, Jason stood over her. He turned the faucet on. She put her shaky hand under the flow to scoop up cold water and rinse out her mouth, soaking her clothes in the process.

He spoke, his voice soft but compelling. "Be careful what you ask for."

She stopped rinsing long enough to look up at him.

His voice sounded sad. "You asked for my help. I helped you. That's what I do."

He stepped away to let her to reflect on his words,

Dish detergent sat on the edge of the counter. Bai slipped her knife into the sheath on her sleeve and poured soap into her hands. She scrubbed at them, determined to rub out the stench of death. As she rubbed her hands raw, flashes of the gangsters' deaths and Mrs. Yan's final gesture kept intruding. The lingering images haunted her.

Bai could hear Jason and Lee talking quietly behind her. She gritted her teeth and turned off the water before pulling down her mask. With no dishtowel in sight, she rubbed her hands on her jeans as she turned around.

She apologized for being such a girl. "Sorry."

Lee smiled behind his mask and shrugged off her apology.

Jason stared. His challenging gaze made her angry. Before she could say anything, he suddenly smiled and turned his attention to their hostage. The girl drew in on herself. Bai watched closely for fear he might shoot the young prostitute.

"There's been a change of plans," Jason said ominously. The girl's eyes widened. "You're going to go upstairs, wake everyone up and evacuate them through the back of the house. There is a back door, right?" He asked the question in a soothing voice, while waving the silenced gun in the girl's face. She nodded up and down like a bobble-head. "Good. You never saw us." He shook his head back and forth for emphasis. "We were never here."

The girl imitated him eagerly, her head swaying in unison with his.

"You smelled smoke," he added. "The front of the house was on fire." Jason mimicked flames by wiggling his fingers. "You ran upstairs to get everyone out of the house. You're a hero." His smile was triumphant.

The girl continued to stare stupidly at him as if mesmerized. He turned the girl around and shoved her in the direction of the door. "Now run, and do what I told you. But remember . . . we were never here!"

The girl glanced back once, fearfully. When she realized Jason didn't plan to shoot her, she bolted. Jason took the green canister out of his pocket, pulled the pin, and tossed it down the stairwell. A sharp bang erupted accompanied by the crackling of wood.

"Time to leave," Jason said as he shepherded Lee and Bai toward the door. "That was an incendiary grenade. In about ten minutes this whole house will be an inferno."

Lee and Bai didn't need further encouragement. They sprinted for the front door. By the time they reached the car, flames licked at the front porch. Layers of crusted paint acted as an accelerant, like gas on dry tinder. Fire spilled across the veranda to engulf the front of the house.

Jason drove away from the conflagration calmly, while pulling the balaclava over his head and running his hand through tousled hair. Lee and Bai followed his example, pulling the masks off and discarding them.

Lee leaned forward from the backseat to speak with Bai. "What did you find in the basement?"

"It wasn't a basement. It was a crawl space." Her voice was raspy from the acid bile. She pulled a stick of gum out of her pocket, unwrapped it, and chewed. "They were using it for a graveyard."

Lee's eyebrows shot up in surprise. "No way!"

"We found Mrs. Yan down there," she added.

Her revelation brought back the image of Mrs. Yan. She lost her train of thought and her heart skipped a beat.

"Holy shit," he mumbled.

"Yeah . . . holy shit," she replied tiredly.

"What else?"

She looked aside at Jason. She wasn't sure how much to divulge. He refused to look at her. "That's all there was," she offered lamely. "It seemed like enough at the time."

She turned around in her seat to meet Lee's gaze. His disbelieving stare questioned her. He always seemed to know when she was lying.

"It would seem that things are about to get interesting," Lee said. "What do you think will happen when the fire department puts out the flames and discovers a body in the rubble?"

She wanted to correct him: *bodies*. Instead, she kept her mouth shut, turned around, and closed her eyes until Jason's voice interrupted her jumbled thoughts.

"Mrs. Yan's body will be burned beyond recognition. It will take weeks, if not months, to identify the remains. If they start digging, they'll find more bodies. It'll become apparent the deaths are gang related. At which point, the police will make things very difficult for Sammy Tu and the *Wah Ching*."

When Bai opened her eyes, she saw that Jason was smiling, happy at the thought of Sammy Tu's problems.

Lee posed a question to Bai. "And what about the girl?"

She couldn't tell him that Jia had been smuggled out of the country without revealing how she'd gotten the information. He would see through any lie she told. Instead, she shook her head and covered her face with her hands. She wasn't prepared to deal with the callous murders in the crawl space. She was still trying to get her head wrapped around the needless violence.

Jason spoke without turning to look at her. "Tell him, Bai."

She turned to look at Jason. He continued to ignore her. She spoke softly. "Two *Wah Ching* were in the basement burying Mrs. Yan. They told us that Sammy Tu has taken Jia to Vancouver to sell overseas."

Lee put his face between the seats again to stare at her in surprise. "You left two men in the basement to burn alive?"

"No," she replied tiredly, leaving it at that.

Lee was silent as he mulled over the information. He turned to Jason. "No prisoners?"

Jason's reply was indifferent. "No prisoners."

Lee sat slowly back in his seat. After a short while, he asked, "Why Vancouver? And why sell the girl overseas?"

"Simple," explained Jason. "She's too close to home in Oakland. She might escape and find help. In Vancouver, they'll sell her off to Asia or the Middle East. There's always a market for young girls. She'll end up somewhere she doesn't speak the language and has no friends—a slave."

"Are we going after her?" asked Lee.

Bai wasn't sure how to respond. She wanted to go after the girl, but she found herself momentarily overwhelmed. Her cases typically involved finding someone who didn't want to be found—a runaway or a deadbeat dad. This was her first foray into the slave trade. It wasn't going well.

Her answer was feeble and she knew it. "We need to talk about it."

She stalled for time, trying to figure out what to do.

Ignoring her indecision, Lee plowed on. "I think we should go after her. 'Failure is not falling down but refusing to get up.'"

His tone challenged her. She didn't have the energy to argue.

"People are dying," she said in her own defense.

"Bad people are dying, Bai," Lee asserted. "That doesn't alter the fact there's a young girl out there who's in for a life of misery if we don't help her."

She nodded in sympathy. She understood what was at stake.

Her cell phone rang. She didn't recognize the number. When she answered, a very officious voice asked, "Mrs. Jiang?"

She corrected the caller. "Miss Jiang."

"I see . . ." said the voice. "This is Mr. Ketchum, provost at Darryl Hopkins."

Her insides went cold. "Has something happened to Dan?"

"No. Dan is fine. The boy she assaulted, however, will require stitches. I think it would be best if we met, Miss Jiang. We need to discuss your daughter's behavior."

She put her hand to her forehead. "I'm about an hour away. Will around two o'clock be convenient for you, Mr. Ketchum?"

"I'm looking forward to meeting you, Miss Jiang."

She closed her phone to end the call. Both Lee and Jason stared at her. "Dan's fine. She beat up a boy."

Lee looked concerned. Jason smiled.

Bai had never named Dan's father. All you had to do was look at Dan and Jason to see the resemblance. She'd inherited his handsome features and, obviously, her quick temper.

"The principal wants to see me." Her words sounded ludicrous after the events of the last hour.

Jason looked aside to smile at her. "Weren't you about Dan's age when you first beat me up?"

She couldn't help but return his smile at the memory, "You deserved it. You pulled my ponytail."

"I couldn't help myself," Jason said in his own defense. "I was in love."

The look he bestowed on her said he still was.

chapter 8

There are always ears
on the other side of the wall

Lee and Jason bracketed Bai as she entered Darryl Hopkins. Arched double doors opened onto an entry hall in the red-brick, deco-styled building. A security desk fanned around the narrow corridor to corral unsuspecting visitors. The only way past the kiosk was through a metal detector.

Two uniformed guards waited behind the desk. They scrutinized Bai and her entourage as she approached. The inspection seemed professional. The faces of the men showed practiced detachment.

"My name is Bai Jiang. I'm here for my daughter."

One of the guards took a small step back, and his hand lifted to rest on the holstered pistol at his side. The other guard smiled tightly and picked up a clipboard off the counter. The guards moved with a precision that indicated training, probably military. Her opinion of them bumped up a notch.

The guard in front pushed the visitor registration sheet across the desk in her direction. "If you'll sign in please, Ms. Jiang. And these gentlemen are . . . ?"

The guard left the question hanging as he eyed Lee and Jason.

She glanced back before answering. "They're my security."

Parents at Darryl Hopkins included diplomats, politicians, the rich, and the very rich. Many of them maintained their own security. Jason and Lee looked the part.

The guard nodded his head in acceptance of her claim. "No weapons are permitted beyond this point." The guard spoke as he turned to open a gun safe at his back. "Any weapons you're carrying will be returned when you leave."

He held his hand out, palm up, and waited.

Lee pulled his Tomcat from his shoulder holster and handed it over. Jason lifted a 9mm from the small of his back, a snubnosed .38 off his ankle, and a throwing knife off of each wrist. The guard eyed the knives speculatively as he deposited them in the weapons case.

Bai removed the blade from her wrist sheath and reluctantly handed it to the guard, who, for the first time, showed surprise. He recovered quickly to issue directions. "If you'll step through the metal detector, Mr. Ketchum and our head of security are waiting for you in the administration offices. The door is down the hallway on your right."

They passed through the plastic stanchions of the metal detector without incident and continued down the empty corridor. The black and white marble on the floor showed wear. The paneling on the walls displayed a patina wood only acquires with age. The building dated from the thirties and had originally served as a fashionable apartment complex before being converted to a private school.

Black lettering on a glass-paneled door informed Bai she'd arrived at the administration offices. She opened the door to find a deserted lobby. The room was spartan. Four backless couches on a polished cement floor hugged the walls. An institutional odor, a combination of stale coffee, ink toner, and moldy building, permeated the air.

Loud voices issued from an inner office. She stopped to listen while Jason and Lee stood in the open doorway at her back. A disembodied voice yelled, "You can't pretend the video doesn't exist."

The reply was conciliatory. "And what would you have me do? This school can't afford a lawsuit."

"I won't allow it, Ketchum. I'm still the head of security at this school and I'm not destroying evidence just to make your job easier. This recording proves the girl is innocent."

"You know that child's background as well as I do. Innocence and guilt are a matter of perception. You just need to do what you're told and let me run this school."

Bai walked over to the door with "PROVOST" lettered in gold on frosted glass. She twisted the knob to fling the door open. Arms held rigidly at her sides, she surveyed the office as a strained hush fell over the room. Two men stood behind a large desk, their expressions frozen in surprise.

A muscle in Bai's cheek twitched. Her nails dug into the palms of her fisted hands. "It's important to remember, gentlemen," she said with venom in her voice, "'there are always ears on the other side of the wall.' And, since you're well aware of my daughter's background, I'm sure you're also mindful I'm not the kind of mother you want to fuck with."

The threat wasn't subtle. The two men facing her stood in stunned silence. Lee and Jason stepped into the room to stand at her side.

Recovering first, the younger of the two men stepped around the desk to greet her with his hand extended. "Miss Jiang, my name's John Race, head of security here at Hopkins. It's a pleasure to meet you. This is Walter Ketchum, our provost."

He introduced the older gentleman, who nodded at her and muttered a brief, "Pleasure," before seating himself behind his desk. He looked as if he'd bitten into something bitter. Bai hoped it was cyanide. She ignored Race's outstretched hand and turned her full attention on the provost.

"Tell me about the recording."

Her eyes bored holes into Walter Ketchum.

Ketchum remained silent as he turned his head to look at Race. Bai watched the interplay with interest. Race shook his head discreetly in denial, a gesture that in turn elicited an angry glare from Ketchum. Red crept slowly up the provost's neck until it covered his face like a bad rash. He continued to stare malevolently at Race until finally, he tossed up his hands. "I was hasty in calling you, Miss Jiang," he blurted out. "We hadn't reviewed the digital recordings before I made the call. It's now evident your daughter was not at fault. She was acting in self-defense. The video clearly shows a case of bullies getting exactly what they deserved."

"I want my daughter brought to me immediately, and I want to see the recording."

A shadow seemed to drop over Ketchum's face. His features became unreadable. He then looked at her in cold evaluation before turning to Race. "If you'll escort Dan to my office, I think that would be best."

She turned to look at Lee and nodded. He understood and turned on his heel to follow Race.

"My security will accompany Mr. Race," she said to Ketchum.

He started to object, but the sound died in his throat when he met Bai's gaze. "Certainly."

The rejoinder seeped out of him as his shoulders slumped. He seemed to deflate as he leaned back into his chair.

She looked around the room. "Where are the boys who were involved?"

Ketchum answered sullenly. "They've been sent home. One required stitches to the inside of his mouth. The other boy was simply shaken by the incident. In hindsight, I suspect he was more frightened of the truth coming to light." He placed a hand over his brow and drew it down his face. "I'm truly sorry for any distress this incident has caused you and your daughter."

Given the circumstances, Bai viewed the apology as a hollow gesture. "Sorry enough to destroy evidence and conceal the truth?"

Her response silenced the provost.

When Dan entered the office, Lee held her hand. Dan smiled when she saw her mother and ran over to hug her. She then stepped around Bai to give Jason a hug. Jason turned his daughter around and put his hands on her shoulders protectively.

Dan was twelve, tall for her age and already a beauty. Long black hair framed a heart-shaped face set off by almond-brown eyes. Every time she looked at her daughter, Bai was reminded of how precious the girl was.

Bai kept her voice light. "We were about to watch a video of your fight with the two boys. Perhaps you could help us understand what happened."

"Sure." Dan seemed outwardly unfazed by the altercation. "But it wasn't much of a fight."

Race swiveled the monitor on Ketchum's desk so they could view the digital recording. The picture on the video was crystal clear. The school obviously employed high-resolution cameras that had captured the scene in full color and graphic detail.

Dan stood in the corridor. Two boys approached. Words were exchanged.

Race paused the recording and turned to Dan. "What are they saying to you, Dan?"

"They kept talking about how I didn't belong here, something about mud people."

Bai intervened. "We'll talk about that later."

She felt it would be better to discuss racial hatred in the privacy of their home where she'd have the time to deal with the delicate subject. Dan was a curious girl and full of questions. Bai wasn't looking forward to the conversation.

Race started the recording again with a pained expression on his face. Words escalated to shoving as the two boys pushed at Dan, one on each side of her. For a moment, all Bai saw was red, her anger so intense she felt the heat of it on her face.

She turned to Jason, who held Dan securely from behind. When she met his gaze, her own anger evaporated out of dread.

Bai turned quickly back to watch the monitor.

One of the boys drew back a fist to strike Dan, who surprised him by stepping inside his swing to use the flat of her palm to strike him under the chin while placing a leg behind his, a maneuver that slammed the boy to the checkered floor. The second boy took a wild swing at her back but met her foot as he stepped forward. The back kick caught him squarely in the mouth.

"Nice form," Lee said, taking pride in her textbook-perfect moves. He was her teacher, her *shifu*.

"Thank you," Dan replied, with a shy smile.

Race offered her more praise. "Nice form, indeed."

"So, we have a hate crime." Bai made the statement as the video played out, her tone matter-of-fact.

Ketchum took offense at the remark. "These are just children, Miss Jiang. I think 'hate crime' is a bit too harsh for what took place."

She looked from Ketchum to Race. "Two boys assaulted my daughter at her school while verbally abusing her with racial slurs. I'm not sure what you'd call it if not a hate crime. If there aren't any consequences for their actions, who's to say they won't do it again? Has a police report been filed?"

Ketchum blustered, "We didn't think it was necessary."

Bai stared at Race. "Who is 'we'?"

He shook his head in denial, and Ketchum backtracked. "Let me amend that. I didn't think it was necessary."

She pulled her cell phone from the pocket of her jacket to call the police. She reported the incident, provided an address for the school, and asked for an officer to respond.

Ketchum stared at her, his expression resigned but oddly defiant. "I should warn you. The instigator of this fight is Anthony Romano, John Romano's son. I hope you know with whom you're dealing, Miss Jiang."

John Romano was a prominent San Francisco attorney with ties to big money. He'd been courted as a conservative candidate for State Attorney General, who professed to be "tough on crime."

Bai shrugged. "John Romano might be an important man with powerful friends," she turned to look at Jason as she continued in a conversational tone, "but I'm fairly certain the same laws that protect Mr. Romano also protect my daughter. For now, let's put our faith in the justice system and wait to see what happens."

Jason met her gaze steadily for several long moments before slowly nodding once in reluctant agreement. His response elicited a sigh of relief that involuntarily escaped her, a breath she hadn't even realized she'd been holding.

chapter 9

Judge not the horse by his saddle

Bai pulled John Race aside to talk in confidence. "I'd like you to burn me a copy of the video."

He looked perplexed by the request. "Is there any particular reason you feel that you'll need a copy?"

He'd posed the question softly while keeping an eye on Ketchum, who viewed them with suspicion from across the room.

"It's just in case the original should somehow get misplaced," she replied.

Race drew a deep breath then looked over Bai's shoulder at Ketchum, and frowned. "Sure, why not? My time here is probably short-lived. There's a good chance I'll be looking for a job before the day is over."

She considered his comment while scrutinizing his face. She liked what she saw. Her hand reached for one of her cards in her jacket pocket. "This is my number. Call me if you need work. I might be in the market for some added security. If you're interested, that is."

He took the card and smiled at the Chinese characters. "What does it say?"

"It says I'm a *souxun*. It means people finder. I'm an investigator, of sorts."

"I'm definitely interested," he affirmed. He looked at Bai and smiled warmly. "If I'm not looking for work, can I still call you?"

He was flirting with her. His smile was nice, and he was good-looking in a blond, Ivy League kind of way—tall, muscular, and boyishly handsome. That he took an interest in her meant he was either reckless or poorly informed. She looked aside at Jason to see if he was aware of the attention she was receiving. He was.

"You're impulsive," she said with a wry smile "which isn't bad in and of itself. I have a tendency to be a little impulsive as well. But you should know being around me can be dangerous, Mr. Race."

Race turned his attention to Jason and Lee. "You do keep dangerous company."

His observation caught her by surprise. "How so?"

"I used to be a soldier, Miss Jiang. I've spent a lot of time around dangerous individuals. Warriors develop an economy of movement and their eyes never stop moving. They place themselves, wherever they are, with the thought of cover and egress. Both of those men are certainly competent. The one in the black suit has trained assassin written all over him."

She felt the need to defend Jason, perhaps out of habit. "He's only dangerous to his enemies. Keep that in mind, Mr. Race."

"I'll definitely keep that in mind, Miss Jiang. But you still haven't answered my question."

She studied him. He didn't show any sign of discomfort at her bold appraisal. His smile widened.

"Call me and see if I answer."

They continued to stare at one another.

He broke eye contact first. "If you'll excuse me, I have a CD to burn."

After Race had left the room, Ketchum excused himself. Bai had a pretty good idea the provost would be making some urgent calls. She suspected that John Romano was about to have an unpleasant discussion in which her name would serve prominently.

Race returned almost immediately and managed to slip Bai the video while Ketchum was still out of the room. She thanked him and handed the disc to Lee for safekeeping. As she was making the hand-off, she heard an unfamiliar voice from behind.

"I'm looking for a Bai Jiang."

"That would be me," she affirmed as she turned around.

The man in the doorway was tall and stoop-shouldered. He wore an old tan raincoat with a torn pocket and too many stains to count. Heavy brogue shoes, scuffed and beaten, matched his face—a face that looked like it might have gone a few rounds before its owner found he preferred alcohol to fisticuffs. Dark, puffy rings under heavily lidded eyes brought to mind a cagey raccoon. A beefy paw swallowed Bai's hand as he introduced himself. "I'm Inspector Robert Kelly. I'm here to investigate a hate crime."

"I wouldn't expect a crime of this nature to rate an inspector," she stated.

"The mayor's placed a priority on hate crimes. That and a misunderstanding between myself and my captain has resulted in my presence here today."

"It must have been some misunderstanding," she observed dryly.

"Ah … well, it seems that the captain's mother wasn't his mother after all—but his wife. And though I'll admit to being under the influence of drink at the time, no amount of Jameson's would have altered my perception to the extent I'd have come to any other rational conclusion. The last, in no way, excuses my having said as much, mind you. My remarks can definitely be attributed to the whiskey. It has a tendency to unleash my tongue and let it wander about aimlessly to leave embarrassing messes behind."

She nodded her head in understanding. Kelly had been banished to the purgatory of hate crimes because he was a garrulous boozer.

She got down to business. "It was my daughter who was attacked. There's a video documenting the assault if you'd care to see it."

Kelly's eyes tracked around the room until they came to rest on Jason. A barely audible grunt escaped his lips. "How do you play in this, Lum?"

Jason was known to the SFPD. They'd never found reason to charge him with anything, but they had plenty of reason to suspect him. He was on their watch list of suspected gang figures. But then, so was Bai. Her file just wasn't as noteworthy.

"I'm a friend of the family," Jason replied.

He wouldn't place the onus on Dan of having him as a father. The relationship was far too dangerous. For her part, Dan was well schooled in the deception. She smiled up at him but said nothing.

Kelly didn't look happy with the answer. A scowl managed to further distort his features. He turned his back on Jason to address Bai. "So we have a juvenile assault, I take it?"

Race answered before she could respond. "That's correct. Dan was assaulted after being verbally abused."

"And who might you be?" the inspector asked brusquely.

"My name's John Race. I'm the head of school security." He offered his hand to the inspector.

"You must be proud." The inspector ignored the proffered hand. "What kind of qualifications do you need to be a kiddy cop around here?"

Race dropped his hand to his side slowly. "I can't speak for my staff, but I was deployed for three tours with Special Forces before being assigned to Quantico to train federal agents."

The inspector nodded his head once and sighed deeply. "I apologize for my wagging tongue. You can't say I didn't warn you." He waited for Race to silently accept his apology with a nod before continuing. "If you have this thing on video, let's see it. I feel another demotion coming on."

Bai stepped over to stand next to Jason and Dan while Race led the inspector forward to view the video. The room was silent as the recording played out. Kelly laughed out loud at the part where Dan took both boys to the floor. When it was finished, he turned around with a sober expression.

Just then, Ketchum returned to interrupt whatever it was Kelly was about to say. The provost introduced himself.

Afterward, Kelly asked in a gruff voice, "So, what part of this is a hate crime?"

Bai spoke up. "Racial slurs and threats were delivered prior to the assault. My daughter can give you the particulars."

Kelly turned to look at Dan. For the first time, his demeanor grew respectful. "Do you feel up to doing that now, young lady?"

Dan looked to Bai for reassurance.

"Just tell the inspector what you told us, Dan."

Kelly took a small digital voice recorder from his pocket and pushed the "start" button. He began the interview by stating the date and time and asking each of those present to identify themselves. Dan then repeated what the boys had said to her to the best of her recollection. When she'd done so, the inspector concluded the recording and turned off the device.

"Well, it seems there's no doubt this constitutes a hate crime." His attitude had become reflective. "There are a couple of ways we can handle this, seeing as how the perpetrators are juveniles. If they were adults, we would simply arrest them. Because of their age, we might, instead, have their parents bring them down to the juvenile authority for booking."

The inspector pushed his tongue against the inside of his lower lip as he gazed at Bai. He seemed to want some assurance his restrained tactics wouldn't meet with her opposition. She was well aware the offenders were children. At the same time, she didn't want to make light of the crime and have it swept away to be forgotten.

"My daughter was assaulted. I want your assurance the boys will be booked into juvenile hall and charged."

"Of that I can assure you," Kelly stated emphatically. "With this video on record there isn't a district attorney in this town who would let these boys slide."

She subtly nodded in acceptance. "I hope you're right about that, Inspector."

Kelly turned to Ketchum without commenting. "I'll need the contact information for the two boys as well as the video of the assault."

Ketchum stalled and puffed out his chest in indignation. "I'm sorry. I can't provide that information. Our school policy is to ensure anonymity to our students as a matter of security. You'll need a search warrant."

Kelly eyed the pompous administrator tiredly.

"I've got a better idea. Since you're interfering with a criminal investigation, I'll just arrest you. A couple of hours in the drunk tank keeping company with perverts who like to puke on expensive-looking shoes like yours should bring you around."

Ketchum looked offended. "You wouldn't dare."

"Just try me."

Kelly delivered his ultimatum wearily, as if he'd said it a thousand times before. The standoff turned into a staring contest. Ketchum looked insulted while the inspector just looked bored.

Finally, Ketchum capitulated. "Very well," he conceded. "I guess there's no point in unnecessarily delaying the matter. I have the names, addresses, and numbers for the two boys in the database. I'll have them for you in a second."

He walked around his desk to print the information. When the printer spooled out the paper, he handed the document to the inspector along with the DVD of the assault.

Kelly stopped to read the names on the paper. "This isn't by any chance John Romano's son, is it?"

"Would it make a difference?" Bai asked.

The inspector looked down at the paper again and shook his head dismally. "I'll pass this on to the DA's office directly, Miss Jiang. And then I'm going to go out, get drunk, and try to forget I was ever here."

"I know you'll do the right thing, Inspector."

"I don't turn the wheels of justice. I am but a lowly servant of the law," the cop answered stoically.

"'Judge not the horse by his saddle,'" Bai observed as he stepped past her.

The big cop stopped just short of the door and turned back to look at her.

"Come again?" he asked.

"I suspect there's more to you than meets the eye, Inspector. I'm putting my faith in you."

"You wouldn't be the first woman I've disappointed," he said with an air of regret before slipping out the door.

chapter 10

You don't punish a dog
by hitting him with a meat bun

Dan spoke softly. "I don't get it, Lee. I don't know those boys except to maybe see them in the hall during passing period. I've never even talked to them before today."

Bai sat in the front of the car with Jason while Dan and Lee occupied the back. Bai leaned back into the soft leather of her seat to eavesdrop. She knew Dan would open up to Lee. He was her sounding board, her closest friend.

When he replied, his voice held sympathy. "Sometimes, there's no rational explanation for the way people act. Fear, prejudice, and hate are all part of the same package. It isn't pleasant, and it doesn't necessarily make sense. Sometimes, it is what it is—a stupid, senseless act."

Dan wasn't so easily mollified. "But those boys aren't stupid. What makes them want to hurt other people? Why me?"

"Maybe it's because you're beautiful and smart and fearless," he offered. After a short while, he asked, "Have you heard of anyone else being bullied at school?"

"No," Dan replied. Her voice sounded angry. "But that doesn't mean anything. If someone gets bullied, they're not going to talk about it. It's embarrassing." Her confession was delivered in a barely audible voice. "I just don't understand why they acted like such jerks."

"You shouldn't be embarrassed," he counseled. "The behavior of those two boys probably has nothing to do with you. You were likely just a target of opportunity. Their victim might just as easily have been one of your classmates."

Bai was about to turn around and offer her opinion when Dan spoke up, her voice filled with resentment. "While I was waiting for

Mom to pick me up, Mr. Ketchum acted like it was my fault. I tried to explain, but he wouldn't listen. He's such a turd."

Jason pulled up in front of Bai's building and hit the brakes. The conversation, along with the car, jarred to a halt.

Bai could sense Jason's anger. She turned in her seat to face him. "Are you coming up?"

He jerked his head once in response but didn't speak.

Dan made an appeal from the backseat. "*Mah Mah* will want to see you. Please, Daddy?"

Mah Mah meant "grandma" and referred to Jason's mother, Elizabeth, who lived with Bai.

Shortly after the death of Bai's parents, Elizabeth had been employed as her live-in governess. Being a widow, she'd brought her son, Jason, to live with her. In a sense, Bai and Jason shared the same mother.

Jason turned in his seat to speak with his daughter. "Perhaps another time, Dan. There are some things I need to take care of first, things that can't wait."

Dan turned to stare at Bai in a silent appeal. The hard set of Jason's features informed Bai it was a lost cause. He hadn't visited his mother in two years. Neither Elizabeth nor he would divulge the reason for their breach.

"Let's agree to let Jason go," Bai suggested. "He'll visit soon. Won't you, Jason?"

"I'll try to make time," he said as he smiled reassuringly at Dan. "I promise."

The promise seemed to appease Dan. She leaned forward to hug her father from behind and plant a kiss on his cheek. Bai glimpsed a brief glimmer of what might have been regret on Jason's face when Dan unwrapped her arms.

As Dan exited the car through the back door, Jason turned to look directly at Bai. "I'll call you later." He then turned his head and spoke over his shoulder to Lee, who had one foot out of the door of the car. "Take care of them."

"As always," Lee replied, before stepping out of the sedan and closing the door.

Bai glanced guardedly at Jason as she pushed open the passenger side door. His face remained passive. As soon as she closed the door, he pulled away from the curb. Her arm rose to wave good-bye before she caught herself and dropped her hand to her side. The impulsive gesture embarrassed her. She turned while shaking her head in silent rebuke to walk up the concrete steps of her home.

She stepped through the glass door to the foyer. Lee and Dan waited for her. The entry was small with a white marble floor and walls painted a stark white. Shiny brass doors belonging to the elevator were to the right. Brass mailboxes lined the wall opposite the entry. To the left was a white steel door that led to Lee's apartment.

The three-story brick building had been gutted by fire. Bai had purchased the burned-out shell and renovated it from the ground up. The top floor was now a luxury apartment shared by Bai, Dan, and Elizabeth. The second story was a private dojo. The bottom floor had a four-car garage facing the back alley and a smaller apartment up front, occupied by Lee.

Bai placed her thumb on the elevator touchpad while shifting around to face Lee. Like all of the security in the building, the elevator lock was a biometric device that scanned her thumbprint. "Shall we meet in the dojo?" She stepped into the elevator and held down the "open" button while she spoke to him. "I could really use a chance to blow off some steam. It's been a strange day."

"Why not," he responded. "A workout might be good for both of us. Can you give me about twenty minutes?"

"Sure, that'll give me time to explain things to Elizabeth. She won't like that I called Jason. And since there's no keeping it a secret, I might as well tell her now and get it over with."

"Good luck with that."

He smiled knowingly and turned to step through the door to his apartment. Bai pushed the "close" button on the elevator door and leaned against the dark wood paneling. Dan stood next to her quietly.

Bai's stomach growled, demanding attention. She put her hand on her abdomen to quell the rebellion. Dan gave her a withering look, a reminder her child was turning into a teenager.

"So embarrassing," sniped Dan.

Bai curled her lip at her daughter and raised her fist in mock anger. Dan rolled her eyes and pretended her mother was invisible. As the doors to the elevator opened, Dan ran past her in the direction of the kitchen. She followed at a more sedate pace, letting her nose lead her. The scent of five-spice pork acted as an irresistible lure.

When she entered the kitchen, she found Dan with her arms wrapped around Elizabeth's tiny waist. The woman was only slightly taller than her granddaughter but exuded a natural elegance that made her seem larger in stature. In her early fifties, she had shoulder-length hair, still black and lustrous, that framed strong features. Her lips were full and shaped like a cupid's bow, her eyes large and brown.

Bai walked over to sit on a stool at the breakfast bar while Dan regaled her grandmother with her adventures at school. Elizabeth listened attentively, providing exclamations of surprise and sounds of approval at the appropriate times. Watching them, Bai recalled her grandfather's house and how Elizabeth had listened to Bai's exploits with the same gentle enthusiasm. It seemed like only yesterday.

When her daughter grew quiet, Bai intervened. "Perhaps you could do your homework before dinner. I need to speak with *Mah Mah* alone."

Dan nodded her head in reluctant acceptance and gave her grandmother a final hug before departing.

Elizabeth waited until Dan was out of earshot before speaking. "So, I hear Jason is involved."

Her implied rebuke came without preamble.

Bai braced herself. "What have you heard?"

"The aunties have been calling all day. Is it true that you got into a fight at the Far East Café? Everybody's saying you assaulted a bunch of young hoodlums and had to call on *Sun Yee On* to bail you out. What's gotten into you?"

"I'm looking for a missing girl, one of Mrs. Yan's children. Her brother sold her to the *Wah Ching*, who took her to Canada to sell overseas. It's possible I'll be leaving tonight for Vancouver."

"And the fight at the café?"

"They started it!"

Even to her, her voice sounded defensive, a juvenile response. It was the same excuse she'd used as a child. Caught off guard by Bai's spontaneous reaction, Elizabeth laughed. Bai could feel the heat of embarrassment on her face as she tried to shrug off the feeble justification.

"Some things never change," Elizabeth chided.

Elizabeth turned away to tend something on the stove.

Bai addressed her back. "Jason's helping me."

Elizabeth didn't turn around. "Is he well?"

"He appears to be well," Bai said, "but I have no way of really knowing. He only lets me see what he wants me to see."

The back of Elizabeth's head nodded to let Bai know she'd heard.

"I asked him to help me get the girl back."

Elizabeth ignored Bai's remark, moving on to another topic. "Was he with you at the school today?"

Bai hesitated. "Yes."

"Reason with him. Don't let him take matters into his own hands."

"I'm handling it. I promise."

Elizabeth turned around. She looked skeptical, one side of her mouth drawing up as she gazed at Bai. "The way you 'handle' him is to bribe him with sex. 'You don't punish a dog by hitting him with a meat bun.'"

Elizabeth huffed out a breath of frustration before turning back to busy herself with dinner, shoving pans around the stovetop as if they'd somehow offended her. Bai waited patiently, aware that Elizabeth wasn't finished with her. When Elizabeth spoke again, her words were more tempered. "He's changed. He's become like his father."

"In what way?" Bai asked.

Elizabeth stopped punishing kitchen utensils long enough to turn and face her. "His father was handsome and dangerous. He didn't know when to be afraid. Or perhaps it was fear that drove him." Her voice sounded distracted as she continued. "Sometimes I think that man rushed toward death as if he were impatient with life and in a hurry to get it over with. It makes me angry. He gave no thought to his wife or son. And now, I see the same man in Jason."

Bai mulled over Elizabeth's words. "He does seem to live for the thrill."

"Yes, just like his father. That's why I don't want you around him, Bai. It isn't safe."

The day's events had shown that to be true. But, in Bai's mind, Jason was still the boy she'd fallen in love with. She didn't want to believe he was lost to her forever. Besides, she rationalized, she still needed his help to find Jia Yan.

"If I leave Lee here with you, can you manage for a day or two?"

Elizabeth stared sadly at her before shrugging. "Don't worry about us. Dan and I will be fine. Do what you need to do." A resigned smile settled onto her face. "I hope you get the girl back safely. I really do."

"I hope so, too. It won't be easy finding her in Vancouver. Jason's working on locating her now."

Elizabeth's voice held a note of reluctant pride. "If anyone can find her, Jason will."

Bai changed the subject. "It might be a good idea to keep Dan home tomorrow."

"Why?"

"I want her safe until I have time to sort out the matter at school. I no longer trust the security at Darryl Hopkins to protect her."

Elizabeth nodded in agreement. "I'm sure she'll enjoy a holiday. And since Lee will be here, she'll be well entertained."

Bai flinched at the thought. "Not too well entertained, I hope. The last time those two went out together they ended up with matching outfits. I think Lee is living out his second childhood with Dan."

Elizabeth chuckled. "Well, we both know there's no controlling Lee."

"I'm going down to the gym to work off some of my frustration. Is Lee invited to dinner?"

"Yes. Tell him I've steamed fresh *shumai*."

The mention of *shumai* got Bai's attention. "Any chance I might get a small sample? I haven't eaten today."

Elizabeth smiled knowingly and turned to open a steamer on the counter. She placed two of the fatty, noodle-wrapped pork dumplings on a napkin and handed them to Bai. "Don't be too long. Dinner will be ready in less than an hour. And be careful. Those are hot."

Bai bit into the first dumpling. The hot pork burned her tongue and the roof of her mouth as the seasoned meat inundated her senses. She sucked cool air into her mouth and chortled in painful pleasure as she turned to leave.

Elizabeth scolded at her back, "You never take my warnings seriously."

It wasn't true. Bai did take Elizabeth's warnings seriously. But in the case of Jason, a little girl's life was at stake. She needed his help. If getting burned again was the price of finding Jia Yan, she'd willingly pay it.

chapter 11

When testing the depths of a stream, don't use both feet

A red neoprene foot flew at Bai's face. With no time to get out of the way, she tucked her arms against the side of her head like a boxer and relaxed the muscles in her legs. When the kick landed against the side of her head, she reeled to the ground and rolled with the force of the blow, letting the momentum carry her out of Lee's reach.

"Shit!" she said, as she rolled back to her feet.

The blow had stung in spite of the neoprene pad on Lee's foot.

"Hurts, I'll bet," he observed wryly.

She could see him smiling inside his sparring helmet. His smugness served as a goad.

He backed off a few paces to give her room as he scolded her. "You committed too soon. Just remember, 'When testing the depths of a stream, don't use both feet.'"

It was her "kamikaze" style of fighting Lee derided. She didn't have the size or upper-body strength to trade punches with a man his size. She relied, instead, on speed and stealth. But, as usual, her impatience had turned out to be her downfall—literally. She'd telegraphed her intentions and given him time to counter her move.

"Keep smiling, Dorothy," she said as she slapped her red sparring gloves together. "I'm about to smack you so hard you'll fly back to Kansas without your ruby shoes."

He opened his mouth to offer a reply. She rushed forward to feint by dropping her left and then her right shoulder before pivoting into a spin kick. He moved to the right in an attempt to block what he expected to be a left hook. Her spin kick landed on his left ear.

The impact didn't fell him, but it knocked him off balance long enough for her to follow the impetus of her kick. She whipped around to duck inside his drooping guard and land a flurry of rabbit punches to his chest. Her foot swept his ankle as she elbowed his ribs to knock him off balance.

In a last-ditch effort, Lee hooked an arm around Bai's neck. He took her down to the mat with him in an uncontrolled fall. She dropped down on top of him with her full weight. He grunted in pain.

Then, there was silence.

"That . . . was . . . really, really . . . smart," she stated.

Her sarcastic comment was muffled by neoprene. Lee's headlock had twisted her headgear around. She peeked out through an ear hole in the side of the soft helmet.

"Not one of my finer moments," he agreed. "Sometimes my instincts just suck."

He attempted to push her off him. "Are you getting heavier, or is it my imagination?"

She rolled to the mat to glare at him. "I might have gained a few pounds . . . mostly muscle."

Her assertion was delivered with a challenging stare. He stared back. She could almost see the rejoinders running through his head.

"Say it and I'll hurt you."

"I was just about to compliment you on your amazing muscle tone. Not often one sees sinew of that caliber . . . nor magnitude. I think the word is 'hefty,'" he appended dryly.

"You're flirting with death."

He smiled through his face guard. "Isn't 'hefty' derived from the word 'heifer'?"

She launched herself at him, pummeling him about the head and shoulders as he laughed.

When she grew tired from hitting him, she asked, "Have you had enough, or do I have to kick your butt some more?"

She removed her headgear by spinning it around to snag her nose on the Velcro fastener She rubbed her scraped nose while Lee laughed.

"I've had enough," he finally admitted.

"Good. Elizabeth invited you for dinner."

"That's the best news you've delivered all day. As days go, this one's been a stinky pile."

Bai was quiet as she thought back over the day's events. Her mind and stomach still churned in the aftermath of the trip to Oakland. She looked aside at Lee. "What do you think I should do about Jason?"

He pulled off his neoprene headgear to stare back at her with a serious expression. "What can you do? If you want to get Jia Yan back, you're going to need his help."

"The help he gave today will probably give me nightmares the rest of my life."

It was Lee's turn to be quiet. He stared at her with a look of discomfort. "Are you ready to talk about it?"

She sighed and tossed her headgear onto the mat. "I'm used to violence. I mean . . . it's not like I haven't been in fights all my life. But what happened in that basement shook me. I could maybe rationalize that those men preyed on young women. But the way Jason killed them . . ." She looked at Lee, meeting his gaze. "It was so casual, so easy."

He dropped his eyes and busied himself by removing his sparring gloves. He shook his head slowly as he pulled the gloves off. "Not very sporting of him." He looked up at Bai and produced a sad smile. "Sorry," he added. "I really don't have any consoling words. Given the situation, I might have done the same thing. Jason's protecting you. He's doing everything he can to make sure there isn't a trail that leads back to you. I can see that. I can understand it."

"I can see that, too," she blurted, "but he doesn't have to kill everybody I cross paths with."

"Who's to say the *Wah Ching* in the basement wouldn't have come after you, Bai. From everything I've seen, they make stupidity its own reward. There's nothing more dangerous than idiots with guns."

The sound of running footsteps ended their discussion. Dan sprinted into the dojo and raced up to stand before Bai. "*Mah Mah* says to hurry! Daddy called and said he would pick you up in thirty minutes. *Mah Mah* says you're supposed to pack a bag. Are you going somewhere?"

"It would seem so." Bai stood to put her arm around her daughter. "Your father and I have to take a short trip. I've spoken with *Mah Mah*, and you're going to be spending tomorrow with Lee."

Dan looked to Lee for confirmation. He smiled wickedly.

His voice was exuberant. "We're going shopping."

chapter 12

The older the ginger, the hotter the spice

Jason took Bai's bag from her and passed it to the driver. She then scooted into the limo and settled into a plush seat while Jason positioned himself across from her. He turned to raise the frosted glass partition between them and the driver to ensure privacy. The smell of cured leather filled the compartment.

She leaned back into the cushioned seat to relax. Her eyes shuttered as she looked out the window. The car cruised through Chinatown and then down to Bayshore, the avenue along the wharf, where the car took a right turn to drive past the Ferry Building.

The Spanish-style structures had once housed the Port Authority and other municipal fiefdoms. Now, upscale boutiques and cafés catered to affluent commuters. The ferries, big, modern catamarans, transported passengers in relative comfort across the bay to Sausalito, Tiburon, Oakland, and as far away as Richmond.

Bai felt a twinge of nostalgia while looking at the renovated structures. She missed the old Ferry Terminal, a cavernous depot with the charm of old San Francisco, before Starbucks was a fixture and cell phones made escape impossible. She missed the wooden benches, worn smooth with age; the hot dog stand and the caramel-corn vendor; and the cigarette and magazine stall where her grandfather had purchased cigars. Mostly, she missed the old ferries, which had been real ships, made of steel and wood, and smelling of salt-dampened air and diesel fumes.

The memories from childhood lapped at her consciousness as the driver moved the car fluidly in and out of traffic. Drowsiness blanketed her as her eyes drooped despite a conscious effort to stay awake.

"Sammy Tu has surfaced in Vancouver."

Jason's sharply delivered announcement roused her. She sat up slowly in her seat to shake off her lethargy. "I assumed we were headed for Vancouver. Is there any word of the girl?"

"No. As a matter of fact, I'm having a problem getting a fix on Sammy Tu. We've heard he's in town. We just don't know where. He's keeping very quiet—strange for someone who's trying to sell merchandise, which could mean the girl has already been sold and he's just making the delivery. Or, it could mean he doesn't plan to sell the girl and has found other uses for her."

Bai didn't like the sound of that. "Other uses" for a pretty, young girl could mean any number of unpleasant alternatives.

She offered another theory. "Maybe he's gone to ground because he's heard his house got burned down. That would certainly get my attention."

Jason looked at her with a bemused expression. "A definite possibility," he conceded. He seemed to contemplate a moment before adding, "My guess, and it's only a guess, is Sammy Tu knows something's gone south. He just doesn't know exactly what. If he can get in touch with his *Wah Ching* associates who were at the café, he'll start putting the pieces together. I think we have to go on the assumption he knows we're coming for him and he'll do his best to avoid us."

"There's no chance he'd just give Jia up and write the whole thing off as bad business?"

Jason grinned, obviously entertained by the thought. "That would be the reasonable thing to do. Nobody's ever accused Sammy Tu of being reasonable. He has a reputation for being greedy."

"Then we do it the hard way?"

"That would seem to be the story."

He seemed resigned and stared at her dispassionately.

She patted the seat next to her. "I need a shoulder."

He took a moment to think about her request before turning to settle in the seat next to her. She leaned into him as his arm wrapped around her shoulders. It seemed like old times. Tears unexpectedly welled in her eyes.

"Where are we flying out of?" she asked.

She didn't really care. The question was tossed out as a distraction. She could feel the heat rising in her chest as her hip pressed against his.

"We're flying out of SFO, a nine o'clock flight on Canadian Air that will put us into Vancouver around midnight. I have people meeting us on the ground."

She snuggled, like a burrowing rabbit, into his shoulder. His suit smelled nice—wool and cologne, with a hint of man. Her eyes closed as she reveled in being held while Elizabeth's warning echoed repeatedly in her head, the words growing fainter with each passing moment.

"How is Dan?" he asked.

She smiled at the thought of her daughter. "She's fine."

She could feel his body tense as she reached over to cup his chin and turn his face toward hers. Her lips grazed his before he put his hand behind her neck and pulled her into him. His tongue found hers, and they were locked together. He leaned back onto the bench seat, and she eased down on top of him. What started out as a gentle kiss quickly escalated. She tugged at his jacket while his hand found its way inside her T-shirt to cup her breast.

She pulled away suddenly to catch her breath. An avalanche of thoughts tumbled through her head. She wasn't a kid anymore. The idea of screwing Jason in the backseat of the limo was, on the one hand, appalling, while on the other hand, enormously appealing. Her rational mind said no! no! no! Her libido said yes, yes, yes. She froze in indecision while Jason's practiced hands melted her resolve.

"This is crazy," she said, as she shrugged off her jacket.

He pulled off her shirt as she sat up to straddle him. Then he leaned back with a smile on his face.

She leaned down to whisper in his ear as he reached around to unhook her bra. "I hope the partition is soundproof. I wouldn't want the driver to get the wrong impression when you start begging for mercy."

She pulled at his belt. He popped the buttons on her jeans, hooked his thumbs in the waistband, and pulled as she rolled off of him. She bounced across the aisle and onto the facing seat to kick off her shoes with her pants around her knees. He grabbed the cuffs of her jeans and pulled, nearly upending her as the pants peeled away. Then he sat back and stared at her with a critical eye.

"You look good," he said appreciatively. "Really good."

"Not as good as I did ten years ago."

She took off her panties and threw them at him. He caught them and tossed them aside.

"No, you don't," he agreed. His smile was wicked as he stared at her. "You look better. 'The older the ginger, the hotter the spice.'"

The flattery had a volatile affect. Bai dropped to her knees on the floor of the car and reached over to grab the waist of Jason's pants to pull them down around his knees. His boxers came along for the ride. Then she got up to straddle him. She leaned in to kiss him and eased herself slowly down. His tongue sought hers while she moved up and down, the motion gaining momentum at his urging, his hands gripping her waist and then moving up to fondle her breasts.

It didn't take long to climax. When Bai peaked, it was violent and frantic. Jason bucked under her. His hands dug into her thighs painfully as she thrust against him, her palms pressed against the roof of the car for leverage. Tremors ran through her body. Blue dots blurred her vision while her back arched in spasms to snatch the breath from her lungs.

Jason's body went rigid before relaxing. They held each other and gasped for breath. His hands loosened their painful grip. He put his arms around her and pulled her close to burrow his head into her shoulder. His voice was muffled against her neck.

"You make me weak," he said as he pulled her face down to kiss her.

She held on tightly, reluctant to move. The warmth of his breath against her neck, the beating of his heart beneath her palm, the feel of his hands on her bare skin—all soothed her. She felt as if she could have stayed like that forever.

She loosened her grip and dropped her head to look into his eyes. "You make me reckless. I guess we're even."

Jason seemed to think about her statement.

"Not quite even." His voice held a hint of mischief. "I think you still owe me for that little stunt in the café today."

Bai rolled off his lap, so she could confront him. "It seems to me your robbing me of any shred of dignity would be sufficient payment. Having sex in the backseat of a car like a teenager should read 'paid in full' on that marker."

Jason looked abashed. "This wasn't my idea."

She stared at him, at a loss for words. He looked back innocently.

Her voice cracked like chipped ice. "Would you like to rephrase that?"

He looked at her, his demeanor thoughtful. "I meant to say it wasn't *entirely* my idea."

His response had the impact of a cold shower.

"Where are my things?" she demanded, searching for her black clothing scattered around the equally black interior of the limo.

"Your pants are over here," he offered, handing her the jeans. "I think your shirt and bra went over my head."

He busied himself by pulling up his pants and straightening his clothes while Bai scuttled to the back of the compartment to look for her shirt and bra. Clothes in hand, she dropped to the floor to find her shoes. She found everything but her panties, which had gone mysteriously missing. It took another five minutes to find them wedged between the seat cushions where they'd landed in the heat of the moment.

By the time she'd dressed, the limo was flying down Highway 101 and nearing the airport. Jason studied her from across the aisle.

His lips quirked up in amusement. "You're not angry, are you?"

"Only at myself," she replied. "Every time I see you I end up naked. I feel like a fool."

"Is ending up naked a bad thing?"

Jason waited patiently for an answer. He looked at her warily.

Bai let out a weary sigh. "I don't really know. I seem to have my life under control, and then I see you and my life's out of control again. I feel like I'm riding a roller coaster."

"It's a fun ride," he quipped.

"That's not the point. We both know it's a fun ride. The sex is amazing. But the thing about a roller coaster is that you always end up right back where you started."

He shrugged off the comment. He didn't seem worried. Maybe the pattern worked for him. It definitely wasn't working for her.

She sat back quietly. Postcoital lethargy quickly caught up with her. If there'd been a bed, she'd have been sound asleep. As it was, she could barely keep her eyes open.

Jason seemed to recognize her condition. "You can sleep on the plane."

He knew her well. Better than anyone, in some ways. She leaned back farther into the soft leather of the seat while choosing to ignore his suggestion. Her eyes closed. The compartment hummed with the muted sounds of the road. Her heartbeat slowed. Her breaths deepened. She drifted.

chapter 13

Even a hare will bite when cornered

Bai blinked. Lights shimmered in her eyes as she tried to focus.

Jason leaned into the car to tug at the sleeve of her jacket. She realized, with a start, she'd fallen asleep. Lethargy continued to cling to her like a needy child. She rubbed at her eyes while clambering out of the double-parked car to stumble upright onto the black asphalt—a less than graceful exit.

Bai watched as Jason retrieved the bags from the trunk of the car before he stopped to speak with the driver. She couldn't hear what was being said over the noise of traffic. The limo sat amid the chaos of the drop-off zone at San Francisco's International Airport. Cars and shuttle buses jostled for space to the tune of honking horns and loud, colorful suggestions offered up by drivers and passengers alike.

Jason and the limo driver turned in unison to watch a black SUV cruise slowly by. Jason then nodded once to the driver before turning to walk toward her with a bag in each hand.

Bai stepped backward toward the curb with her attention focused on Jason. She almost fell over a woman exiting a cab behind her. A matron with gray hair and rounded hips turned with a startled expression to stare at her, dumbfounded, no doubt, to find a stranger, first tripping over her then clutching at her to keep from falling.

"I'm so sorry," Bai said in apology while trying to straighten the woman's sweater she'd accidently tugged aside.

The matron brushed Bai off with obvious annoyance and walked away wordlessly. Before Bai could give the angry woman another thought, Jason stepped up beside her.

"I think that's everything," he said.

Her attention was pulled back to the SUV exiting the terminal. She nodded toward the departing vehicle. "What was that all about?"

He shrugged the question off. "It's probably nothing. We can discuss it when we're inside."

Shifting a bag to his other hand, he latched on to her elbow to guide her through the glass doors of the terminal. She allowed herself to be steered through the yawning building. Passengers, most of them trailing wheeled luggage, scurried in all directions as Jason deftly led her through the crowd to the Air Canada ticket booth. They bypassed the lines to walk up to the first-class counter, where their passports were given a cursory glance before tickets were dispensed. Thirty minutes later, they made their way through the security gate and into the boarding area.

Jason touched her arm to get her attention. "We might as well wait in the first-class lounge. We have a while before our flight leaves. I'm buying if you're drinking."

"This is new," she said. "You usually get me drunk before you have your way with me. Now I'm confused."

"Think of it as priming the pump," he grinned.

"I'd suggest you think of it as a dry well," she responded as she waltzed past him.

Strategically placed leather chairs and glass coffee tables filled the lounge. The seating arrangements were placed just far enough apart to provide privacy as long as conversations were conducted in a discreet manner. He followed her to an unoccupied nook where she took a seat.

He dropped the bags into a corner chair. "What are you having?"

"Glenlivet over ice. The older the better."

As he turned toward the bar, she opened her phone to retrieve her forwarded messages. The first two messages were from her lawyer, Robert Hung. He informed her that the negotiations on the real estate exchange—the one with *Sun Yee On*—were shaping up as anticipated. The second message asked that she meet with him in person as soon as possible on an urgent matter. The third message proved to be even more disturbing. The caller, a man who didn't identify himself, delivered a threatening, profanity-laced tirade. The caller didn't just threaten her; he threatened her daughter.

She closed the phone, her temper vacillating between red hot and deadly cold. Jason returned a few moments later and placed her scotch on the coffee table next to her. He seated himself adjacent to her as she picked up the drink. She swallowed deeply before opening her phone to replay the last message for Jason's benefit, sitting silently as the voice ranted. When the message ended, she closed the phone and sat back to wait for his reaction.

He took a deep breath and spoke in a clipped voice. "We were followed to the airport."

Jason's composure never wavered. His eyes were distant as if he were looking for something on the horizon. When he tilted his head, he focused his attention on Bai, and she drew back reflexively at the anger behind his unblinking pretense. He frowned when he saw her reaction but didn't say anything. His fury wasn't directed at her.

She finally asked, "Did you recognize them?"

His eyes dropped. "No. They picked us up at your place and followed us as far as the terminal. I got a look at the passenger when the car passed us in the white zone. He was Anglo."

Bai sat quietly and sipped her drink. She couldn't think of anyone who might want her followed. Sammy Tu, even if he knew she was looking for him, wouldn't hire muscle to follow her. The attack on Dan at school didn't warrant that level of response. It was kid's stuff.

She shrugged her shoulders, at a loss. "That was the black SUV you were watching in the unloading zone?"

He nodded.

"Should I hire additional protection for Dan?"

"It's already done. I have men assigned to her around the clock. Lee's been made aware, as has Tommy. I'd hoped to spare you the details."

"So, that was the conversation you were having with the driver?"

Jason nodded and looked at Bai soberly. "I didn't want instructions going out over a cell phone. It's not safe."

"I owe you. Again." The words were spoken softly.

He shook his head. "She's my daughter, too. Anybody even thinks of touching her, and I'll kill them."

"I can't wait until she's old enough to date."

He smiled bitterly. "I've already explained the situation to Dan. We'll discuss dating when she turns thirty."

"I seem to remember we started dating considerably younger."

He didn't answer. He simply raised his eyebrows and stared at her.

"Point taken," she conceded, sipping her scotch.

"Do you want another drink?" he asked, while getting to his feet.

"Why? You still hope to get lucky?"

"You and I both know luck has nothing to do with it. I have skills," he bragged.

"I'll pass on the drink. I'm still thinking about the other." Jason was cocky, but he was also right. The man had skills. She smiled, in spite of her lingering resentment. "While you're getting another drink I'm going to check my makeup."

Jason nodded in acknowledgment then raised his empty glass to let Bai know where he was headed. He turned his back to her and walked toward the bar. Picking up her bag, she headed in the opposite direction toward the restroom just around the corner.

She pushed open the door of the ladies room. The amenities for first-class fliers were sumptuous by airport standards—it was more of a lounge, really. There was a seating area with divans and a row of vanities stocked with miniature deodorants, hair sprays, and face creams. In the back was a separate area with showers.

She stopped to look at the products in the vanity area before strolling around the corner to look at the showers. Curiosity compelled her to draw the curtain aside.

The click of a shutting door caused Bai to cut short her inspection. The sound of a stall door opening and closing suggested she was no longer alone in the lounge. She didn't pay the entrant any attention until she heard the clacking of a second stall's door being shoved open. A third slapping door elicited a twinge of apprehension.

Bai retraced her steps to the partition wall separating the showers from the toilets. Turning the corner, she watched as the matronly woman, the one she'd tripped over earlier, pushed at another stall door.

Bai witnessed the disappointment written across the woman's features when she found the stall empty.

She must have sensed Bai's presence because the woman slowly turned to face her. A smile spread across her face as she spoke in a reassuring voice. "There you are, dear. I've been looking for you."

Bai stared at the woman and pointed to her own chest while thinking the woman must have been mistaken. "Me?" She cleared her throat. "Why would you be looking for me?"

The matron smiled and stretched out a hand toward Bai. "I was so rude outside, earlier. I wanted to apologize. My behavior was inexcusable."

"You had every right to be upset," Bai replied. "I was careless, not looking where I was going. It was my fault entirely."

The woman's hand, which Bai ignored, slowly dropped to the matron's side. Bai felt uneasy. The notion of the elderly woman's following her to apologize, though plausible, didn't ring true. Bai's gut was telling her that something was very wrong.

"If you'll excuse me, I have a plane to catch," Bai explained as she sidestepped toward the door.

The woman took two quick steps to block Bai's path. Her smile widened as her arms spread to herd Bai back toward the vanities. "You can't leave yet, dear. We've barely become acquainted."

She advanced rapidly toward Bai with her hand stretched out as if to take Bai's arm. Bai slapped the hand away and rabbit-punched the woman in the face with a closed fist, a reflex. The woman's head snapped back as she stumbled before regaining her balance. Bai darted toward the door again, but the woman moved fast and jumped into the aisle to block her escape.

"They didn't tell me you were a fighter." The woman spoke with a clinical detachment while steely eyes betrayed her anger. She stared malevolently at Bai while she wiped blood from her lip. "They said you were an easy target, a civilian. The Major will have some explaining to do."

"Who are 'they'? Who's the Major?" Bai asked. "Why are you doing this?"

The woman smirked and ducked her head. "It's just a job, dearie. We all do what we must. It doesn't mean we can't be civil, does it?" Her words sounded consoling. "What's really important is that you stop all this foolishness. I just want you to take my hand and trust me."

The woman stretched her hand out to Bai and smiled. Her blood-stained teeth gave the woman a predatory look.

"Does that line really work for you?" Bai asked in amazement.

The matron's grin widened as she gestured with outstretched palms. "More often than you might think." She edged closer to Bai as she spoke. "Most people are sheep. If you treat them kindly, they're remarkably cooperative."

Bai stepped away from the vanities to the center of the aisle where she'd have more room to maneuver. She dropped her bag to the floor to free her other hand and started to reach for her knife. Then she stopped. The knife was at home in her closet where she'd left it, knowing she couldn't take it through security. "Shit," she uttered, as she raised her fists and settled into a fighter's stance.

Bai backed away. The matron followed, heavy brogues edging forward cautiously on the tile floor. Her feral smirk remained fixed in place as she stalked Bai, like a grinning wolf.

Bai studied the woman while retreating one step at a time. She attempted to return the woman's smile but had difficulty making her face muscles work. She quickly dampened her fear as she noted every detail of the woman's appearance in an attempt to fully assess her assailant.

The gray hair was obviously a wig that had been knocked slightly askew by Bai's punch. Padding had been added to the woman's waist and hips. A gray sweater and gray skirt, worn loose, would allow freedom of movement. The heavy brogue shoes added two inches to her height and considerable weight to her feet. From the obvious attempt at disguise, Bai surmised the woman was both younger and faster than she'd at first thought.

The woman spoke to Bai in a lulling tone. "I wasn't supposed to fulfill the contract until you reached Vancouver, but then they didn't say anything about your having a professional with you."

"You mean Jason?"

"Is that his name? I didn't know. I've only been told he's triad and dangerous. I needed to separate the two of you to remove you quietly. I couldn't believe my good fortune when I saw you wander off to the restroom."

"What do you want with me?" Bai asked, fearing the answer.

Her adversary simply shrugged and smiled the same enigmatic smile.

"'Even a hare will bite when cornered,'" Bai warned.

Gliding away from the stalls, the matron reached to her waist to unsnap the buckle of her belt. A wide fabric strap with interlocking plastic clasps came free in her hand. Her fingers stripped away the decorative stitching to expose a heavy line that sparkled under the fluorescent lighting. She snapped the metal buckles before Bai's face to reveal the garrote.

"For every hare, there is a snare."

Bai walked backward slowly while trying to reason with the woman. "I don't suppose we could talk this over." Her words didn't seem to penetrate the woman's awareness. "You really don't have to do this."

The assassin stopped to stare at Bai with a look of chagrin. "Of course, I have to do this. I don't get paid unless you die. Besides, you hit me in the face, you yellow bitch."

Bai refused to be cowed. "What happened to 'let's be friends'?" she asked.

Bai's hip unexpectedly bumped up against the vanities, startling her. The matron rushed her.

Despite her earlier scrutiny, Bai had underestimated the bulky woman. The matron leapt into a flying spin kick that very nearly took Bai's head off. Bai arched her back over the vanities to duck under the sensible, matronly shoes as they flew past her nose. As she tipped back, Bai's hand brushed against a small can of aerosol hair spray. As the woman turned back to confront her, Bai snatched up the can and lunged forward to spray her attacker in the face.

The killer stifled a scream, turned, and lurched away, tears streaming from eyes that blinked spastically as she wiped at them.

Bai attempted to run past the blinded woman who jolted aside, as if by instinct, to ram her. With the woman's shoulder jammed into her ribs like an NFL linebacker, Bai stumbled back toward the vanities. The assassin pinned her against the counter while Bai frantically fumbled for a weapon. She grabbed a long-tailed comb lying on the vanity. With adrenaline-fueled strength, she stabbed the comb down at the woman's exposed back.

The matron must have sensed something coming. She jerked her head around and looked up at the last moment, eyes bleary with tears. The tail of the comb hit her in the eye and kept going, burying itself until Bai's hand bounced off the woman's forehead.

Bai froze in shock.

The matron's body went rigid. She stood up straight and turned as her arms jerked out. Rocking on her heels, she shuddered, gurgled, and dropped like a felled tree. When her face smacked the tiles with a sickening crunch, the business end of the comb snapped off to skitter across the floor like a giant cockroach.

The woman convulsed once and then became very still. A deafening quiet filled the room.

Bai's mouth hung open. It took her a moment to realize she wasn't breathing. She gasped for air while her pulse thundered in her ears. She stooped to put her head between her knees, willing herself not to get sick.

As her thoughts started to sort themselves, she looked up to scan the restroom. Her body trembling, she stood up to cross the room and discovered a plastic jam lock on the door, the kind travelers carry with them for extra security in hotel rooms. The killer must have placed it there.

Bai turned back to grab the woman under the arms and drag her back to the showers, where she dumped the body unceremoniously into an empty stall. Rifling the woman's pockets, Bai found an Irish passport, a prepaid cell phone, and nine $1,000 packets of freshly minted 100s. She stuffed the woman's possessions inside her jacket.

She stepped out of the shower and reached back to turn on the hot water by brushing the handle with her knuckles. Blood from the gouged eye stained the floor pink as water pooled around the woman's outstretched legs. The gray wig slipped aside to reveal blonde hair. In her hand, the matron still clutched her garrote.

Bai pulled the curtain closed using the edges of her hands. She'd seen enough.

Hastening back to the vanities, she picked up her bag and stopped long enough to grab a tissue to clean up a small amount of blood on the tiles as well as the broken end of the comb. She stuffed everything in her bag along with the can of aerosol spray she'd used to temporarily blind the matron.

Before leaving, Bai examined herself quickly in the mirror. When she was satisfied she didn't carry any trace of the encounter, she walked over and released the jam lock and put it in her purse. A paper sign taped to the outside of the door stated the bathroom was closed for maintenance and would reopen in fifteen minutes. She left the sign in place and ran her hand over the handle of the door to smudge any prints.

She walked slowly back to where Jason waited. He saw her coming and stood up.

She leaned in to speak to him. "I think we should board the plane now."

"We still have fifteen minutes."

She leaned in closer to whisper in his ear. "I killed a woman in the restroom. We really, *really* need to leave."

He examined her face carefully but didn't question her further. He put his arm around her waist to lead her out of the lounge and down to the gate where the plane waited. A gate agent halted the line of economy passengers so the two of them might board.

When they were seated, a flight attendant asked Bai if she'd like a drink. She ordered a double scotch. When it came, she tossed it back and closed her eyes. She stayed that way until she could feel the tires of the plane lift off the ground. Only then did she let tears of relief roll down her face.

chapter 14

A bride is like a horse; you break her in by constantly mounting her and continually beating her

Bai closed her eyes and tried to find her spiritual center. Her thoughts were in an uproar. Images of the matron's body, a comb garishly sprouting from her eye, kept intruding. She squeezed her eyelids tight as she relived the short skirmish, all the time wondering if there wasn't something, anything, she could have done differently to avoid the deadly exchange.

After hours of soul searching, Bai concluded it was best to avoid public restrooms.

Jason turned to her with a questioning look every time she opened her eyes. Unwilling to talk, she shook her head repeatedly to stave off his curiosity. She hadn't yet come to terms with killing someone.

Eventually, the wheels of the plane thumped against tarmac. The jet rolled down the runway to a terminal gate. The interior cabin lights brightened. Like zombies, passengers stood to shuffle down the narrow aisle of the plane before being herded into a cold, clammy boarding tunnel redolent of machine oil.

Jason and Bai walked straight to customs with passports in hand. A uniformed agent asked for their documents, questioned whether they had anything to declare, and then mumbled, "Welcome to Vancouver," before ushering them through sliding glass doors that led to a passenger loading zone.

A white limousine waited. The driver recognized Jason and bowed before quickly opening the rear door. Jason stood back to allow Bai to enter first then followed her into the car. She scooted across the seat to make room for him. On the other side of the aisle sat a large man. He seemed to fill the bench seat. A blue suit, stretched to its limit, did little to mask his massive musculature. His eyes studied her as the car door closed. She didn't recognize him, and, from his puzzled expression, he didn't know her either.

Jason reached over to give the man's beefy hand a cursory shake but didn't say anything. The giant pushed a button on a small device held in his lap, and a low-frequency hum filled the compartment.

The man nodded in Jason's direction. "It's safe to talk now."

The sound of his voice was surprising—pitched about three octaves higher than Bai had anticipated. The tinny voice seemed out of place resonating from such a huge figure. She cracked a smile despite an attempt not to.

Jason made the introductions. "Bai Jiang, this is Shan Hong, our manager here in Vancouver."

The man puffed out his chest, preening. Bai put her hand to her mouth to hide her amusement and nodded in acknowledgment. Shan immediately bristled at the casual greeting. His fat lips tightened before twisting up into a sneer. He showed his contempt openly. His eyes sent a silent inquiry at Jason as he handed him a leather briefcase.

Jason ignored the unasked question. He put the briefcase on his lap to open the combination lock. Inside were a signal scrambler, a brace of automatic pistols with spare clips, a pair of throwing knives, and a large manila folder. Taking the folder out of the case, he closed it and snapped the latches down.

As Jason looked over the contents of the folder, Shan's gaze drifted back to Bai. His eyes narrowed as he took stock of her. She kept her face blank but didn't avert her gaze. Her forthright attitude seemed to annoy him.

Shan turned his gaze to Jason. "There was a killing at SFO. The body of a woman was found in the first-class lounge. They didn't release much information. I only mention it because of the time of the death . . . around the time of your departure."

He was fishing for information.

Without bothering to look up from the papers before him, Jason shrugged. "It has nothing to do with us."

Jason finished perusing the papers in his lap and then handed the folder to Bai. They were reports, Canadian police reports, on Sammy Tu. It seemed Sammy Tu was well known in Canada. His rap sheet detailed arrests for pimping, procuring, and assault and battery.

When she looked up, she realized Shan was still staring at her. He looked angry.

"Are you sure it's a good idea to let this *woman* read the reports? Our sources are confidential."

Shan's question was directed at Jason, though his baleful stare remained fixed on Bai. She ignored him and continued to read the material. He wasn't the first sexist pig she'd run into. He might, however, have been the largest sexist pig she'd ever run into. The man seemed to fill the compartment of the limo.

When she was done, she handed the reports wordlessly back to Jason, who then proceeded to put them back into the briefcase. He hadn't bothered to answer Shan's question. His was a silent rebuff that hung in the air between the two men like a lingering stench.

Jason broke the silence, his voice sounding tired. "Do we know where Sammy Tu is?"

Shan answered reluctantly. "There's been a sighting. He showed up at the Palace Hotel a couple of hours ago and was seen entering an elevator. It stopped at the twelfth floor. Our contact in the hotel lost him, and he's not registered there, at least not under his own name. We have a man posted on the twelfth floor. We're waiting for a visual confirmation."

"Have you checked the register for all of the floors?" Bai asked.

Shan ignored her question.

She tried again. "If Sammy knows we're looking for him, and he does, he'll attempt to avoid us. If the elevator indicator said twelfth floor, he's probably somewhere on the eleven floors below that. He wouldn't walk up when he could walk down."

Shan folded his arms across his chest to stare straight ahead. "'A

WHITE GINGER

bride is like a horse; you break her in by constantly mounting her and continually beating her.'"

In the silence that followed, Bai felt her face grow red, not from embarrassment but from anger. She turned away to look out the car window at the scenery—trees, snow, buildings, darkness.

Just when she thought Shan's insult would go unanswered, Jason spoke. "She's right. Check the register again. Also, look under known aliases." His voice was calm but steely. "As a matter of fact, let's save time by going there now. The Palace is a nice hotel, and we might as well be comfortable while the search is under way."

Shan's jaw clenched at the rebuke. He shot Jason a look that bordered on insolence. Bai glanced aside at Jason to read his reaction. He stared straight ahead, his face inscrutable.

Shan was disrespectful in an organization where face was everything. Loss of face, more often than not, meant loss of life. The two men sparred with words and unspoken insults. Bai had seen the signs before. Jason and Shan were locked in a complex and deadly dance for power.

Shan turned around to slide open a partition at his back so he could speak with the driver. Sticking the upper half of his body through the opening, he motioned insistently with his hands, the hammering gestures an indication of his anger. She noticed Jason smiling at the exchange. His grin quickly slipped away as Shan turned back to face them.

"We're only a few minutes from the hotel," said Shan. "A suite is being reserved for you under the name of John Wang."

A small, self-satisfied smile played across Shan's lips at one of the oldest jokes in existence. Jason didn't return the smile.

"Your predecessor made a point of ridiculing me in public." Jason's voice was controlled and calm. "He didn't like the fact I was young for such a position of authority. He didn't like that I kept my own counsel and did things my way. You'd do well to keep in mind what happened to him."

Jason let the silence endure as he turned to look out the window.

Intrigued by the exchange, Bai studied Shan. His eyes glittered with anger and his face hardened. He turned and became aware of her silent scrutiny. She recognized the malevolence on his face and smiled, a gesture that only seemed to make him angrier.

Jason addressed Shan without turning to face him—another slight. "Drop us at the front entrance of the hotel, then wait five minutes before following. I don't want to be seen with you. I'm not well known in Vancouver, and I don't want to attract any more attention than necessary. Call me in my suite when you've narrowed down Sammy Tu's whereabouts."

Shan didn't reply. He sat rigidly in the seat like a ticking bomb. With a barely perceptible movement, he nodded to acknowledge the directive.

The limousine came to a stop under a lighted hotel portico. A man in red livery walked toward the car to open the passenger door. Jason slid out of the limo, briefcase in hand. When Jason's back was turned, Shan took the opportunity to put his hand on Bai's knee and squeeze. His grip was painful.

She backhanded Shan with a balled fist. The sound of smacking flesh resounded like a rifle shot, twice—once when Bai's knuckles met Shan's jaw and once when his head slammed back against the glass partition. He sat stunned as she scooted out of the car.

As she bounced out of the limo, Jason closed the door and turned to her. "What was that all about?"

"He put a hand on me. I put a hand on him."

Her anger was controlled but no less virulent. Jason nodded silently and took a deep breath. He put his hand on her elbow, ostensibly for support. She suspected it was to keep her from jumping back into the limo and having another go at Shan. Her hands shook with anger.

The driver retrieved the luggage from the trunk and would have given it to the bellman had Jason not intervened. He grabbed the two small bags and took Bai's arm to walk with her into the brightly lit, opulent lobby of the hotel. At the registration desk, she stood to one side while he spoke with the clerk.

When everything was in order, they walked to a bank of elevators. "We're on the twentieth floor, Mrs. Wang."

"You know, of course, you're going to have to put Shan in his place."
She spoke while they waited for the elevator. "His disrespect for you is a
challenge. His disrespect for me is an affront."

Jason's reply was resigned. "He's one of the reasons I'm here in
Vancouver. You don't have to concern yourself with him. He's already
signed his death warrant."

She was curious. "What's the other reason you're here?"

She turned to face him. He reached up to touch her face gently
with his fingertips. "You," he said, his eyes searching hers, "I'm here for
you."

chapter 15

Dead songbirds make for a sad meal

Jason slid the key card into the slot on the door, and the indicator light turned from red to green. He pushed the door open and ushered Bai into the room. She flipped on the light switch as she walked past him, entering a sitting room furnished in hotel chic—beige couches, brass and glass coffee tables, and a wall of windows overlooking the city.

The view drew her across the room.

"It's beautiful," she said, staring out over a tapestry of lights, the night bright and clear.

Jason came to stand behind her. He put his arms around her shoulders and pulled her into him. His strength folded around her like a comforting blanket. The embrace made Bai feel safe, protected. Turning around in his arms to hold him closer, she pressed her face into the curve of his neck.

He whispered in her ear. "How tired are you?"

His lips brushed her earlobe. Bai tilted her head up to kiss him deeply as she reached up to put her arms around his neck. She needed him with a sudden urgency. She'd spent the day surrounded by danger and death, and she wanted desperately to feel alive. A leg wrapped around his. He grabbed her thighs to lift her as she wrapped both legs around his waist while he carried her to the bedroom.

The next couple of hours were spent rolling each other from one end of the bed to the other. It was exhausting but fun. When she had nothing left to give, she lay on the bed, a little light-headed but blissfully sated. He lay on his back to catch his breath. He wasn't going anywhere in a hurry.

She reluctantly decided it was time for show-and-tell. "There's something I need to show you."

Jason propped himself up on one elbow and raised a finger to ensure her silence. He then roused himself to pad back to the sitting room. His slender, muscular body moved with the natural grace of a feline.

When he returned, he put the black box, the electronic scrambler, on the nightstand and turned it on. "I thought we might need this."

Bai got out of bed without replying and went into the living room to retrieve her bag. She pulled out the assassin's passport, phone, and money to drop them on the bed.

"I took these off of the woman at the airport, the one who tried to kill me. I was hoping you might be able to use them to find out who she was and who hired her."

She seated herself next to Jason, leaning her head against his shoulder as he picked the items up to inspect them.

"You really killed her?" His tone held a professional curiosity.

"She didn't give me a choice," she said bluntly. "She was determined to kill me. The woman had a garrote. The whole thing was like something out of a spy movie."

He closely examined the passport, then the bundled money, and finally the phone.

Jason spoke to her as he examined the phone. "You said she used a garrote. Can you describe it?"

"I suppose so. Why? Does it matter?"

She was hesitant to go over the attack in detail. The memories were still too fresh and too disturbing.

"Assassins have favorite tools," he explained. "If we can identify the weapon, we may be able to identify the assassin. If we can identify the assassin, we may be able to trace her back to the person who hired her. It's a chain, one link leading to another."

She nodded in understanding. Closing her eyes, she visualized the woman holding the garrote, trying to focus on the instrument and not the assailant.

"She disguised the garrote as a belt. The buckle was two interlocking plastic rings. A heavy nylon string, maybe fishing line, sparkled when the light caught it."

"What an interesting choice of weapons." Jason seemed intrigued. "My guess would be a diamond-encrusted filament. Excellent for removing limbs cleanly. A bone saw. Cuts through skin and bone like a hot knife through butter. It's also good for chopping off heads."

Bai's hand went instinctively to her throat. The thought of being decapitated sent cold shivers through her. She trembled. The assault suddenly seemed real, and terrifying, and sickening.

"I think I need a hot shower."

Jason reached out and put his arms around her. "You did well. You did what you had to do—survive. It's not your fault."

"I killed somebody."

Tears ran down her cheeks and along her nose. She snuffled and reached up to wipe her nose with her hand.

He turned her to look at him "'Dead songbirds make for a sad meal.' All of us have a song—some prettier than others but none without purpose. The woman you killed would have silenced you if you hadn't silenced her first. You acted in self-defense. Don't beat yourself up."

"Give me a minute," she said as she disentangled herself and stood up to stumble into the bathroom.

She closed the door behind her and stepped into the shower. Her hand fumbled at the handle on the faucet valve. She swiveled it to hot and adjusted the water until it burned her skin. Turning her back on the streaming water, she braced her hands against the ceramic tile and cried—gasping for air between convulsive sobs, keening as her chest heaved. She let the emotional floodgates open. It was the only way she'd be able to function. She couldn't carry her feelings around all bottled up the way Jason did.

She lost track of time. She didn't know how long she stood in the shower and sobbed. It must have been a while because when she raised her head to look around, the bathroom was swamped in thick steam. She soaped and rinsed quickly before turning the faucet to cold to let the spray wash over her face to take the swelling and redness from around her eyes. She didn't want the world to know she'd been crying.

When her teeth started to chatter, she turned the shower off and reached for a towel. The heavy bath sheet felt good against her chilled skin. She scoured herself with the soft, fluffy cloth then wrapped it around her waist.

With her bare hand, she wiped a swatch of fog away from the steamed mirror. She ran her hands through her coarse hair to pull it away from her face and studied her reflection in the mirror. The image staring back at her didn't look any different than before. But she could feel she was changed, and the change was irrevocable.

She shook her head in sorrow. The image in the mirror mimicked her. She forced a smile onto her face. *She was alive*, she rationalized. That mattered.

Drawing a deep breath, she turned away to open the door to the bedroom. She expected to find Jason in bed waiting for her. He wasn't. The sitting room was empty as well, but the phone at the desk blinked, flickering orange in the dark. She picked up the receiver and pushed the button to retrieve the message. Jason's voice, clear and precise, let her know he was in the coffee shop, and she should join him when she felt able.

She took about five minutes to get dressed. She pulled on her leather jacket and made sure she had everything she'd need. A key card to the room was in her pocket. Jason must have put it there.

Bai opened the door and checked the hall, wary, out of habit, of strangers. It was around two in the morning. The corridor was deserted. Pulling the door closed behind her, she stood in the alcove and considered taking the elevator at the other end of the hall. A door directly across from her led to the stairwell. She decided, on impulse, that what she needed was physical exertion to clear her head.

She pushed open the heavy fire door and stepped into the stairwell. The air was cold in the unheated shaft, courtesy of the wintry Canadian night. Littered with cigarette butts and smelling of tobacco, the cement landing obviously served as the unofficial smoking room. Steel railings spiraled down the concrete steps while round, matching handrails lined the unfinished concrete walls. Muted light came from caged glass fixtures shaped like beer cans that protruded from the walls overhead.

Once again, she stopped to listen. When she was satisfied she had the stairs to herself, she started running. Taking the steps two at a time, she ran down the stairwell until she reached the bottom. Turning around, she started running up the steps. Thighs burned as she raced up the stairs. Her breathing became deeper, her mind more focused as she ran. When she reached the top of the stairwell again, she stopped to lean against the cement wall, drawing cold air into her lungs as she let herself cool down, her face hot and flushed.

Shoes scuffed against concrete stairs. The sound echoed as a door slammed shut. Bai had no way to determine how far below her the sound originated. As she listened, a second door on a landing below opened and closed. She pressed herself against the exit with one hand on the door breaker.

Steps receded as someone started down the steps while the first set of steps grew closer. She stayed where she was out of curiosity. She wanted to know who else felt compelled to use the stairs in the middle of the night. It didn't take long for the footsteps to converge.

"I told you to wait in the room." The reedy tenor surprised Bai. It was Shan. "You could have been seen."

A second man replied. "Relax. Nobody uses the stairs in the middle of the night."

Click. Bai recognized the sound of a lighter flicking then a deep inhalation.

The second man continued. "I need to know what's taking so long. When do you plan on killing them?"

"Soon. I want them together. I want Jason to watch his whore die. I need to see his face. I'll make it slow and painful. I'll make the snooty bitch scream."

She froze. Common sense told her it was time to leave, but curiosity kept her in place. Her shoulder rested against the steel door as she leaned back to listen.

"I didn't sign up for any triad killings." The other voice was decidedly unhappy. "This was just supposed to be a decoy job. We get the woman out of town and let someone else do the dirty work. The whole idea was to avoid involving *Sun Yee On*. This shit is most definitely not what I signed up for."

"The woman's not the problem," said Shan, dismissing the other man's qualms. "I've told you I'll take care of her. I don't know why Jason's here, but this may be the opportunity I've been waiting for. I can kill them both and make it look like a contract hit. The woman's death will look like collateral damage—she was in the wrong place at the wrong time. But you're going to have to disappear afterward. The *Shan Chu* won't let this go. He'll be looking for answers. He'll be looking for you."

Silence followed. She suspected the other man wasn't satisfied with Shan's response.

"Have it your way," the other man said begrudgingly. There was defeat in his voice—and perhaps fear. "When this is over, I'm done here. My house is gone anyway. That crazy bastard burned me out. I'm going south. So far south nobody will ever find me."

"Then we don't have a problem, Sammy. You go your way. I go mine. Both of us will be a little richer."

Bai's eyes widened. Could it be Sammy Tu that Shan was conversing with? She was confused. What did they have to do with each other?

The voice corrected Shan before she could speculate further. "A lot richer!"

"Maybe by your standards, Sammy, but then you have small expectations. That's why you're a gutter pimp, and I'm about to move up to *Hung Kwan* of the brotherhood. There are going to be some changes in *Sun Yee On.*"

"Sure, sure. Whatever you say. Just don't try and pull me into your war. I don't want any part of it. Like I said, when this is over, I'm gone. You never saw me. I was never here."

"It's better for everyone if you disappear."

Shan's voice held a note of finality. He'd just pronounced Sammy Tu's death sentence, and Sammy was such a tool he failed to recognize the peril. She could almost feel sorry for the man.

A door opened and closed. Thinking the men had left the stairwell, Bai reached for the breaker bar on the door. Her hand rested on the handle when she heard the sound of footsteps on the stairs again. She froze, afraid to even breathe. Time seemed to pass slowly as the footsteps faded. She waited until she heard the sound of another door opening and closing before she pushed the door to the stairwell open and sprinted for the elevator.

chapter 16

Kill one to warn a hundred

Bai fidgeted while the elevator seemed to take forever to descend. Her nails tapped nervously at the brass handrail. Their clicking was rapid, like the thumping of her heart. When she stepped out into the lobby, she paused just outside the shiny brass doors as they slowly closed behind her.

Soft light filtered down from crystal chandeliers. Overstuffed, ornate furniture occupied the lobby in small groupings, anchored by artificial bamboo trees that sprouted from large ceramic vases. A bellhop, idly reading a magazine, leaned with his ankles crossed against the closed concierge desk. On the other side of the room at the reception desk, a young black woman in a red blazer typed at a terminal, clearly engrossed by the task.

A nighttime maintenance crew vacuumed the carpet, polished the furniture, and wiped down the mirrors and glass. They were all Asian, all men. She watched them apprehensively as she angled across the room toward the coffee shop. Frayed nerves made her suspicious of everyone.

A sign at the entrance to the coffee shop asked that patrons wait to be seated. She ignored the request and brushed past a hostess who approached with a stack of menus. Her behavior was rude, but she was past caring. She just wanted to find Jason and get out of there.

Tall booths upholstered in a dark red material divided the room into sections. The stalls acted as barriers to obstruct her view. Pacing the aisles, she looked for Jason as she walked past booths filled with boisterous late-night diners. Waitresses hustled trays piled high with hot, loaded plates.

Bai finally found him seated in the rear with his back to a wall. He waved to her. Her face must have telegraphed her mounting anxiety, because his lips dropped into a frown at her approach.

She halted abruptly in front of the booth. "We need to leave."

"Sit," he said, standing up to let her into the booth next to him.

She didn't want to sit and returned his frown while shaking her head. He took her by the arm and forced her into the booth then slid in next to her. Turning over an empty mug, he poured steaming coffee from a plastic carafe.

"There isn't time for this," she objected, pushing the cup away. "I overheard Shan and Sammy Tu speaking in the stairwell. They plan to kill both of us."

He glanced at her, raised an eyebrow, and put the cup in her hand. "Drink."

She took a sip to appease him. The coffee tasted good. She took another sip.

"How do you always manage to end up in the wrong place at the wrong time?" he asked. "You seem to have this gift. It's almost like you're an irresistible trouble magnet."

"So now this is my fault? Didn't you hear me? They plan to kill us! We need to get out of here!"

Raising a hand, he lowered it slowly to indicate she should similarly lower the volume of her voice.

"Just tell me what you heard, and everything will be fine."

Bai stared at him. He seemed calm, unruffled. She felt like screaming.

Taking another sip of the hot coffee, her gaze slipped over the room nervously. "They said something about killing me and making it look like collateral damage. Do I look like collateral damage?"

He smiled. "What else did they say?"

She scowled at him. "Sammy Tu didn't expect you or *Sun Yee On* to be involved. Shan sees this as an opportunity to take your place and move up in the organization. I'm beginning to get the impression he really doesn't like you."

He grunted in amusement and made a rolling gesture with his hand to indicate she should continue.

"And he said he was going to make me scream and make you watch."

She took another sip of the coffee. Her hand trembled to betray her anxiety. The smile on his face vanished. His eyes veiled like a curtain being drawn. For a moment, she thought he might show his anger, but the moment passed.

His hand moved across the table to rest on hers. "Relax. He won't try to kill us here. There are too many witnesses. Reinforcements are on the way. They'll be here soon."

"The cleaning crew," she blurted. "I saw them in the lobby. Who are they?"

Jason shook his head and bit down on his lip to hide his amusement. "They're the cleaning crew. They clean the hotel. Don't let your imagination get the better of you."

"I can't help it. I'm new to this. People may not like me, but no one has ever tried to kill me. Being a nosy bitch never got me into this kind of trouble before."

"You get used to it," he stated blandly.

"What are you saying? I don't want to get used to it. This is crazy!"

He pursed his lips and pulled something out of his jacket. He slipped it under the table to her. She put her hand under the table to feel the plastic grip of an automatic pistol. It was still warm from resting against Jason's chest.

She pushed the gun away. "I don't want it."

"Are you sure?" he looked surprised. "This isn't the time to stand on principle. I have another."

"Yes, I'm sure. Besides, I don't have any place to put it. In case you haven't noticed, this jacket isn't exactly cut to hide my assets."

The asymmetrical leather jacket hugged her curves. The garment was chic but left nowhere to hide a gun.

Jason smiled and drew his hand back to place the gun back in his jacket. "Believe me, I've noticed."

He thought a moment and then reached inside his cuff before placing his hand beneath the table again. "If you won't take a gun, at least take this."

He passed her a throwing knife, a finely balanced blade with razor-sharp edges.

"You still know how to use one, don't you?" he asked.

She frowned at the insinuation. "Don't be insulting."

She carefully slipped the knife into the sheath built into the sleeve of her jacket. The knife was reassuring. She hadn't felt fully dressed without one.

"Hopefully, you won't have to use it," he said. "I have my own people on the way. I'm just not certain how many of my brothers in Vancouver Shan has managed to turn."

"I don't get it. Why would anyone follow him? He's a bully and a fool."

Jason waved away the criticism. "He has his talents and his allies. There's a faction in *Sun Yee On*, an old guard, who is determined to return to the 'old ways.' They believe in a lot of sentimental nonsense . . . like the 'old days' were really all that great. Shan's even been talking to the Big Circle Boys about forming a new alliance of triads that would revert to drinking one another's blood and vowing blind fealty."

Bai was mystified. "The Big Circle Boys used to be Red Guard. They've always been our enemies. What do they hope to get out of an alliance?"

"They probably want nothing more than to start an internal struggle within *Sun Yee On*. Whatever makes us weaker makes them stronger. But Shan can't see the danger. The man's blinded by ambition. He's also a bit delusional, if you haven't noticed."

Jason grimaced. Bai was familiar with that look. It was regret.

"Why does Shan hate you?" she asked.

He let out a puff of air and seemed to gather his thoughts before answering. "Because I treat him like the fool he is, for one thing. And, I killed his sponsor, a man who challenged my authority as *Hung Kwan*. The death seemed necessary at the time."

"'Kill one to warn a hundred'?" she asked, quoting an old proverb.

His voice was sober. "Something like that."

Bai had difficulty sympathizing with Jason's failed management style. She was more concerned with the present.

"So, what do we do now?" she asked.

"Now, we eat. This is the safest place for both of us. The longer we wait here, the longer my men will have to get in place. Besides, I'm hungry. Being with you gives me an appetite."

The smile returned to his face. She was tempted to let his reassurance lull her. Her better judgment kicked in to ward off the enticement. Jason was thinking on his feet and improvising as he went. That he seemed to be enjoying himself didn't lessen her anxiety.

She didn't return his smile but picked up a menu anyway. She ordered a salad and fettuccini with pesto; he ordered a steak. They settled on coffee and water. Given the circumstances, getting drunk seemed like a bad idea.

When the waitress wandered off to see to other customers, Bai leaned into him to speak in confidence. "I thought the attempts to kill me had something to do with *Sun Yee On*. Now I'm not so certain."

"You may be right. A lot of unanswered questions still need to be addressed. It would be nice to have a word with Sammy Tu to get the whole story." Jason's musings seemed to be as much for his benefit as for hers. "Plus, we still need to find out if he has the girl."

The waitress approached with their salads. When she'd delivered the plates to the table and informed them, playfully, that she was just a shout away, she departed. Bai's nerves were starting to settle and her appetite to return. Usually, her appetite was the last thing to desert her in times of stress.

Jason's mood seemed annoyingly light. He grinned at her. "Anyway, getting back to your problem, I dispatched the money and phone to our headquarters here in Vancouver. We should know by tomorrow what bank dispensed the money. There's no way to tell who the money was given to, but the sequential numbers will definitely point us to a specific region—If not a specific bank branch. The fact that somebody paid in sequentially numbered bills leads me to believe they don't make a habit of hiring killers. It's blatantly stupid."

Bai agreed with him but also knew it was dangerous to make assumptions. "That's only if the money was in payment for the hit."

He raised his fork to emphasize his point. "That's true. The money could be a red herring, but it never hurts to follow a lead. The phone is a burn phone, prepaid with only one number programmed into it. And, again, we won't be able to trace who purchased it, but we will be able to find out where it was sold. If the money and the phone come from the same region, maybe those responsible are somewhere nearby. We also have the phone number, likely belonging to another burn phone. But it never hurts to call and let them know their assassin is dead, and we're on to them. Might light a fire under them. Make them do something hasty, something stupid."

Bai was less than happy with that thought. She looked at him doubtfully. "Something 'hasty' like try to kill me again, you mean. Thanks, but let's give that one a little more consideration. I'm not really sure I want to be bait. Besides, the trail may only lead back to an agent."

It was a given that contracts, more often than not, went through intermediaries. Lawyers had proven to be perfect go-betweens since client confidentiality provided a screen for the culprits to hide behind. Overseas agencies also provided a similar service for a fee. Assassination, like many businesses, had gone global.

"If the contract has been processed through an agent," Jason acknowledged, "we won't have a problem." He sounded confident in his statement. "We're not the law or the government. If the agent doesn't want to talk, I'm sure I can persuade him otherwise."

She stared at him. There he sat, blithely discussing using her as bait to draw out assassins and then torturing someone to find out who was behind the attempts on her life. She appreciated his efforts but wondered where the man she'd fallen in love with had gone.

He must have seen something in her eyes because he put down his fork and reached for her hand. "I'm sorry." There was genuine regret in his voice. "Sometimes I forget myself."

Returning his gaze, Bai searched his eyes for an innocence that wasn't there anymore. It broke her heart.

"I'm sorry, too."

chapter 17

If you're going to bow at all, bow low

Jason sipped his coffee as a thoughtful expression shaped his features. "The fear and anxiety that you're feeling ... you can control those emotions, even use them to focus."

"I don't understand," Bai replied. "I was pumped full of adrenaline when the woman at the airport attacked me. My body reacted even though I was scared and angry at the same time. But now that I know I'm being hunted, I'm a nervous wreck."

"You have to change your mindset. You've had too much time to dwell on the possibilities. We're predators, animals at heart. You need to tap into that primal energy and use it. Don't be the hunted, Bai. Be the hunter."

She wasn't sure she could follow his advice. She'd spent all of her adult life attempting to become a better person. Being a hunter felt like a repudiation of everything she believed.

"I'm not sure I'm that kind of an animal," she replied tiredly. "I like to think of myself as more of a grazer—protect the young and helpless, help the aged and infirm. Being a predator isn't my thing. "

He leaned back in the booth and dismissed her qualms with a wave of his hand. "I know you. When the time comes, you'll do what's necessary to stay alive. You've already proven that." His smile was a subtle taunt. "You have an amazing capacity for survival. It's in your blood. You come from a long line of predators."

His assertion made her uneasy. She didn't want to be a killer. Her first impulse was to deny his claim, but she knew it would be a waste of time. He wanted to believe she was like him. He wanted her to be a part of his world.

"And what's in your blood, Jason? What's with this reckless thirst for danger? You knew, even before you came here, trouble was brewing, yet you walked into a trap and dragged me into it with you. And you're enjoying it."

The smile drifted from his face. "You're right about my dragging you into this. It was a mistake to bring you here. When I realized Sammy Tu was headed for Vancouver, I should have found a way to leave you behind. But I wanted to be with you. I can feel you slipping away."

She could see the pain in his eyes. She looked down, unable to meet his gaze. "We're not kids anymore, Jason. Maybe this isn't the time or place, but the fact is, as much as I love you, I can't go on like this. You drop in and out of my life without warning. I want more. I want to come home to a husband who loves me and warms my bed every night. What we have isn't enough for me."

He opened his mouth to respond but was interrupted by his cell phone. He put the device to his ear. His widening smile seemed to indicate good news.

"I have to leave now," he said brusquely. "Keep those thoughts on hold. We'll finish this conversation later."

He glided out of the booth in one fluid motion, stopping only long enough to put his hand on Bai's cheek and caution her. "Stay here. You'll be safe in the café until this is over. If someone is stupid enough to come in here and threaten you, don't hesitate to use the knife."

Grabbing hold of his hand, she looked up at him. "Don't be in a hurry to die. You have a daughter who needs you."

Jason stopped and looked at her, his smile vanishing as his features took on a more serious expression. He nodded once, turned, and walked in the direction of the lobby. She sat at the table and watched his retreating back.

As Jason walked out of the restaurant, four men, one of them Shan, emerged from a booth on the other side of the room. Their eyes followed Jason. Bai's heart skipped a beat. She found herself scrambling out of the booth, her fear forgotten. Four against one was too many even for Jason. She needed to even the odds.

Her voice carried across the restaurant. "Shan!"

Shan turned her way with a surprised look on his face. He hesitated, his head swiveling between Bai and Jason as indecision knotted his features. She strolled toward Shan, smiling, while sweat trickled down the small of her back and fear wrenched her gut.

Turning abruptly, Shan gestured to two of his men. They peeled off to follow Jason while Shan and another man waited for Bai. Her smile broadened. She'd managed to split the opposition and give Jason a fighting chance. Now all she had to do was survive her own reckless ploy.

Shan forced a smile onto his face as she approached. His contempt bled through the brittle grin. Bai had to squelch the instinct to run in the other direction.

He extended his hands, palms up. "How fortunate. I was just looking for you." His tinny voice ingratiated. "I tried your room, but no one answered. I have the man, Sammy Tu, you've been looking for. But we have a problem. He says he'll only talk to the *souxun*."

There it was—a deadly game of cat and mouse. She studied his face for any sign of compassion. His cold expression regarded her as if she were a different species, a bug to be squashed. She could see he meant to kill her.

"That's good news," she replied, working hard to maintain her smile. "Where is he? Do you know if he has a girl with him?"

"We have him in a room on the seventh floor. I didn't see a girl, but Mr. Tan, here," Shan gestured to the man standing deferentially at his side, "will take you to him. I, unfortunately, have other duties to attend to."

On cue, Tan stepped forward and bowed slightly. The tenuous bow was too shallow to be a sign of respect. Bai's grandfather had always advised, "If you're going to bow at all, bow low." It was obvious Tan had never met her grandfather, by virtue of the fact that he still breathed.

Bai stared him in the eye with an unrelenting gaze. Her scrutiny seemed to unsettle him. He looked away and then down at his shoes.

"I'll be happy to accompany Brother Tan," she said.

Tan turned his head away as what might have been guilt flickered across his features. He might follow Shan's orders, but he didn't appear to be especially happy with the situation. She hoped she might use Tan's shame to drive a wedge between him and his boss.

Shan flicked his hand at Tan and turned away from Bai, a rude dismissal. Tan took the cue to usher her toward the lobby. She went willingly. If nothing else, she reasoned, she'd finally get the chance to meet Sammy Tu.

As they walked into the lobby and past the concierge desk, Bai waved at the lazing bellhop. He waved back reticently with a look of confusion. Tan turned to see who, or what, had drawn Bai's attention. While he was distracted, she took the opportunity to slip her knife from its sheath and hold the razor-sharp blade between her finger and thumb, the hilt hidden within the sleeve of her jacket.

Tan walked straight to the bank of elevators and stopped to push the "up" button. She turned to him and smiled brightly. His expression remained wary.

The elevator door opened. Tan waved Bai into the lift. She stepped into the elevator and waited until he lifted his hand to punch the button for the seventh floor. Before the elevator door closed, she had the knife poised under his eye. The sharp blade drew a line of blood across his cheek.

She whispered into his ear. "Did you really think I'd be so gullible?"

"I don't know what you mean. I'm taking you to see Sammy Tu. That's all."

Perspiration ran down his forehead. He swallowed convulsively, his Adam's apple bobbing up and down. She could almost smell the fear on him. She wondered if he could smell the fear on her.

"Flinch, and you're dead," she warned.

She pulled his jacket back with her free hand and ripped the automatic weapon from his shoulder holster. Her thumb flicked off the safety and cocked the hammer as she pressed the barrel into his back. His body went rigid. As she drew the knife away from his face, he let out a long sigh of relief and slowly braced his hands against the elevator doors to take deep breaths.

She slipped the blade carefully back into its sheath before frisking him for more weapons. As the elevator dinged at the seventh floor, the doors started to slide open and he raised his hands. It was then she discovered a solid object—hard and heavy—holstered to Tan's back. She flipped up the back of his coat and pulled out a throwing hatchet.

"Are you serious?" She looked at the archaic weapon. "Really? You actually want to go back to being known as 'hatchet men'? When Jason finds out about this, he's going to chop you into little pieces with this relic."

Bai demonstrated by waving the ax in front of Tan's ashen face.

"I wasn't given a choice," he pleaded. "Shan made an example of those who refused to carry the ax. I'd rather be killed by the *Hung Kwan* than by Shan. It would be a cleaner death."

Given Shan's behavior, Bai conceded Tan might have had a valid argument. "What if I can get you out of this mess?"

Her offer was genuine. She needed an ally.

He turned his head to look at her with interest. "How?"

"Nobody's going to blame you for staying alive by playing along with Shan. But now it's time to choose sides. You help me out, and I'll square things with Jason."

"Or what?"

He fished for alternatives. Bai looked at him and shook her head in frustration. "Do you really want to try bartering with an angry woman holding a gun? Are you that stupid?"

He shrugged, leaving her to form her own opinion.

"Listen," she said in exasperation, "you can start running now and see how far you get. You're a dead man if Shan finds out I took away your toys, and you're a dead man for crossing the *Hung Kwan*. It would seem keeping me alive is your best chance of surviving this mess."

He contemplated her offer. The frown on his face said he wasn't happy with either choice.

"Given the alternative," he said reluctantly, "I'm your man."

He held out his hand for his weapons. Bai smiled at his audacity.

"Your enthusiasm is inspiring," she said, slapping his hand away with the blunt side of his hatchet.

She released the tension on the hammer of the gun but kept it leveled. "Trust comes in small increments. Let's start with your telling me everything you know about Sammy Tu."

"I don't know very much," he admitted. "Shan introduced me to him this evening. He's down the hall in room 724. My impression, so far, is that he slithered out of a swamp."

"Is there a young girl with him?" she asked.

"No. At least, I haven't seen a girl." He stopped to ponder a moment. "It's strange, though. Shan said something to Sammy Tu earlier. Something about the young needing discipline. I didn't understand what they were talking about. The comment just struck me as odd."

"To say Shan is odd is an understatement. His hatred for women runs deep."

Tan averted his eyes. He seemed to be hiding something.

"Is there something you'd like to tell me?" she asked.

"There are rumors, but that's all. It's probably nothing."

"What kind of rumors?"

"That Shan likes to hurt women. I don't know if it's true. I've never even seen Shan with a woman, let alone seen him hit one."

"Do you have children, Tan?"

His features became guarded "I have two daughters. Why?"

"What would you do if someone tried to hurt them?"

He replied without hesitation. "I'd kill them."

"I'm starting to like you better all the time, Mr. Tan."

His smile was hesitant. "Do you want me to take you to Sammy Tu now?"

"After you," Bai said, pointing down the hallway with the ax.

He nodded then turned to walk down the corridor. She followed, tucking the ax handle inside the belt at her waist as she walked.

Turning a corner, Tan stopped before room 724. He knocked and called out. "It's Tan. Open up."

Smiling into the peephole, Tan put on a good show. She still had the pistol at his back, but it wasn't pointed at him. At some point, she realized, she had to trust her instincts.

The door rattled as the safety chain was released. A thin man with a crimped face stood in the doorway with both hands poised on his hips, like a comic book hero.

"And who do we have here?" His voice was that of the man from the stairwell. Amusement distorted his face. He looked like a happy clown.

"I'm the *souxun*." Bai brought the gun up to point it in his face as she ratcheted back the hammer. The chatter of the automatic weapon managed to grab his attention. He froze. "You, Sammy Tu, have been found."

chapter 18

A courageous foe is
better than a cowardly friend

Tan shoved Sammy Tu into the room and threw him up against the wall to check for weapons. Sammy Tu wasn't carrying, which suggested he was either very trusting or a fool.

Bai kicked the door closed behind her. "Take a seat, Sammy." She waved the gun in the general direction of a desk chair. "We have some things to discuss."

Sammy Tu's eyes dodged from side to side while his tongue licked his lips nervously. He looked like an animal caught in a trap as he feverishly looked for a way to escape his predicament.

The room was a hotel standard: a double bed, two upholstered chairs, and a small writing desk against the wall. Unless Sammy Tu was willing to take a header out the window and drop seven stories to the ground, he had no place to go.

She scowled. "Just sit down, Sammy, before I shoot you."

He stared at her. Her words didn't seem to penetrate his bewilderment.

"That's not to say I won't shoot you anyway," she informed him as she raised the gun to point it at his chest.

Tan put a hand on Sammy Tu's shoulder and pushed him down into the chair. He kept a hand on Sammy Tu to dispel any notion of his getting up again.

Before she could question him, Sammy Tu started to blab. "I knew, I knew it, I knew it! That asshole Shan set me up, didn't he? He used the girl then sold me just like a whore. I'm a fucking whore. That's what I am. I'm nothing but a fucking whore."

She couldn't entirely comprehend Sammy Tu's rant, but reference to the girl got her attention. "Tell me where Jia Yan is."

He shot her a furtive look. It was obvious to Bai that lies were running through Sammy Tu's head like shoppers on Christmas Eve. Reaching into her sleeve, she pulled out Jason's knife and handed it to Tan.

"See if you can prick Sammy's memory," she suggested.

Taking the knife, Tan quickly sliced through Sammy Tu's ear. He tossed the bloody trophy into the pimp's lap before Sammy Tu even realized what had happened.

A howl erupted from Sammy as he stared at the severed ear in horror before grabbing at his bleeding head. Every foul word in his vocabulary spewed from his mouth, including a few Bai hadn't heard. As Sammy ranted, she watched him dispassionately, surprised at her own detachment. Her reasoning told her she should have been horrified by the callous violence. Oddly enough, she wasn't, and momentarily wondered why.

She waited until the cursing subsided to incoherent whimpering. "Where's the girl, Sammy? If I have to ask again, Mr. Tan will be obliged to cut off something even more sensitive."

He twisted around to stare fearfully at Bai. Tears streamed down his face. "What's left of her is through that door." He nodded at the access door to the adjoining room. "Shan's been at her since yesterday. I'm not sure there's much left." He wept and his face crumpled. "He said he was going to pay me for her. But he never gave me a fucking dime. It was all lies, nothing but lies."

The pimp folded up and whimpered.

Bai looked at Tan to catch his attention. "Keep a close eye on him. Cut him if he tries to run."

Tan grimly nodded in response.

She walked around the bed to open the door to the adjoining room. It was unlocked from the other side. She couldn't see much. The lights were off and the curtains drawn. She found the light switch next to the door and flipped it on.

Jia Yan was curled into a fetal position on the bed. She was naked, bruised, and covered in blood. Bai walked over to lean down and touch the girl's wrist to check for a pulse. Jia mewled like a kitten. She was alive, but just barely.

Standing there, Bai felt like a failure. Tears filled her eyes as she stared at the broken child. She was afraid to touch her again for fear of hurting her. There was no way to tell how many broken bones or internal injuries Jia suffered. Bai couldn't fathom the cruelty inflicted on her.

Anger quickly replaced guilt. She hated Shan. She trembled with rage as a molten fury exploded within her. For the first time in her life, she really wanted to kill someone.

She stormed back into the room where Sammy Tu and Tan waited. Tan looked at her with apprehension. Words spilled from her mouth in anger. "I'm going to find that son of a bitch and I'm going to kill him."

"The girl?" Tan asked.

Bai stared blankly at him and realized she'd lost it for a moment. "Right . . . ," she nodded, reordering her priorities, "the girl's alive, but she needs medical attention."

He looked to her for instructions. His questioning presence forced her to stop and think. It wouldn't do her or the girl any good if she flew into a rage. She needed a plan.

"First," she said, "I want you to get on the phone and arrange for an ambulance. Have them come through the back. There must be a facility *Sun Yee On* uses."

"Yes, there's a private hospital, a good one," said Tan. "No questions asked."

"Good. After that, I want you to call Shan. Tell him that I'm in the room next door with Sammy Tu. Tell him you listened at the door. Tell Shan you heard us say the girl is dead. I want you to tell him I've bought Sammy Tu. You heard us negotiating a wire transfer for a million dollars. We plan to pin Jia's murder on him. That should bring him running— and alone. He won't want anyone else to know about the girl or the money."

Tan looked worried. "Are you sure you want to bring him here? You shouldn't underestimate him. He's dangerous."

"Don't worry. Just make the calls."

She walked over to put the barrel of the gun to the side of Sammy Tu's head. She played with the idea of pulling the trigger. The pimp continued to weep. When he felt the barrel of the gun against his temple, he jammed his eyes closed with fear and cringed.

After a tense moment, she decided he wasn't worth the bullet—or the burden on her soul. She settled for slamming the barrel of the pistol down on the back of Sammy's head. He slumped forward, unconscious. Bending over, Bai pulled the laces out of his shoes and used them to bind his hands and feet. She didn't want him going anywhere until she'd had another chance to question him. She still needed to find out who'd hired him. And why.

Speaking heatedly into the phone, Tan arranged for an ambulance. Then he called Shan. She listened as he sold the story convincingly.

When he hung up, he nodded to her. "He's in the elevator now."

"Good." Her anger had grown cold—but no less potent. "I'll be in the hallway waiting."

"Don't you want me to come with you?"

"No. Stay here." She cast a glance at the doorway to the adjoining room. "You take care of the girl. If I don't come back, get her out of here and let Jason know what happened. If he doubts your story, you tell him I swore on my daughter's life. He'll understand."

She could see that he wanted to argue with her, but she didn't give him the chance. She handed him the gun. He looked at the weapon and then bowed deeply from the waist, demonstrating the respect he'd neglected earlier.

She pulled Tan's hatchet out of its resting place in her belt. "Don't shoot Sammy, no matter how tempting it is. I need him."

Her feet carried her swiftly across the room. She looked back once as she closed the door. Tan's eyes followed her with a worried expression.

Turning the corner in the corridor, Bai ran toward the elevators, her body racing with adrenaline. The lights above the elevator doors informed her it was on its way up; the number 4 was lit. She skidded to a stop fifteen paces from the elevator and waited. Her life would depend on her sense of timing.

As a child, Bai had practiced with hatchets as part of her martial schooling. She recalled throwing the heavy blades and the resulting feeling of satisfaction upon hearing the crack of wood when the hatchet split a target. She hoped her muscles remembered the experience as well.

She held the ax at her side as she wiggled her arms to loosen her shoulders. She flexed her legs by bouncing in place. The elevator dinged to signal its arrival at the seventh floor. She took three fast steps as she swung the hatchet behind her. On the fourth step, her arm arced the hatchet over her head. She released her grip with the fifth step and watched the blade spin away as she slid to a halt.

The hatchet somersaulted through the air with a whirring sound.

The elevator door started to open. Through the widening crack of the door, she glimpsed Shan waiting impatiently. He looked up to see her bent over, her hands on her knees. She notched her head up to meet his gaze.

Their eyes met. She witnessed the hatred on Shan's face before his expression flicked to surprise. He'd seen the hatchet. His eyes became saucers. Hands flinched up to fend off the blade. Too late.

The hatchet barely cleared the opening doors before it slammed into his forehead. The impact snapped his head back violently. His feet flew out from underneath him. He flopped on his back in the elevator with his arms and legs splayed. His body twitched for a moment before going completely still, the hatchet protruding from his forehead.

Bai walked up to the elevator to stop it from closing. She didn't want Shan's body traveling from floor to floor with a hatchet covered with her fingerprints embedded in his head. Pushing the "open" button inside the elevator, she grabbed the cuffs of his trousers and pulled. He was a big man. She strained as she tugged on his pant legs. His body was halfway out of the elevator when the doors tried to close. They caught Shan at the waist and rebounded while the elevator bell dinged repeatedly in protest.

She jumped at the sound of a voice. "Could you use a hand with that?"

She turned frantically to find Jason flanked by four men, some of whom she knew from San Francisco. He smiled. The other four men looked concerned by her activities.

"And this, gentlemen," Jason pronounced, addressing those standing around him, "is what happens when you piss off the *souxun*. I want you to keep this in mind the next time you're tempted to mess with her."

He gestured with his hand, and two of his men moved to gather Shan up and drag his limp body down the hall toward the back stairwell.

She grabbed Jason's arm to lead him back down the corridor. "Your timing is a little off. I could have used you about ten minutes ago."

He looked at her and shook his head in frustration. "I thought you were safe in the restaurant. It wasn't until we saw Shan bolt for the elevator that it occurred to me you might do something stupid, like follow me."

"I didn't follow you. I drew Shan and one of his men away. I thought you might be in trouble."

He turned aside to look at her. She could tell he was exasperated. "You're a hard woman to protect."

She smiled at him. "I never said the job was easy."

She stopped in front of room 724 and knocked. "Tan, it's me, Bai. Open up."

A few seconds later, the door swung open to reveal Tan. The automatic weapon still rested in his hand. It was pointed at the ground. Tan recognized Jason behind her and stepped away from the door to bow low as Jason stepped into the room. Jason's men followed like shadows.

She looked across the room and saw Sammy Tu was coming around. He was drifting in and out of consciousness, his head lolling.

She pointed at the pimp. "Meet Sammy Tu."

As Jason stared at Sammy, she turned to Tan. "What about the ambulance for the girl?"

Tan seemed shaken. His face looked pale. "They should be here any minute."

"Did you look in on her?" she asked.

He nodded in response and took a deep breath. "I wish I hadn't. Is Shan dead?"

"He's dead all right," offered Jason, interrupting their conversation, "but that doesn't explain what you're doing here with a gun in your hand, Tan."

She jumped into the conversation by placing herself physically between the two men. "He only served Shan to protect his daughters. He helped me escape and worked with me to kill Shan. He did what he had to do until the time was right. He should be forgiven. After all, 'a courageous foe is better than a cowardly friend.'"

The look Bai bestowed on Jason didn't brook any argument. While looking at Tan, Jason's expression remained unreadable. Sammy Tu moaned softly in the background as Jason stared. No one moved.

Finally, he relented. "I'll expect full cooperation on weeding out any of Shan's followers."

The question wasn't rhetorical. Everyone in the room waited for the answer.

Showing respect, Tan again bowed low. "You'll have it, *Hung Kwan*."

"In that case, welcome back, Brother. You can thank Bai for your life."

Jason turned to one of his men and nodded. The man pulled a phone from his jacket pocket and made a connection. The call would take Tan's name off the list of those to be hunted down and killed.

There was a knock on the door. One of Jason's men answered with his gun drawn. Two men in emergency response uniforms stood in the hallway with a wheeled gurney.

"Let them in," Bai urged.

As they wheeled the gurney through the door, she directed them into the next room where a young woman clung tenuously to life.

chapter 19

Forget injuries, never forget kindnesses

Tires squealed as the ambulance turned a tight corner. Bai's hands gripped the sides of the gurney for support while the vehicle pitched and swayed as it raced through the streets of downtown Vancouver.

Bai hovered over Jia while feeling helpless, unable to do anything to aid the injured girl. A paramedic attempted to insert an IV drip into Jia's arm but seemed to be having a problem. He shook his head in frustration as he labored over her while talking to Bai. "We need to hydrate her, but her blood pressure is so low the veins have collapsed," he explained. "Wait a minute! There you are, you little bugger." He looked up with a grin. "I got it!"

The paramedic was young, exuberant, and freckle-faced. He looked like he was twelve years old. Bai nodded in encouragement and felt like a lame cheerleader.

"We can't give her anything for the pain," he added. "We don't know enough about her injuries. I'm afraid anything we give her might stop her heart. She's weak; her pulse is thready." He attached an intravenous drip and hung the bag on an overhead hook where it rocked back and forth. "We'll just get some fluids in her and wait for the doctors to make the hard calls."

"How far to the hospital?" Bai asked.

"We're almost there. Our trauma team is really good, and they're fully staffed."

"Has it been a busy night?"

"It's been a crazy night," he asserted brightly, then seemed to regret his choice of words. "That's to say, we're getting more calls than usual. There seem to be a lot of gun-related incidents tonight."

"Seems to be a lot of that going around," she agreed.

The ambulance swerved suddenly, throwing Bai to the side before coming to an abrupt halt. She felt the vehicle back up then stop again. The rear doors flew open. Men dressed in blue scrubs reached in to tug at the gurney.

Bai jumped out of the back of the ambulance and into frigid air as men wheeled Jia through a set of automatic doors that swooshed open at their approach. A current of warmer air, smelling of disinfectant and floor cleaner, enveloped them.

Orderlies rushed the gurney down a brightly lit hallway with Bai right behind them. Walls of white tile flew by as they ran. Wheels rattled and clattered when the gurney slapped through another set of metal doors and into a room of curtained cubicles. Jia's gurney was smoothly eased into the nearest open bay where people in green and red scrubs dropped on her like raptors on roadkill.

A blood-pressure cuff was hurriedly strapped to her arm. A trauma nurse pressed a stethoscope against her chest while another clipped a pulse monitor on her finger. To assess her medical needs, they quickly checked her temperature and respirations; drew blood; and peered into her eyes, mouth, ears, and every other orifice.

Jia fought them feebly. Pitiful moans escaped bruised and swollen lips while Bai's stomach clenched in empathy as she watched from the sidelines. She couldn't help the feeling it was *her* child lying on the gurney.

Almost immediately, Jia was pulled out of the cubicle as doctors and nurses raced the gurney down another hallway, all the while spouting medical jargon. Bai tried to follow, but a woman in a white doctor's coat put an arm out to hold her back. The physician was taller than Bai and very white, with alabaster skin and red hair. She was striking.

The doctor gripped Bai's shoulders. "You'll have to wait here."

Bai tried to push past her. "I need to be with Jia."

The doctor refused to let go. "There's nothing you can do but get in the way."

Bai turned and almost struck the woman. The doctor must have seen something in Bai's expression because she flinched but, to her credit, didn't let go. Bai took a deep breath and a step back. She faced the doctor and brought her emotions under control.

"I need to be with her," Bai repeated.

"I'll come and get you as soon as we've done x-rays and ultrasound. We may have to run a CAT scan as well. You're better off in the waiting room until we can assess your daughter's condition."

The doctor's tone left no room for argument. Her stare was direct and commanding.

Bai thought the woman was a bitch—and liked her for it. She acquiesced to the doctor's orders, even though it pained her to do so. She wanted access to Jia. If that meant giving a little to get a little, she'd play the game.

She didn't bother denying she was Jia's mother. "You'll let me know as soon as you have something?"

"Of course I will."

Bai stuck her hand out. "My name's Bai. You do everything you have to do to make that girl whole. I don't care what it costs or what specialists you need to call in. Do we understand each other?"

The doctor looked at Bai's hand and then took it in a firm grip. "I think we do, Bai. My name's Shannon, Doctor Shannon Brian. Now if you'll excuse me, I have a patient to see to." She turned and walked away without a backward glance.

Bai followed the signs to the emergency waiting room. It proved to be an antiseptic purgatory complete with blue plastic chairs, dog-eared magazines, and scuffed linoleum floors. It was also, thankfully, unoccupied.

She wandered out into the hall and found a coffee machine. After feeding the mechanism a dollar, it sloshed out a cup of lukewarm mud that tasted like shoe polish. Thinking it might have enough caffeine to keep her going, she tried to drink it. She made it halfway through the cup before she gave up and tossed it in the trash, where it landed on a small mountain of mostly full coffee cups.

Walking back into the waiting room, she settled into one of the disgusting blue chairs to wait. Time dragged. She checked her cell every five minutes and felt as if she'd been caught in a time warp as the minutes ticked away like hours. Just when she thought she couldn't stand it anymore, Shannon returned, her face grave. Bai braced herself for bad news.

Shannon's voice was harsh. "What exactly happened to your daughter?"

"A sadistic man beat her repeatedly."

The color in the doctor's neck turned from white to red.

"Where is he?" she demanded.

"Where he'll never hurt anyone again."

Shannon stopped herself. Whatever she'd been prepared to say was abandoned as she stared at Bai and tried to read her. Finally she nodded. "Good!"

It was a terse but heartfelt endorsement.

"What about Jia?" Bai asked.

"We're prepping her for surgery now. She'll probably lose her spleen. I don't think we can save it. Her kidneys are bruised, and she has internal bleeding. We'll know more once we've opened her up." She paused for a moment as she looked at her clipboard. "Her right wrist is fractured. Repairing that can wait until she's out of surgery. We'll set it while she's still sedated. Four of her ribs are fractured, but her lungs, miraculously, are all right—no punctures we could see. Her breathing is good, given the circumstances. Other than that, she has facial lacerations, a couple of loose teeth, and a hairline fracture of her cheek that will have to heal on its own. Oh, and a dislocated shoulder that's got to hurt like hell. We're packing it in ice to get the swelling down before putting it back in place. She may require follow-up surgery if the tendons are too severely damaged."

She dropped the clipboard to her side. "I can't say for sure your daughter's out of danger. She's sustained a lot of tissue damage. There's always the danger of clotting. But she's young, and that will work in her favor. We'll know more in a few hours. Right now, she's stabilized." She paused a moment before continuing. "Even if she makes a complete physical recovery, the long-term psychological damage may prove more difficult to repair. The prolonged abuse she's endured can have lasting effects. You should see to it she gets professional help."

Bai looked at Shannon and asked the question candidly. "Was she raped?"

"No. And that's even stranger. Usually when girls are brought in with these kinds of injuries, sexual penetration is the first thing we look for. Your daughter's hymen is still intact, and she appears not to have been molested."

Bai digested that bit of information as she reflected on Shan's hatred for women. She took into account his high voice and his raging temper. Her observations led her to speculate that he might have been abusing steroids. Shrunken testicles from prolonged steroid use would explain a lot of his symptoms.

"Can you refer me to a good therapist in San Francisco?" Bai asked.

"Not offhand, but I can make some calls. We've still time for that. Your daughter won't be leaving here for a few days, at the very least."

"When do you expect she'll be out of surgery?"

"If everything goes well, you can see her in a couple of hours. Your daughter's been assigned a private room with two beds for pediatric patients. Why don't I have an orderly take you up and get you situated? She'll be wheeled up as soon as she's out of recovery. I'll give you an update before then."

Bai thought about the offer. She had a number of things to attend to, but she was dead on her feet. She'd been up for nearly twenty hours, killed two people, and seen another two executed. Mrs. Yan still waved at her every time she closed her eyes. Her nerves were so frayed she felt like she was rattling.

"That's very kind of you."

Shannon waved aside the courtesy "Forget it. You look like you could use some rest."

"My people have a saying, 'Forget injuries, never forget kindnesses.'"

Shannon looked at her with a thoughtful expression. "I'll have to remember that."

The doctor smiled for the first time, and Bai was taken by how beautiful she was.

"Follow me," Shannon said, and turned to walk down the hall.

She led Bai in the opposite direction of the emergency room. At the first nursing station, Shannon turfed Bai to an orderly who took her to the third floor and deposited her in a room with two hospital beds, the kind with metal rails. A drape, suspended from a rod on the ceiling, divided the room. A utilitarian bath with a shower was accessible through a door near the entry. The walls of the room were painted with clouds and rainbows, but the room still smelled of disinfectant and floor wax, the unmistakable aroma of hospital.

Bai sat on the bed farthest from the door. She leaned back to rest her head against a starched, brittle pillowcase, thinking she might rest her eyes for a moment. And slept.

chapter 20

Do good, reap good; do evil, reap evil

Bai awakened to someone's tugging on the sleeve of her jacket. Jason stood at the bedside with her overnight bag in his hand. It took a moment for her to remember where she was. She sat up groggily.

"I thought you might need this," Jason said, holding up her bag.

Bleary-eyed, she looked at him. "You just can't stand it when I sleep. Is that it?"

He smiled and put the bag down at the foot of the bed. "Since you've obviously decided to move on, I don't see any reason to be nice to you, unless, of course, you'd consider changing your mind."

He walked around to put his hands on her shoulders and knead the muscles of her back. She almost purred. Despite the rude awakening, his flirtation brought a smile to her lips. She turned her head to look out of the window. Dawn was breaking. Crimson rimmed the horizon.

She put a hand on Jason's, which continued to rest on her shoulder. "You must have news, or you wouldn't have wakened me. What's going on?"

"While you slept," he prefaced, "I've been working on extracting the truth from Sammy Tu. No easy task given his penchant for lying. I've met some terrific liars before, but nothing compares to the ingenuity of his stories."

"You woke me up to tell me he's a big fat liar?"

"There's more to it than that. It turns out he did hold a contract on you. But it wasn't to kill you. His job was just to lure you away from the protection of *Sun Yee On*."

His comment grabbed Bai's attention. She sat up straight to wipe the sleep from her eyes as she thought out loud. "Did you get the name of the contractor?"

He walked around to sit on the bed and face her. "That part was easy. You ever hear of the law practice of Hung and Chin?"

"Hung and Chin are my attorneys! There's no way Benny and Robert would handle a contract on me. We've known each other since we were children. The idea of their being involved in this is preposterous."

He smiled and shrugged his shoulders. "They may not knowingly have handled the contract. And this is where it gets really interesting. It seems the contract was a blind document handled by Hung and Chin without their being privy to the contents."

"Does that make any sense to you?" she asked.

"That's something you'll have to ask them. I'm not an attorney."

A sardonic, lopsided smile twisted his features. He seemed amused by the turn of events.

"Do you think this is funny?" she asked.

"Maybe a little. Not like laugh-out-loud funny, but the situation does reek of irony. Think about it—your childhood friends unknowingly assisting in your demise."

She dismissed his warped idea of humor with a flick of her hand. "I'd liked to have been there when you questioned him. Are you absolutely sure he told you the truth?"

Jason dropped the smile and spoke candidly. "Trust me; you wouldn't have wanted to be there."

Seeing his features harden, Bai understood. It would have been impossible for her to stand by and watch someone tortured for hours on end. Then again, she'd been the one to hand Tan the knife that severed Sammy Tu's ear. She was beginning to have serious doubts about who *she* really was.

She took a deep breath and let it out before asking, "Did he have anything else to say?"

"He had plenty to say—mostly atrocious lies. At one point he swore he was an undercover DEA agent. Then he tried to convince me he was an unwilling pawn. That Shan had set you up. The only interesting information was a story about Jimmy Yan. Sammy Tu sent one of his girls to entice you into looking for Jia. It seems Jimmy had been coached to tell you Sammy Tu had left for Vancouver. The idea was to draw you away from Chinatown and *Sun Yee On*. Jimmy got caught up in his own macho bullshit and got kicked in the balls before he could deliver his lines. How's that for a classic cock-up?"

She shook her head in amazement. "The trip to Oakland should never have happened."

"Sammy Tu went ballistic when he found out *Sun Yee On* was involved and we'd burned down his house. Now that, you've got to admit, has really good potential for humor. This whole setup was pretty much a comedy of errors. The fact we still ended up coming to Vancouver gave him the impression we'd already exposed his involvement. He thought *Sun Yee On* was gunning for him. That made him nervous enough to call on his best client, Shan, for help. It seems Sammy Tu's been providing girls to him for quite some time."

She took a moment to sort out the interwoven relationships. She was starting to think she might need to draw a flow chart. "So Jimmy was involved in this from the beginning? Does he know his mother's dead?"

"That's another macabre story." Jason's smile faded as he seemed to gather himself. "According to Sammy Tu, Mrs. Yan balked at Jimmy's selling his sister to gain admittance into the *Wah Ching*. Sammy Tu told Jimmy to take care of it. He lured his mother over to Oakland and went after her with his pocket knife, the preferred weapon of newbie tough guys. Sammy Tu said Jimmy chased the old lady around for about twenty minutes before she grabbed her chest and fell over dead. Sammy Tu professed regret at not killing Jimmy then and there. It seems he couldn't stop laughing long enough to pull the trigger."

Bai put her head in her hands. Jimmy, as it turned out, was an even bigger idiot than she'd imagined.

"And you're certain he was telling the truth? It all sounds so crazy."

"In the end, he gave us everything he had. I feel confident he told the truth. And, like all good deeds, his part in this won't go unpunished."

"You didn't kill him, did you?"

"No. I'll leave that to someone else."

She couldn't bring herself to feel sorry for Sammy Tu. He'd sold girls to Shan, sending them to a brutal death.

"'Do good, reap good; do evil, reap evil,'" she said sadly.

Jason chuckled at the adage. "Let's hope not." He brushed a bit of imaginary lint off his shoulder and smiled at her. "How's the girl?"

"They think she'll live. She's probably going to lose her spleen. I hope that's the worst of it. The doctor said she'd come by when Jia came out of surgery. That was a couple of hours ago."

"Did they say how long she'll be hospitalized?"

"They think a couple of days, at least. Why?"

"Because our private jet is headed back to San Francisco in a little more than an hour and I'd like you to be on it."

She couldn't understand his motive for hastening her departure. "What's the rush to get rid of me?"

"It's not me," he said as he put his arm around her shoulders. "I like having you around. It's just that when you buried the hatchet, so to speak, with Shan, you did two things. You eliminated the leader of the faction that has been questioning my authority, and you did it in a way that embarrassed the hell out of his followers."

"You think they might come after me?"

He hugged her affectionately. "You do seem to arouse the most passionate feelings in men."

She ignored his jibe. "Who's going to look after Jia?"

"The girl isn't your problem. You've found her. Job well done," he said dismissively.

She turned to glare at him, stunned by his callousness. "The hell she isn't my problem! She wouldn't be here if somebody hadn't decided to use her as bait to kill me. I'm the *souxun*. I found her. Nobody else seems to want her. Her mother's dead, her brother sold her, and her other siblings are in no position to care for her. As far as I'm concerned she's mine. You got that?"

Her anger was instantaneous and blistering.

He threw up his hands, "OK, I get it. I didn't know you felt that way. Give me a minute to think. There's got to be a way to make this work."

She watched him guardedly as he put his hand to his chin in thought. His eyes became distant before he finally turned back to her. "What do you think of this? Dan and my mother fly back to take care of Jia. Tommy's bringing the jet back today to meet with the *Fu Shan Chu* who's flying in from Hong Kong. Tommy could keep Dan and Elizabeth here for a few days with him. They'd be safer with Tommy than they would be at home, and the girls can look after Jia. I'll even volunteer a private jet to fly everyone back to San Francisco when Jia's well enough. In the meantime, you'd be free to pursue matters with Hung and Chin and follow up on the information from the cell phone and the money you took off the assassin at the airport." He put his hand over hers. "All I ask in return is you don't do anything rash until I get back in town. By 'rash,' I mean you and Lee don't go vigilante and try to confront whoever is behind your problems on your own."

She gently removed his hand. "I seem to be doing a pretty good job of taking care of myself."

"I never said you couldn't take care of yourself." He looked genuinely concerned. "I would just prefer you didn't go off half-cocked and get yourself killed. You are the mother of my child. I would be a poor substitute should anything happen to you. Keep that in mind."

She dismissed his remark but had to admit his offer made sense. Being with Tommy would afford Dan and Elizabeth better protection than she could provide on her own. He would be traveling with a small army of soldiers. Furthermore, she wanted to get back to Chinatown to find out what her attorneys knew about the contract they'd handled, since she'd been the intended victim.

Still, it galled her that he was right. "All right, it's a deal."

He glanced at his cell. "You have about an hour before the plane leaves."

Shannon Brian walked into the room. She was dressed in surgical greens. The color set off her red hair and pale skin. Jason looked up from his phone and his eyes widened.

Bai introduced them. "Shannon, this is Jason Lum, a friend."

"I've already met Mr. Lum. I take it that knife wound healed without any problems?" As she asked, she looked at him speculatively.

"Good as new," he replied. "I didn't realize you were the surgeon on Jia's case."

He looked nervous. Jason never looked nervous.

"I happened to be on call in the E.R. when she came in."

He turned to Bai. "Jia's a lucky girl. Shannon's the best surgeon in the city."

"Really? I'm glad to hear it," she said. She studied the interaction between Shannon and Jason. "And how is she doing?"

"Better. She's in recovery, and her vitals are strong. We've removed the spleen, patched her kidneys, set the bones in her wrist and her dislocated shoulder. She's still heavily sedated and will stay that way for several hours. Her eyes are open, but she's not coherent. You're welcome to go see her."

"Thanks, Shannon, for everything. It seems I'll be returning to San Francisco soon. My mother and daughter will be flying in to care for Jia. Whom do I see to make arrangements?"

Jason spoke up before Shannon could answer her question. "I can take care of that. We have a hospital liaison to handle these kinds of situations. Why don't I do that while you see Jia? When you're finished, I'll give you a ride to the airport."

"Fine," Bai said, standing up.

"I can take you to see her," Shannon offered. "I'm on my way back to the recovery room now."

She followed Shannon into the hall. Jason turned in the opposite direction as the two women walked along the corridor to the elevators.

While they waited for the lift, Shannon asked, "Is Mr. Lum a relation?"

The question seemed innocent enough, but Bai could detect an underlying tension. "No, he's an ex."

Shannon seemed uncomfortable with the answer. "That's interesting. You're no longer involved then?"

Bai avoided the question. "Would you be willing to take some unsolicited advice?"

"Probably not, but go ahead anyway."

"Jason's beautiful, dangerous, and exciting. Hooking up with him is like flying a kite in a thunderstorm. It's just a matter of time before something bad happens."

"That's good advice."

"Yes, and I wish I'd taken it when it had been given to me." She glanced aside at Shannon, who seemed amused. "But there are some things you just have to find out for yourself."

chapter 21

A child's life is like a piece of paper on which every person leaves a mark

Jia Yan's face, bruised purple and yellow, looked like spoiled fruit. Brown eyes sunken within folds of puffy, half-closed lids followed Bai's movements. The girl appeared to be semiconscious. Still, Bai had no way of telling how much, if anything, Jia understood. The urge to cry at the sight of the broken child left her fighting to control her emotions.

She leaned over to speak softly into Jia's ear. "My name is Bai Jiang. I'm the *souxun* sent to find you. I want you to know that the man who hurt you is dead. You have nothing to fear from him, or anyone else for that matter. You're under my protection. You're safe now."

She looked down on Jia's battered face and thought of something her grandfather had shared with her. He'd said, 'A child's life is like a piece of paper on which every person leaves a mark.' Bai wanted nothing more than to take an eraser and obliterate the last few days from Jia's page. The least she could do, she vowed, was to make those responsible for the child's suffering pay.

"In a few days," she said, her voice cracking with emotion, "when you're well enough to travel, you'll be coming home with me. All you have to do now is mend. Don't worry about anything else. I'll take care of you."

She wanted to wrap the girl in her arms and comfort her, but that was out of the question. Jia's left arm was in a fresh cast. The smell of curing plaster lay thick in the air. Her right arm was strapped to her side with an elastic bandage. Bai settled for touching the tips of Jia's fingers lightly. She leaned down to deliver a light kiss on the girl's forehead while trying not to shed tears in the process.

As Bai turned away, she wondered distractedly how Dan would feel having another girl in the house. Bai had no qualms about taking

149

Jia home. She'd found the girl. As far as Bai was concerned, hers was a clear case of "finder's keeper's." Jia belonged to her now.

Jason was waiting for her outside the recovery room. She stopped to look him in the eye. "I want her guarded until Elizabeth arrives. I need to know you'll keep her safe."

"If it'll make you feel better, I'll leave two of my best men here to watch her. I'd stay myself, but there is pressing business that requires my attention."

"Anything I should be concerned about?"

He shook his head in denial. "I can assure you she's safe here. Word of Shan's deviant behavior is spreading rapidly. Those who supported him will find it difficult to defend a man who beats children to death. I just need to tie up some loose ends before Tommy arrives."

He paused, his lips pinched together in thought. "As you can imagine, it's become common knowledge that Tommy is coming to Vancouver to clean house. I have men deployed to watch some of our more restive associates. It's especially important I don't lose any of *Sun Yee On's* assets. Tommy's made it clear he doesn't want to finance a bunch of dissident rivals."

"If Shan's any indication of what infests *Sun Yee On*, a house-cleaning is long overdue," Bai observed.

"Shan was an aberration," he said defensively, "but there's no denying a bit of restructuring is in order." He put his arm around her shoulders to steer her away from the recovery room. "The car's waiting under the front portico."

She walked with him down a long hallway to the hospital lobby, then out glass doors to a tall, covered driveway. A black limousine waited with the engine running. White exhaust plumed in the chill.

She stopped to look around. A light mist hugged the ground to mute the lush, green foliage of the hospital grounds. Dew-laden grass scented the morning air. "It smells cleaner here, different from the city."

"Not as many people peeing on the sidewalks," quipped Jason, taking some of the magic out of the moment. "Canadians, in general, seem to be better about that sort of thing."

She stared at him in despair. "You really know how to kill a mood."

"Among other things."

He opened the door of the car as the driver came around to take her bag. She stepped into the car with Jason right behind her. Two of his men already occupied the opposite seat. One of them cradled a pump-action shotgun across his lap while the other listened to an MP3 player with his eyes closed.

She spoke to them. "Hello, Jon. Art. You two are a long way from home."

She recognized the men from long acquaintance in San Francisco. They were older than she and had served under Tommy when he'd been *Hung Kwan*. Both men were experienced enforcers and reputed to be very good at their jobs.

Art, the one listening to music, pulled his earplugs out and smiled at her. "There's a story going around that you went *mano a mano* with Shan and put a hatchet in his head."

The two men beamed at her.

She frowned at the comment. Without anger fueling her blood-lust, she'd started to second-guess her homicidal behavior. Even though she couldn't work up any remorse for killing Shan, she couldn't take pride in her actions either. Mostly, she just felt empty.

"The first one's the toughest," Art offered solicitously.

"Hopefully, it'll be her last," Jason stated, not bothering to mention it had been her second killing of the day.

Art was going to say something else, but Jason intervened. "I think a little contemplative silence would be good."

His suggestion was met with obedient nods.

The car pulled slowly away from the hospital. They rode quietly toward the airport as the sky lightened by shades. Weak winter sunlight quickly burned off the mist. By the time the car reached the fenced area of the airport where *Sun Yee On's* private jet waited, the sky had turned a vibrant blue.

Jason got out of the car to walk Bai to the ramp of the plane. Jon and Art followed, their hardware concealed beneath open trench coats.

When she reached the ramp, Jason held out her bag. "Remember, you don't do anything but ask questions until I get back. Whoever initiated the contract on you is obviously dangerous. I don't want you and Lee tackling this without me."

She nodded in understanding and bestowed what she considered her sincerest smile on him. He scowled in return. His expression suggested he wasn't convinced by the easily won concession. He probably feared she'd keep pushing until something gave, regardless of the danger. It was her nature.

She placed her hand against his cheek before turning to walk up the ramp. Stopping at the door of the plane, she turned around to see him staring up at her with a deep frown etched on his face. She smiled and waved. He shook his head and turned away to walk back toward the waiting limo.

She stepped through the hatch of the plane and made her way toward the cockpit.

The walls of the jet were paneled in a glossy red wood. Oversized recliners in dark blue leather provided individual seating for eight. She appeared to be the only passenger as she sat in a seat situated mid-cabin over one of the stubby wings.

"Would you like something to drink?"

She started and turned to find a woman standing behind her. A lovely smile accompanied the inquiry. The stewardess was petite, Chinese, and wore a black skirt with a starched white blouse. A small set of silver wings glistened on her collar.

"Coffee, if you have it," Bai replied. "Am I the only passenger?"

"Yes, it'll just be the two of us and the pilots. My name is Mei. We'll be taking off in about ten minutes. In the meantime, I could bring you an espresso, cappuccino, café mocha, or just coffee. Which would you prefer?"

"Just coffee, thanks. Black. Is it all right if I use my cell phone?"

"As long as we're stationary. Once we're in the air, we have phones onboard you can use while in-flight. Just let me know what you need, and I'll be more than happy to provide it."

"Thank you."

The young woman bowed and turned away to walk toward the back of the plane where a partition door stood ajar. Bai assumed there was a galley behind the screen. The hidden compartment explained the young woman's sudden appearance.

She tossed her bag into the seat next to her then pulled her cell phone out of her jacket pocket. She called Lee, fully aware he wouldn't be thrilled to hear from her so early in the morning. The phone rang for a long time before he finally picked up.

His voice was slurred. "Did somebody die?"

The question startled her. "Why? Did you hear something?"

"Wait a minute! Somebody really did die? What time is it, anyway?"

"It's six o'clock. Answer my question."

"What?"

"Why did you think somebody died?"

"What other reason would you have to call someone in the middle of the night?"

"The sun is up! It's six in the morning."

"Just because the sun is up doesn't mean it's day. Only barbarians are awake at this hour. Are you in some kind of trouble?"

"More than you could ever imagine," she divulged. "There's been a change in plans. I'm flying home. I'll be there in about three hours. Dan and Elizabeth will be flying out with Tommy this morning. You and I have some work to do, and it may be dangerous."

His voice dropped an octave. "Tell me."

"Someone's trying to kill me, Lee. And I haven't the slightest idea who or why."

"What do you need me to do?"

She smiled. She knew she could depend on him. It wouldn't have mattered what she'd asked of him.

"For right now, get Dan and Elizabeth ready to travel. The tricky part will be not alarming them. Tell them I need them here in Vancouver to take care of Jia. Also, I need you to make an afternoon appointment with Hung and Chin. Robert left a message yesterday saying he had something urgent to discuss, and I need to speak with them about a contract they handled."

"Evidently you found the girl."

"I found her, but she's in bad shape. She's been nearly beaten to death. That's why I need Elizabeth and Dan here to take care of her while you and I take care of matters at home."

"Got it," Lee affirmed. "Will you need a ride from the airport?"

"No, don't worry about me. Just take care of them. I'm pretty sure Tommy will have an armed escort waiting for me. *Sun Yee On* has taken an interest in my problem. That's part of the story I'll have to explain in person. It gets a little sticky."

"Sticky" was their code word meaning "bloody." Lee would understand.

"I'll be waiting," he replied with a note of worry in his voice.

"See you soon."

She ended the call just as her coffee arrived in a large ceramic mug. She dipped her nose into the cup to smell the bitter fragrance before taking a long, slow sip. It was surprisingly good. The plane started to vibrate, so she pushed the seat into a reclining position as the jet taxied out to the runway. There, it turned on the tarmac and gained speed as the whine of the engines turned into a roar. The plane began to ascend. Bai felt herself pressed back against her seat as the jet leaped into the air.

Bright sunlight from an oval window warmed her shoulder. Putting her coffee cup on the tray next to her, she looked out the port-hole to marvel at the brilliant winter day. Fluffy white clouds dotted a pastel-blue sky. She reflected on the beauty of the world around her. There was nothing, it seemed, like a near-death experience to give one a new appreciation for life.

chapter 22

Govern a family as you would cook a small fish—very gently

The plane rolled to the end of the runway at San Francisco International and slowly turned away from the passenger terminals. Taxiing to a hangar on the other side of the tarmac, the jet lumbered noisily between massive doors as the light outside dimmed. Overhead lights flickered on to cast a stark white light over the parked jet while leaving the rest of the cavernous structure in shadow.

Bai waited for the engines to wind down before unlatching her seat belt. The young stewardess was already pushing open the door of the plane. Bai grabbed her bag and walked toward the exit. The flight attendant smiled warmly and bowed.

"Thanks for the ride," Bai said over her shoulder as she stepped onto the ramp.

She negotiated the narrow metal steps one at a time until she reached the bottom, where a customs agent dressed in a black uniform waited. The officer smiled. It was a more gracious reception from customs than she was accustomed to.

"May I see your passport?" he asked.

She fumbled her identification out of her pocket. When she handed him her passport, her hand trembled, surprising her. She'd naturally assumed her body would follow her will despite being sleep-deprived, neglected, and generally abused. The tremor served as a warning. Her body plotted rebellion.

She looked up to see if the customs agent had noticed her quivering fingers. He seemed preoccupied. His eyes dropped to glance at her passport. "Anything to declare, Ms. Jiang?"

"No, nothing."

The cavernous hangar echoed with emptiness. Her voice sounded hollow in her ears.

While she stared at the agent, it occurred to her she did have something to declare, though it was nothing he'd be interested in. She wanted to tell someone she was being hunted like an animal by an unknown adversary. She wanted to say she didn't have the slightest clue as to why. Instead, she swallowed her anxiety and took a deep breath.

The agent pressed an arrival stamp onto her passport and handed it to her with a deferential nod of his head and a brief "Thank you."

The sound of tires scrunching against cement drew her attention. A black limousine glided out of the shadows to park a few feet from where she stood. A man she knew, a member of *Sun Yee On*, got out of the driver's seat to open the rear door for her. It appeared Tommy had thought to send a car after all.

She greeted the driver. "Hello, Martin."

"Good morning, Bai. Did you have a good trip?"

He made a chopping gesture with his open hand to mimic a hatchet. Apparently, her adventures in Vancouver were already a hot topic of discussion at *Sun Yee On*. She'd hoped to beat the rumors home. She feared Dan and Elizabeth might hear the stories before she had a chance to explain herself.

She shook her head in exasperation at Martin's grisly taunt and slipped silently into the back of the limo without offering a reply. To her surprise, Tommy waited for her inside.

He smiled. "Did you have a pleasant trip?"

"Is it safe to talk?"

He nodded. "Yes, the car is shielded."

"Two attempts on my life were made in less than twelve hours. I have reservations about defining it as a pleasant trip. What do you think?"

His lips quirked up in amusement. "I think you're alive to tell of it, so it isn't all bad. Those years of training finally paid off. And, I hear you got the girl back, which is reason to celebrate. I'm proud of you." He beamed at her and shook his head, marveling, she supposed, at her good fortune at having survived. "I heard about how Shan died," he added as an afterthought. "His seems a fitting end. I'm only sorry I wasn't there to see it."

She wasn't cheered by Tommy's fatherly pride. The killings left her feeling raw and confused. She changed the subject. "There's still trouble brewing in Vancouver."

"Yes. It's kind of you to remind me." His tone was sarcastic as his mouth screwed up in annoyance. "It's obviously past time I paid a visit to Vancouver. There's nothing like a little bloodletting to instill allegiance in the ranks. Loyalty seems to be a thing of the past. It was different in my day."

He folded his arms across his chest.

"Are things that bad?" she asked.

He looked at her and waved his hand to dismiss his own misgivings. "No, not really." He produced a reluctant smile. "I think maybe I'm just getting old. I grow tired of the squabbling over territory and tribute. Self-interest has infested *Sun Yee On*. The brotherhood has changed, just like the rest of the world." He continued in a confidential manner. "I have to confess. I don't seem to have the people skills Ho Chan possessed. Your grandfather always seemed to find a way to avoid these messy confrontations."

"Grandfather always said, 'Govern a family as you would cook a small fish—very gently.'"

Tommy looked like he'd taken a bite of something unpleasant.

"I'm not Ho Chan," he reminded her. "And concessions now would only be seen as weakness. If *Sun Yee On* is to change, that change must come from a position of strength. Anything less would be suicide on my part. Brutality, I'm sorry to say, is the order of the day."

She felt sorry for those who opposed him. She suspected the lessons Tommy would be dishing out would be of a dire nature.

"But enough about my problems," he said, a smile sliding onto his face with practiced ease. He clasped her hands in his. "I have good news for you. We've traced the serial numbers on the bills Jason provided. They were issued to a bank in Stockton, First Bank of Commerce. The phone you recovered was sold in Sacramento by a major electronics retailer. There's no way to trace it beyond the point of sale, but the two cities are both in the Central Valley—not more than about fifty miles apart."

She tried to conjure up a connection to the valley towns but came up blank. "I don't know anyone in either of those places who would have a reason to put a contract out on me."

"It could be coincidence," he suggested.

"Did you manage to learn anything from the men who followed us to the airport?"

"Sadly, they disappeared. We tracked the plates on the car to a rental agency at the airport. The car had been returned."

"Were you able to find out who'd rented the car?"

"It was paid for with a company card. The company is registered in the Cayman Islands. It's another dead end."

"What was the name of the company?"

"It's called Havemore Enterprises and exists only on paper. My people haven't been able to find a company by that name doing business anywhere in the world. Whoever wants you dead is being careful to cover their tracks. I'm sorry I don't have more information for you."

She put her hand on his arm. "You've done enough already. And thanks for offering to take Elizabeth and Dan with you to Vancouver. Knowing they're safe allows me the freedom to find out who's behind all of this."

He placed his hand over hers. "Just be careful, Bai. Don't do anything foolish."

"I've already been lectured to by Jason. You don't have anything to worry about. I don't have much to go on. The phone and sequential numbers on the money were my best leads."

He looked at her and squared his shoulders. "Then I suggest you do what Ho Chan always advised me whenever I was stuck for answers."

She looked at him, perplexed. "What's that?"

"Follow the money," he said as he sat back and nodded his head knowingly.

"That seems a little simplistic."

"And so I once thought. But time and again, I found there aren't a great many things that will compel a person to kill. One is love. But I think we can rule that out. Another is jealousy. Have you jilted any lovers lately?" A wicked smile accompanied his question.

She smiled at the thought. "That would be wishful thinking. Recently, I've given thought to becoming a Buddhist nun. How do you think I'd look with a shaved head?"

Tommy appraised her head seriously before rendering an opinion. "Not much different from the way you look now." He made a habit of bemoaning the fact she didn't work at being more feminine. "But that's beside the point. Have you slighted anyone or done them irreparable harm?"

"I'm a *souxun*, Tommy, not a killer—not until yesterday, anyway. None of my cases lately have involved anything even remotely dangerous, unless you consider tracking down a deadbeat dad perilous."

He shrugged off her comment. "Then we come back to money. Because money, though not evil in itself, can make people do evil things. Go back over the last year and look at your investments. See if there isn't something there that might give you reason for concern."

"It's timely advice," she admitted. "I'm going to see Hung and Chin later today. They handle most of my business. Maybe they'll know something I'm not aware of. I've been relying on their services for years." She looked searchingly at him. "In hindsight, perhaps I've placed too much faith in them."

"Perhaps," he said, smiling crookedly, "but don't jump to conclusions. So far your adversary has proven especially canny. The attempted hit smells of money, Bai. Big money. Professional killers aren't hired off the street. The woman you killed at the airport was one of the best. Interpol has been trying to get their hands on her for years."

The revelation startled her. She reflected again on the fact that she was lucky to be alive. "That's all the more reason to get Dan and Elizabeth someplace safe," she said. "I don't want them in danger because of me."

He patted her hand in assurance. "They'll be safe enough with me. You just be careful and watch your back. If they come at you again, they will probably come in force. They've come to a crossroads, metaphorically speaking, which means they'll either step up their game or walk away. I doubt they'll walk away."

The look he cast her way was cautionary.

She nodded to let him know she understood the danger. "Thanks, Tommy. I owe you."

"In the meantime," he continued, "I've placed guards around your home." He looked at her and smiled. "Consider it repayment for Shan. I've detested that man for years and couldn't find a way to discredit him. You've done me a huge favor. Not only did you eliminate him, you also exposed him. He was a monster."

Bai looked down at her lap. She'd killed a man in a fit of rage. Despite the accolades, she couldn't feel good about what she'd done.

Tommy leaned forward to knock twice on the frosted glass separating the passenger compartment from the driver. The engine of the limousine immediately turned over, and the car pulled slowly forward to pass through the open hangar doors. As they exited, two black SUVs joined in escort, one in front and one behind. She rode in silence as the limo whisked her back to San Francisco, back to Chinatown. Where, only a day before, she'd managed to be bored.

chapter 23

Outside noisy, inside empty

Tommy dropped Bai at the curb in front of her home. He promised to return in an hour to pick up Dan and Elizabeth.

The morning was cold. The street quiet. A light fog crept in from the ocean. Damp air clung to Bai's cheeks with a silky wetness. She tucked her hands into the pockets of her jacket to keep them warm.

Two men, sitting in black sedans and parked on opposite sides of the street, nodded to her when she stopped to stare at them. They weren't trying to hide. Their presence was a show of force, and a warning that her home was under the protection of *Sun Yee On*.

She turned to take the front steps of her home two at a time, quickly entering the building and ducking into the elevator. While pressing her finger against the thumbprint sensor, she forced a smile onto her face. When the door opened on the third floor, Dan, Elizabeth, and Lee stood in the entry. Mute stares greeted her as she stepped out of the elevator.

"What happened?" she asked.

Elizabeth's reply held reproach. "We were worried about you."

Dan ran toward Bai and threw her arms around her mother's waist to cling to her.

Bai turned her head to eye Lee suspiciously. "What have you told them?"

He raised his hands in mock surrender and shook his head in denial. "I haven't told them anything!"

"Nobody needs to spell it out for us," Elizabeth interjected heatedly. "It doesn't take much imagination to put two and two together. Not when we get a call to pack our bags and run off to Vancouver with Tommy. You're in trouble, and you're trying to protect us. But we're a family, Bai. Our place is here at your side."

Bai put her hands out to forestall an argument. "You've got it all wrong. There's a girl in Vancouver who needs your help. I'd have stayed with her if I could, but I have business to attend to here. All I'm asking you to do is go to Vancouver to care for a badly injured child until I can clear up a few business transactions."

Dan stepped away from Bai but continued to stare at her mother with a fierce intensity. "Who is she, Mommy?"

"Her name is Jia. She's fifteen years old and a really bad man beat her up. She's in the hospital. She's alone and frightened. She really needs a friend."

Dan turned to look at her grandmother. Elizabeth looked somewhat mollified by the explanation, but her stiff manner suggested she wasn't entirely sold on the story. Bai produced her best happy-but-tired smile to seal the deal.

Elizabeth scowled in return. "Are you sure that's all there is to it?"

Bai nodded fervently. "That's all there is to it. I promise." She turned to look at Lee for support. "Lee and I have an appointment with Hung and Chin today. You can call to check if you don't believe me."

Elizabeth turned to glare at Lee. "Is she telling the truth?" She raised her finger to shake it at him before he could answer. "And don't you dare lie for her."

He appeared taken aback by her distrust. His face formed a mask of hurt and denial. "We have a two o'clock meeting with the lawyers. I swear."

His hand went up in the Girl Scout three-fingered pledge. He'd managed to deftly assure Elizabeth while deflecting the question. Bai was impressed.

"And tomorrow," Bai said, "or the next day, we'll hopefully finalize our business. After that I'll join you in Vancouver. Or, if Jia is well enough to travel, I'll see you here at home. I just need a couple of days."

Elizabeth didn't look happy with the explanation, but Bai could see she wavered. "Very well, I suppose. Dan and I can give you a hand. How badly is this girl hurt?"

"I want to prepare you both." Bai put her arm around Dan's shoulders to walk toward the kitchen where she hoped to find breakfast. "Jia had to have her spleen removed, and she's got some broken bones. Her face is so swollen and bruised it hurts to look at her. It's going to take time for her to heal. When I bring her home she's going to need therapy, both physical and mental."

Elizabeth seemed surprised. "You're bringing her home?"

Bai opened the door to the refrigerator and stuck her head inside. Her action was brainless. She'd managed to avoid Elizabeth's question but found herself taking refuge in a cold box, like a kid with a guilty conscience, while her mind raced to come up with a rational reason for bringing Jia home. The problem was . . . her reasons weren't rational. They were emotional. She'd bonded with the child. She was running on pure instinct.

"You can't hide in there forever," Elizabeth stated at her back.

She cringed; Elizabeth was right. Her nose was already turning red. Pulling out a carton of eggs and some Chinese sausages, she reluctantly turned around while bumping the refrigerator door closed. She laid the sausage and eggs down on the counter next to the stove.

Not two feet away, Elizabeth and Dan stared at her with questioning looks. Lee found himself a corner stool at the breakfast bar and stared at nothing in a nonverbal declaration of neutrality.

"Of course, that would be a family decision." Bai backpedaled swiftly upon observing their unsmiling faces. "Which is something 'we' should decide after you've met and had a chance to get to know Jia." Her voice trailed off to nearly a whisper. "I'm just saying that I think it might be a good idea."

Elizabeth walked up to stand before her. "We'll talk about it later."

Some of the frost had melted from her stance as she took the sausage out of Bai's hands. "Sit down before you hurt yourself. I'll make breakfast."

"Don't you and Dan have to pack?" Bai asked.

Elizabeth shooed her out of her way as she grabbed the cutting board and a sharp knife. "We're already packed."

Bai retreated to the breakfast bar to take a seat next to Lee. Dan joined them as they watched Elizabeth expertly slice the sausages, along with some green onion. She then shredded cheddar cheese before pouring oil into the wok and setting it on the stove over a blue flame.

First, the julienned sausages were dumped into hot oil to sizzle and brown. Then, in went a dozen eggs and the green onions as Elizabeth whipped at the concoction until the scramble was fluffy. Last to go in was the cheddar to let it melt without burning. She portioned the contents into three bowls and set them on the bar with chopsticks.

"No rice?" Bai asked.

"You're pushing your luck," Elizabeth said, trying hard to hide a grin.

Bai turned to Dan, who seemed unusually quiet. "Are you all right?"

"I'm just thinking. It's OK to think, isn't it?"

The reply seemed a little testy. Her child wore a frown. It didn't take a mother's intuition to know something was wrong.

"I'm just not used to your being quiet," Bai observed.

Dan turned to look at her mother. "'Outside noisy, inside empty.'"

Bai nodded in understanding. It was a familiar proverb that had been hammered into Bai's head as a child. Her grandfather had shown little tolerance for noise. "So, there isn't anything bothering you?"

Dan continued to stare at her bowl and play with her chopsticks. When she spoke, her voice was hesitant. "Will I have to share my room?"

"Would that be so terrible?"

Dan thought about the question, her face drawn into a frown. "I guess not," she offered. "I don't really know. I've never shared a room."

"Well, let me put your mind at ease." Bai kept her voice soft. "If we decide it's a good idea for Jia to come stay with us, we'll turn my office into a bedroom. I never use the office anyway. Everything I need is on my laptop."

Dan nodded and looked up at her mother. "I don't think I'd really mind sharing a room."

"I know, sweetie, but you don't have to worry about it. A girl needs her space. I'd guess Jia feels the same way."

Her words seemed to cheer Dan. A smile worked its way back onto the girl's face as she picked distractedly at the scrambled eggs.

Having averted a family crisis, Bai turned her attention back to her breakfast. The eggs were fluffy and light, the sausage sweet with just enough green onion to delude one's self that the dish was healthy. She shoveled eggs, while Elizabeth poured mugs of hot green tea and put a cold glass of milk in front of Dan.

All too soon, Bai's cell phone rang. Tommy waited downstairs.

Lee carried bags as everyone crowded into the elevator. Bai felt sad to see her family leave. She missed them already.

"You two be sure to let me know if you need anything. I'm only a phone call away," she advised.

Elizabeth brushed aside her offer. "We'll be fine. Vancouver's a big city. If we've forgotten anything, we know how to find a store. Don't we, Dan?"

"Sure, *Mah Mah*, and Jason's going to be there, isn't he?"

Elizabeth glanced at Bai with a stern look of disapproval.

Bai kept her response light. "He might be there, Dan, but I'm not sure you'll see him. He's there on business."

As they stepped out of the elevator and down the stairs to the sidewalk, four men in black suits flanked the limousine. They gazed away from the vehicle with hands held inside open jackets to conceal drawn weapons. Black SUVs blocked traffic at both ends of the street.

Elizabeth took note of the security measures and stopped dead in her tracks. She looked at Bai with fire in her eyes, and Bai knew there would be hell to pay when Elizabeth got her alone. She took comfort in the thought that the occasion wouldn't present itself anytime soon.

She smiled stiffly at Elizabeth and forged ahead. She held Dan's hand firmly. If Elizabeth wanted to berate her she'd be forced to follow Bai to the waiting car.

Tommy stepped out of the limousine to intercept Elizabeth.

"So good to see you both," he said as he put his hand out to take Elizabeth's arm while pulling Dan in for a hug. "What a treat," he said, "to travel with two such beautiful women."

Tommy was a charmer. He gathered Elizabeth up and guided them both into the car. "Sorry to rush you," he said, as he stepped into the car, "but we're running a little late."

He winked at Bai before closing the door. She owed him another one. Bai put her hand on the window as the car pulled away from the curb. Then she and Lee turned to walk quickly back inside.

"Now to business," she said as she punched the elevator button for the third floor.

chapter 24

Deep doubt, deep wisdom;
little doubt, little wisdom

Once inside the apartment, Lee turned to Bai. "Do you want to tell me what went down in Vancouver?"

Bai held up a finger to silence him and then went into the living room to turn on the stereo. She cranked up the volume on the Rolling Stones to drown out their conversation. As Mick refused to be a "beast of burden," she explained how she'd managed to kill two people—one in self-defense, the other in a fit of rage.

When she'd finished, he stared at her. His mouth hung open as if he'd been hit with a stun gun. It took him a while to react. "Are you all right?"

She shrugged and let out a deep breath. "I'm not really sure. I cried like a baby after killing the woman. After I killed Shan, I didn't feel anything. I was just empty. It was like all of my anger, all of my feelings, had been buried with that hatchet." She put her head down. "No . . . that's a lie." She looked up at Lee, tears in her eyes, and whispered, "It felt good."

He smiled at her hesitantly. "Catharsis."

"What?"

"Catharsis is when someone purges all their emotional tension. The act of throwing that hatchet set you free of all the hate you were harboring. You unburdened yourself, an act that was good for you but, obviously, not all that great for Shan."

Looking down at her hands, she tried to find a sense of guilt about Shan's death. She couldn't. Her lack of remorse continued to trouble her. She didn't want Jason to be right about killing's being in her blood. Her father had been a killer, as well as his father before him. They were violent men who'd managed to compartmentalize their lives, taking a life then coming home to dinner with the family.

Lee stared at her with concern. "What are you thinking?"

"I won't be like my father or my grandfather. I won't be a killer. It's not what I am."

She was afraid. It was hard for her to admit, but she was afraid of herself.

He tried to reassure her. "It's not as if you went looking for trouble."

"That's just it. I did. I went looking for Shan. I wanted to kill him, and I killed him. It wasn't out of fear. I still don't feel guilty. That's wrong, and I know it's wrong." She looked at him plaintively. "It's . . . just . . . wrong."

He reached out and put his hands on her shoulders to turn her, so she was facing him. "If I'd been there, I'd have killed Shan. Any decent person would have killed that bastard. You did the world a favor. We should throw a party, except, as twisted as I am, even I know that would be wrong." He paused to smile. "Wouldn't it?"

His questioning expression made her smile.

He put his hand on her cheek and said, "I think you think too much, but that's what makes you special. 'Deep doubt, deep wisdom; little doubt, little wisdom.'"

"Is there any occasion in life for which the Chinese don't have a proverb?"

He smiled gently at her. "I haven't found one yet."

Her phone rang to interrupt their conversation.

She looked at the display. "It's John Race."

Lee raised his eyebrows as the phone rang again. "Aren't you going to answer it?"

She vacillated before responding. She wasn't sure she wanted more complications in her life. Race, being available, handsome, and interested, represented excellent potential for becoming a complication. Then again, he was handsome.

"Hello."

"Is this Bai Jiang?"

"Yes."

Her voice was hesitant, nervous. She cleared her throat while mentally castigating herself for acting like a schoolgirl.

"This is John Race ... the man you met yesterday at Darryl Hopkins."

"I remember. What can I do for you, Mr. Race?"

"I'll get right to the point, Miss Jiang. Is your offer of employment still open?"

His voice sounded uncertain. She could almost feel his reluctance. He was asking for a job from a woman he'd shown interest in. She could empathize with his dilemma, and yet she knew almost nothing about him other than that he was boyishly handsome and disarmingly direct.

"Let's meet to talk about it, Mr. Race. Are you available for lunch?"

He quickly grasped at the opportunity. "That would be fine."

She smiled into the phone at his eagerness. "I'll make the reservations for twelve o'clock at Boulevard Restaurant."

"Twelve o'clock at the Boulevard. That's over on Mission, isn't it?"

"Yes, the corner of Mission and Steuart. You can't miss it."

"I'll see you there at noon. Thanks."

"Don't thank me yet, Mr. Race. Let's wait and see how we get along. Oh ... and bring your resume if you have one available."

His voice sounded more confident. "I have one with me, Miss Jiang. That's not a problem."

Bai ended the call and looked up.

Lee stared at her with folded arms and tight lips. "Do you think he can be trusted?"

"I'm not sure. I guess we'll find out. I'd like to see what his background is before I turn him down. We may need more security, especially for Dan, at least until we can find out why someone wants me dead. Regardless, you'll get a chance to grill him. You're joining us for lunch."

She picked up her cup to sip the hot tea while she thought about Race. He seemed competent and had demonstrated integrity when he'd defended her daughter. She remembered he had combat experience, which suggested he knew how to take care of himself. She also remembered he had the most amazing blue eyes.

chapter 25

If you pay peanuts, you get monkeys

Bai reached into her safe and grabbed her automatic weapon by its pebbled grip. The nine-millimeter smelled of gun oil. She sniffed and frowned. She didn't like carrying a gun. Under the circumstances, she couldn't justify not carrying one.

She'd showered and changed her clothes. Her form-fitting leather jacket was replaced by a black leather blazer to accommodate the gun. Her flats had been abandoned for more practical leather trainers, in case she needed to run for her life.

The gun slipped into the holster tucked into the small of her back. More modestly sized than a regular Beretta, the Compact fit her hand while still carrying thirteen bullets in the clip and one in the chamber. Her proficiency with a gun was such that fourteen bullets were superfluous—just because she didn't like guns didn't mean she didn't know how to use one.

Lee waited for her in the living room where he surfed the web on his phone. "I have something to show you."

She stepped around the couch to look over his shoulder.

"It's John Romano," he explained. "He's giving a speech. I thought you might want to see who he is since you're almost certain to meet with him over the incident with his son."

John Romano had perfectly styled, dark wavy hair and a barrel chest. His complexion suggested he spent too much time in a tanning booth. A strong chin and a straight nose rested beneath heavily lidded eyes topped by a unibrow. He appeared formidable.

"Turn up the sound, I want to hear what he's saying," Bai said.

When Lee punched up the volume, she instantly recognized the voice. "Son of a bitch!" Her temper flared as she reached for her cell phone and flipped to the voice messages. "Listen to this."

She played the obscenity-laced message for Lee. The two voices were identical. He turned his phone down to listen to Bai's message. When the voice mail ended, Lee's expression was grim.

"I know someone who can positively identify the voice on that recording by matching voice prints," he stated.

"What's a voice print?"

"Everyone's voice is unique because of differences in vocal cavities and the way each individual moves his mouth when he speaks. Those unique speech patterns can be translated into what's called a spectrogram that can be used to positively identify a speaker. I have friends in the recording industry who can make a spectrogram of the message you just played and compare it against one of Romano's speeches. If it's a match, you'll have evidence of harassment that will stand up in court."

She looked at Lee blankly. "What do I need to do?"

"Just forward your voice message to my phone. I'll handle it from there."

She nodded and did as he suggested while he stood to accompany her. They were late for their downtown appointment with Race. They walked to the elevator and took the lift down to the garage.

Bai didn't often drive in the city. She preferred taxis, but the attempts on her life made her wary of being trapped in a vehicle she didn't control. As a precaution, she chose to drive her MINI Cooper Clubman. The car was parked between Elizabeth's BMW, a present from her son that, to the best of Bai's knowledge, had never been driven, and Lee's sixties-vintage, red Cadillac convertible with a white leather interior.

She fired up the MINI and hit the button on the dash to open the garage door as Lee folded into the passenger seat next to her. Bai hit the gas, and the car scooted into the alley, where she braked hard. Her finger tapped the button again to close the garage door as her foot slipped onto the gas pedal. She turned left into the alley and screeched to a halt, bumper to bumper with a black sedan blocking their way.

One of Tommy's men waved at her before starting his car to back out of the alley. She followed the car and waved back as she peeled around the corner. When she looked again in her rearview mirror, the black sedan followed.

"We have an escort," she said, glancing aside at Lee.

"That's comforting."

She looked at him sheepishly. "There's something you should know before we leave Chinatown." She paused to find the right words. "I'll understand if you want to go home and sit this one out."

"Are you going tell me it's dangerous? I already know that."

"Tommy thinks whoever's trying to kill me will come at me in force. I fear he may be right."

"And your plan is . . . ?"

"I'm going to find out who they are and take the fight to them."

"Use attack as the tactic of defense. It seems like as good a plan as any. So what's the problem?"

"I just want you to know you don't have to get involved in this. I'll understand if you want out. Say the word, and I'll take you home."

He looked at her and scoffed. "Don't be stupid. I was the one egging you on. Telling you to go to Vancouver to get the girl. If you'd gotten killed, I'd have blamed myself. There's no way you're getting rid of me now. We're in this together, whatever 'this' is."

She smiled and turned her head to glance his way. He sat with his arms folded, a determined look on his face.

"All right! Strap in," she said, as she twisted the wheel to spin the car into an alley, "it's going to be a bumpy ride."

The Works model Clubman had a supercharged engine and racing suspension. The engine roared like a lion as the car scampered around curves like a hamster on speed. She drove down familiar back alleys to avoid traffic and quickly made her way to Grant Avenue. She followed Grant through the heart of Chinatown, past the dragon gates, to turn left onto California headed toward the Embarcadero.

The trailing car stopped and turned around.

"Tommy's protection only extends as far as the boundaries of Chinatown," she noted.

"You can't really blame him. His resources are stretched pretty thin. I imagine he has a lot of men in Vancouver to back him up."

Bai nodded in agreement. She was grateful Tommy had spared the men to secure her home, despite her sometimes ambivalent and out-spoken attitude toward the brotherhood. It seemed that being the granddaughter of Ho Chan Jiang still carried some cache within *Sun Yee On*.

A right turn at the Hyatt Regency Embarcadero brought them within two blocks of the restaurant. She made two green lights and pulled around the block to the front door of the Boulevard where she skidded to a stop at valet parking.

Stepping out of the car, she handed a man in a red jacket a twenty-dollar bill. "Keep the car next to the front door and don't let anyone near it."

The young man smiled as he pocketed the bill. "No problem. I'll make sure nobody messes with it."

Lee joined her at the entrance to the restaurant. They stopped long enough to watch as the valet backed the Clubman to the curb next to his stand.

Bai then turned to push at the old-fashioned revolving door to enter the eatery. The restaurant reverberated with the sounds of clinking glasses and animated voices. Air, redolent with aromas of garlic and roasting meats, made her mouth water.

Boulevard Restaurant was housed in a Mansard-style building. The structure dated back to before the earthquake of 1906 that had left most of San Francisco in ashes. Ironwork, intricately tiled floors, beautiful coving, and handblown glass fixtures perfectly complemented the wood paneling lining the interior of the restaurant. White tablecloths and brick walls helped create a feeling of sumptuous warmth.

A familiar face smiled at Bai in greeting. The young woman picked up a couple of menus and gestured for her and Lee to walk past the group of people gathered around the small reception kiosk.

The hostess spoke to Bai as they skirted the crowd waiting for tables. "Your guest has already arrived," she said as she led the way to the back of the restaurant. "I hope you don't mind that I seated him?"

Bai spoke over the subdued din of the restaurant. "Of course not, Shell, and thanks for getting us a table on short notice."

"For you, anytime, Ms. Jiang."

Smiling, Shell stood aside to allow them to take seats at a table where John Race stood at their approach. He leaned over to pull a chair out for Bai.

She slipped into the seat, tilting her head to look up. "Thank you."

Race nodded a silent "you're welcome" before taking a seat across from her at the square table. Lec sat on her right with his back to the wall and a clear view of the street. His eyes moved restlessly. He appeared relaxed. She could tell he wasn't.

Diners, despite the hum of the restaurant, turned to take note of the striking trio. One look from Lee's intimidating gaze and they hurriedly turned away.

She looked across the table at Race, who met her gaze and said, "It's nice to see you again." Turning to Lee, he added, "Both of you."

Lee nodded back, his face bland, the tightness of his shoulders and back almost antagonistic.

Pulling a folded sheet of paper out of his pocket, Race handed it to her. "Here's the resume you asked for."

She unfolded the paper and scanned the resume. It surprised her. The document described an experienced and highly decorated soldier, an officer. She handed the resume to Lee before turning her attention back to Race.

"It says you held the rank of captain in the Rangers, Mr. Race. What made you leave such a promising career in the military?"

"I served three tours, Miss Jiang. I've seen enough of war. It's not that I didn't enjoy being a soldier. I'd just had enough."

"What did you think of the war?"

He looked uncomfortable with the question. "I like to win. I'm not sure there's ever a winner in a civil war."

"Do you consider yourself a patriot?" she asked.

"I've fought for my country, and I would do so again. Why do you ask?"

"Because it's easy to know a man's face but more difficult to know what's in his heart. I need to find out what kind of man you are, Mr. Race."

He looked at her, sizing her up. "How old are you, Miss Jiang?"

She smiled. She understood what he was trying to get across. "I'm aware that people lie, Mr. Race. I'm not naive. As to your question, have you ever heard the expression 'A woman who tells her age is either too young to have anything to lose or too old to have anything to gain'?"

It was his turn to smile. "I would assume, Miss Jiang, you fit into the first category."

Holding her gaze, he openly flirted with her. She found him attractive but wasn't sure that was a good thing, given the nature of their potential employer and employee relationship. She didn't want any complications, especially when she was entertaining the thought of entrusting him with her daughter's life.

Lee interrupted. "You obviously know how to handle weapons, Race, but would you be willing to use them to protect Bai and Dan? Would you be willing to kill in their defense?"

He looked surprised by the question. "Do you anticipate the need for that kind of protection?"

Bai raised her eyebrows as she pondered his question. She needed to level with him or at least provide enough background to give him a clue about what he might be dealing with. At some point, she would either have to trust him or cut him loose. She didn't have much middle ground with assassins on her trail.

"Someone is trying to kill me," she stated bluntly. "There was an attempt on my life last night. I expect there will be more. So the answer is 'yes,' I do anticipate the need for that kind of protection."

Sitting back in his chair, he seemed startled by her confession.

The waiter arrived to stand at her elbow.

"A bottle of your ninety-eight Montrachet," she said without looking up. The waiter nodded and walked away to retrieve the wine. Race sat silently across the table from her with a troubled look on his face.

Lee goaded him. "Do you have the stomach for it, or don't you?"

Race turned to him. A glint of anger flashed in his eyes before he managed to quell it. His emotional discipline served as a point in his favor. She didn't have any use for a man who couldn't control his temper.

Taking a deep breath, he turned to her while ignoring Lee. "I have the stomach for it. I'll do whatever it takes to keep you safe."

"Do you own a gun?" she asked.

"I do."

"Do you have a concealed carry permit?"

The look on his face was troubled. "I'm afraid not. I haven't needed one up until now."

Lee spoke to him. "It's all right. You're big. You can stop bullets the old-fashioned way."

Bai put an arm out to stifle Lee. "I'd apologize for Lee, Mr. Race, but if I started I'm not sure where it would end."

Race looked at her and shook his head. "Is he always this irritating?"

She looked aside at Lee. "No. He's really quite sweet. He's had a bad day and feels responsible for me. He's baiting you to see if he can anger you. Lee constantly tests people, often out of curiosity. He wants to know how you'll react."

"I'm sitting right here. You don't have to talk around me," Lee stated.

He didn't look fazed by the subtle reproof. Instead, he turned to Race. "She's right. I need to know what will set you off. I have to know what your weaknesses and strengths are so that if we're in a dangerous situation together, I can base my response on yours. I don't want you around Bai and Dan if you're some kamikaze warrior bent on going out in a burst of flames. We already have one of those."

Lee turned his gaze on her and left little doubt as to whom he was talking about.

The waiter arrived at the table with the French burgundy swathed in an ice bucket. He proceeded to open the bottle, a distraction that gave everyone a chance to chill. The wine proved to be delicious. The waiter left to allow them time to peruse the menu.

"This must be a misprint. There aren't any prices on my menu," Race observed.

She couldn't help but smile at his confusion. "You're my guest. Your menu isn't supposed to have prices."

He looked at her a moment. He seemed a little unsettled by the idea.

She turned to Lee. "Do you have a pen?"

Lee retrieved a pen from the pocket of his blazer and handed it to her.

She turned to face Race. "May I see your menu for a moment?"

He handed her the menu with a confused look on his face.

She wrote a number on his menu and handed it back to him.

"What's this?" Race seemed perplexed by her gesture.

"That's the monthly salary I'm prepared to pay you to work for me."

Race stared at the menu again. "That's a lot of money, Miss Jiang."

"'If you pay peanuts, Mr. Race, you get monkeys.'"

chapter 26

All people are your relatives,
therefore expect only trouble from them

Over coffee, the conversation turned more personal.

"Where did you grow up, Mr. Race?" Bai asked the question while lifting a cup to her lips.

"Please, call me John."

She nodded in acceptance of his offer. "Only if you'll call me Bai."

John nodded and replied, "I was born and raised in Cleveland, Bai. My parents still live there."

"Any brothers or sisters?" she asked.

"Just a sister. She's married and lives overseas with her husband, who's in the Air Force."

"Are you carrying, John?" Lee asked casually.

"No, I didn't expect I'd have to kill my lunch." He seemed amused by his little joke. "Besides, I already told you I don't have a concealed weapons permit."

Lee appeared perplexed. "Would that really stop you from carrying?"

"I take the law seriously." His demeanor was serious, his face a sober mask.

Lee looked aside at her and tilted his head. "I see a problem."

She didn't take the bait, determined to ignore his sarcasm.

He smiled sweetly and turned back to Race. "You were an Eagle Scout, weren't you?"

"You make it sound dirty." Race smiled, but his expression seemed forced.

"Have you always been a tight-ass?" Lee asked, grinning. "Not that I have a problem with a tight ass." His smile broadened. "I'm just curious."

Race's face darkened. She decided it was time to change the subject and intervene before he could respond to Lee's jibe. "Before you make a decision as to whether or not you'll accept a position with me, you need to be made aware of some things. The nature of that discussion requires a more private setting. Would you mind taking a ride with us after lunch?"

He turned to her with one eyebrow lifted. He appeared intrigued by her request. "It would be my pleasure."

"So what happened at the school?" Lee asked.

The lines around Race's eyes grew tight. "Let's just say that my lack of fervor in covering Ketchum's ass was seen as a sign of disloyalty. He had my final check waiting for me at the end of the day." He shrugged his shoulders. "Obviously, I won't be using him as a reference."

Bai's cell phone rang. She reached into her jacket while excusing the interruption. The number displayed wasn't one she recognized. She accepted the call out of curiosity.

"Miss Jiang, this is Inspector Kelly." His voice sounded muffled. "Listen, I don't have much time, but I wanted to call you before you heard it from someone else. The case against Romano's son has been dropped."

The news stunned Bai.

"How can they get away with that?" she demanded in a hostile tone. "The incident was caught on camera. There's a recording of what happened."

"The recording disappeared from evidence lockup. Nobody's willing to admit it ever existed. I tried to look into it and was warned off. I'd like to do more, but my hands are tied without some kind of evidence to back up the story. I'm sorry."

She dropped her head a moment to let her temper cool. When she spoke, her voice was more tempered. "Does Romano have that much juice in this city?"

"I wouldn't think so," said Kelly, sounding unsure. "I really don't know where this is coming from. I'm sorry I can't be more help, Miss Jiang. I'm taking a chance just calling you. I've been assigned to desk duty and I've had a hard time getting away to call. I'm being watched."

"It's OK, Kelly. I understand. Thanks for trying."

When the call ended, she was left wondering how deeply into city government Romano's influence reached. She looked across the table at her lunch companions, who'd only had the benefit of half the conversation.

"The recording given to Inspector Kelly has mysteriously disappeared." Her mind raced with the implications. She looked at Race. "Ketchum doesn't know you burned me a copy of the fight, does he?"

"No, and he doesn't know I burned a copy for myself either." He looked angry. "If you'd like, I can walk another copy downtown and deliver it for you."

She was tempted to take him up on his offer but hesitated.

"No, I don't think it would do any good. They'd just make that disk disappear and then come after you to make sure no more copies were floating around. We have other, more pressing matters than John Romano and his jerk kid. When we're ready, we'll take on Romano. He's made it personal."

She turned to make eye contact with the waiter. One sign of a good restaurant is the staff is only present when needed. Her subtle glance brought him immediately to the table. He handed her the bill that she paid with cash.

"Are we ready, gentlemen?"

Lee stood up first, followed by Race. Stepping out ahead of her, Lee walked swiftly to the front entrance. Race insisted she precede him and followed at a more leisurely pace.

"Why's Lee in such a hurry?" he asked.

"He's checking the front of the restaurant to make sure it's safe. Then he'll look under the car for explosives. He's protecting me."

She glanced back at Race, who looked a little discomfited by her answer.

"You're new to this kind of work. But your training should serve you well. You just have to put yourself back into a patrol mindset. Just assume the enemy could be anyone."

"Do you suspect everyone?"

She laughed. "The Chinese have a saying, 'All people are your rela-
tives, therefore expect only trouble from them.' Does that answer your
question?"

"I think I get the gist of it."

His eyes scanned back and forth to take in everyone within his line
of sight. As she stepped through the door, she glanced back to see him
with his back to her, protecting her. He was on patrol.

When they exited the restaurant, Lee had the car running. He
climbed out of the driver's seat and got into the back as she walked
around the car to drive. When Race got into the passenger side, she
immediately put the car into gear and shot out onto Steuart Street,
took a fast right on Mission, and headed up Embarcadero.

Race was pressed back into his seat by the rapid acceleration. He
struggled to get his seat belt fastened with a surprised look on his face.

She talked while she speed-shifted gears. "Before you accept a position with me, you need to be made aware of a few things. First, you
need to understand my father was triad, his father was triad, his father's
father was triad, and so forth. I have triad associations, though I don't
participate in triad business. Would those associations make it difficult
for you to work for me?"

He turned in his seat to look at her as he clung to the suicide strap
over the door with a startled look on his face. "So you're some kind of
mafia princess or something?"

She smiled, thinking the comparison ludicrous but was amused by
the idea. "Something like that."

He hesitated before answering. "I look at it this way, Bai. We all
have family, for better or worse. We deal with it. What your family does
is none of my business. My business will be protecting you and Dan
even if that means protecting you from your own family. It's all the
same to me."

"Then I would ask that anything you hear or see while in my employ
remains confidential. I'm afraid that if you fail to keep your word in this
matter, your indiscretion may prove fatal. Do you understand?"

"Are you threatening me, Bai?"

He seemed taken aback by her warning.

She briefly glanced his way and smiled. "Not me. But there are others who wouldn't hesitate to eliminate you, should you prove untrustworthy. I don't mean to scare you, but you need to think carefully before you accept the position."

"I can keep a secret, Bai."

She glanced back at Lee. He shrugged, leaving the decision up to her.

"Welcome aboard, John," she announced. "We're going back to Chinatown for an appointment with my lawyers if you'd like to join us."

"What's the appointment about?" Race asked.

"I'm not entirely sure. My lawyer requested we meet as soon as possible. While we're there, I have questions of my own. The attempt made on my life produced some clues as to where the contract might have originated. I need to speak with them about that."

"Are they involved?" he asked.

"I hope not, for their sake."

She was certain that if they were involved, Jason would make short work of them.

chapter 27

Gold is tested by fire, man by gold

Robert Hung waited for them in the reception area of his law offices. A tall, thin man with a gaunt face, he appeared immaculately dressed in a three-piece suit. His thinning hair was parted with laser-like precision to lay flat against his scalp.

He ran forward to clasp Bai's hands when she walked through the door. "I'm so glad you're here!"

As John Race stepped through the door behind her, Robert did a double take, his head turning from Bai to Race. "Who are you?"

Bai vouched for Race. "He's with me."

Robert turned to her. He looked confused, his eyebrows drew up, and his mouth fell into a disapproving scowl. "Are you sure that's wise, Bai?"

Robert eyed Race suspiciously: he was white and therefore suspect. She was all too familiar with the reaction, a reminder that racism wasn't the purview of whites alone. She reached out to grab his chin and turn his head to face her. "What's going on, Robert? This isn't like you."

He had a hard time meeting her gaze and backed away a step. "Right, then," he said, pulling at the lapels of his suit jacket to straighten them as he produced a tepid smile. "I think it might be best to have this conversation in the conference room. We'll have more privacy there."

He executed an about-face to march through the small lobby and down the hall, his back ramrod straight. His arms swung stiffly at his sides as if he were leading a parade.

Lee turned to Bai to mouth a silent "What the fuck?" before preceding her down the hall.

She turned to look at Race and tilted her head in the direction of the conference room. "Shall we?"

"Can it get any stranger?" he asked, as he walked with her down the hall.

She assumed the question was rhetorical. Inwardly, she wondered the same thing.

Robert waited in the conference room. He was seated at the oval table, his hands folded before him on the tabletop. His eyes were cast down.

"Where's Benny?" Bai asked.

Benjamin Chin, Robert's partner, was a round, unkempt man who habitually wore rumpled white shirts and dark slacks. He looked more like a bartender than an attorney and was as gregarious as Robert was reserved, making them an odd couple. But they'd been best friends since grade school. The relationship seemed to work for them.

"That's just it, Bai. I don't know where he is." Robert's face fell into his hands. He took a deep breath before pulling them away. "It gets worse," he added sorrowfully. "There's more than five million dollars missing from your accounts."

The room was silent as they all felt the impact of the statement.

"Well, that sucks," Bai pronounced in a massive understatement of her true feelings. "Grandfather always said, 'Gold is tested by fire, man by gold.' Just as a matter of curiosity," she asked, "how much more than five million?"

He threw up his hands. "Five million and one dollars—to be exact."

Lee walked over to perch on the edge of the table near Robert. He sat close enough to make Robert draw back and look up at him. "When was the last time you saw or heard from Benny?"

"I saw him three nights ago when we left the office around six. He was fine. He said he was working on something and he'd tell me all about it the next day. When I got into the office the following morning, he'd left a voice message on my phone saying he had some really good news to share and he'd be a little late. He never showed up."

"Have you reported him missing?" she asked.

"I filed a missing person's report yesterday morning. The police made me wait forty-eight hours before they'd officially consider him missing. I knew something was wrong almost immediately. We had a lunch date at Yank Sing, you see, and he loves dim sum. He wouldn't miss lunch unless something was really, really wrong." He paused to look at Bai beseechingly. "I can't believe he would steal the money and run away. That just isn't Benny."

Bai dropped into a chair and took a deep breath. She closed her eyes to think.

When she opened her eyes, everyone looked at her expectantly. "Let's go with the assumption he didn't steal the money." She looked around to see if anyone objected to her line of reasoning. "I can't believe he would steal from me. We've known each other since grade school." Her gaze was met with silent stares. She continued. "So, assuming he didn't steal the money, what use would he have for 'five million and one' dollars?"

"He liked to gamble," Lee interjected, not ready to sign off on Benny's innocence.

Robert rushed to Benny's defense. "He liked to gamble, but he wasn't compulsive. He bet on mah-jongg for heaven's sakes. He didn't play the ponies."

She put up a hand to quell the bickering. "Just humor me for a minute, gentlemen." Her sharp tone demanded attention. "What I was trying to ask was, why the one dollar?"

The dollar bothered her. If someone intended to steal five million dollars, why bother with a lousy buck?

Race finally offered up an offhand remark with a shy smile. "eBay."

She stared at him, befuddled by the answer.

He explained. "It's what I do when I want to hedge my bet on an auction. If I think the competition will bid fifty dollars, I'll offer fifty-one. It could make the difference between winning the item and losing it."

Lee looked skeptical but kept his thoughts to himself. Robert appeared thoughtful.

She asked, "How did he move the money, Robert?"

How the money had been transferred from the account might shed some light on his intentions. If the money had been wired out of the country, for instance, there was a good chance both Benny and the money were gone. If he'd taken five million in cash he couldn't have gone far. Five million dollars in thousands would still add up to five thousand bills, a hefty load to carry.

Robert shook his head in frustration. "He took the money out in a cashier's check. That's what worries me. I don't want to admit to myself he stole the money, but I don't know what else to think."

Bai offered a different scenario. "See if this makes sense," she said, easing back into her chair. "Suppose he went to a sealed-bid auction. They require cash at most of the bank-sponsored sales, so he would have to take a cashier's check, which is the same as cash. But if that were the case, what was he trying to buy?"

Robert jumped on the answer. "Real estate! Benny's crazy about real estate. He's always looking for the big score. And if he succeeded in winning the auction, he'd have immediately recorded the deed."

She thought about Robert's assumption. "It might be worth a trip downtown to the recorder's office to see if he's filed any paperwork. But before we leave, there's another matter to discuss. It's been brought to my attention that you handled a contract through this office for a Mr. Sammy Tu. What can you tell me about the agreement?"

He looked at her, a blank expression on his face. "I don't know what you're talking about. I've never heard of Sammy Tu. To the best of my knowledge, our offices have never handled any business transactions associated with that name."

Her eyes bored into his, looking for any indication he was lying. "Is there any chance someone else might have handled it? Think carefully, Robert. This is very important."

He pressed his fingers against closed eyes to ponder her question. When he pulled his hands away, he asked, "When was this contract initiated?"

"I'm assuming it was in the last couple of days."

"The only people here were me and Park."

"Where is she?" Lee asked.

Park was the receptionist and secretary. She'd been a fixture in the office for several years. Bai knew little about the woman other than her first name. Park appeared to be middle-aged and of average appearance. Bai considered her nondescript but likeable.

Robert turned to answer him. "She didn't come in today, and I haven't been able to reach her. She's not answering her cell or her home phone."

"Is that unusual?" he asked.

"Somewhat," he replied, looking a little abashed. "There've been times in the past when she would drop out of sight for a day or two. She's a member of Alcoholics Anonymous." He paused before adding in a confidential manner, "She's had a few lapses. I'm afraid Benny's disappearance may have tipped her over the edge."

"Do you know where she lives?" she asked.

"Of course," he replied.

Bai stood. "Then I suggest we take a little trip to make sure she's all right. If we've time, we'll swing by the County Recorder's Office to see if Benny registered any property."

She was anxious to find out what Park knew, if anything, about the contract placed on her. The missing money was important, but at the moment not nearly as important as her life. She reasoned that she could always make more money.

Lee and Robert got up from the table and walked out of the conference room while Race waited for her at the door. "Even if your attorney purchased property with the money, it doesn't explain his disappearance."

She nodded in agreement. The fact Benny hadn't surfaced in almost three days was worrisome. He was impulsive and often clueless. She hoped he hadn't gotten himself into trouble.

While ushering her out the door, Race talked at her back. "It could be he's out celebrating the good news he mentioned on the phone. He could be holed up somewhere with a girl and a bottle."

"You don't understand," she remarked over her shoulder. "His idea of a good time is a quart of Ben & Jerry's ice cream and a *Star Wars* video. He lives with his mother and would never leave her alone without making arrangements."

Race looked somewhat sobered by her comments.

Bai turned to face him. "There isn't any need for you to accompany me to see Park. Why don't I call you tonight, and we can sort out the details of your employment. That will give me time to think about schedules and so forth."

"That's fine with me," Race replied. "I have a few loose ends to tie up as well. And thanks again for lunch. Next time it's my treat."

He turned to precede her out of the office. Bai watched as he walked away. He looked as good from the back as he did from the front. She still wasn't sure hiring him was the smart thing to do. But then, she had to admit, she'd never been smart when it came to men.

chapter 28

A day of sorrow is
longer than a month of joy

Bai found a parking space on the street in front of Park's building. The receptionist lived in a run-down, three-story tenement next to an alley. Beige paint peeled away from clapboard siding like sunburned skin. A Laundromat on the ground floor vented damp air redolent with the scent of fabric softener onto the sidewalk.

She got out of the car and was met by the sound of tumbling dryers. The churning hum reverberated through the plate-glass window of the coin-operated laundry. At the corner of the building, Robert pulled open a rickety wooden door and waited.

Park lived on the third floor, two flights up. Wood runners sagged and squeaked in protest as they ascended. The stink of mold, rotted wood, and cooking oil permeated the narrow stairwell.

"Sounds like we're kicking rats," Lee quipped as worn treads squealed underfoot.

"It's cheaper than a burglar alarm," Bai noted. "There's no way anyone's going to sneak up these stairs."

It was difficult to see in the dimly lit stairwell. By the same token, she surmised they were better off not knowing everything that the dank, narrow space had to offer.

Lee turned to scowl down at Robert, who followed them up the stairs. "How much do you pay Park? Not that it's any of my business, but you'd think you'd want your employees to be able to afford decent housing."

Robert sounded sheepish. "You're right. It isn't any of your business." He was silent a moment before adding, "I pay a fair wage."

Bai wondered what he considered a fair wage.

"It's the door on the right," he offered lamely as he pointed to one of two doors on the landing.

"You've been here before?" Bai asked.

He shrugged. "This isn't the first time she's failed to show up for work."

She eyed him with curiosity.

"It's not what you think. She and I have a purely professional relationship."

"I wasn't thinking anything of the sort."

It was a lie. The thought had crossed her mind.

"Methinks he doth protest too much," added Lee.

Robert didn't offer a reply. Sniffing at the rank air and ignoring Lee's taunt, he turned his face away in denial.

Lee stood on the landing to knock on the door while Robert and Bai waited below on the stairs. There was no answer. He knocked again, louder, before trying the door. It was locked.

Lee looked back at her. "What do you want to do?"

"Pick it," she said. "We need to see if she's all right."

"You can't do that," Robert protested. "That's illegal."

She turned on him with an exasperated look. "I'd suggest you close your eyes and put your hands over your ears. See no evil. Hear no evil."

Startled by her suggestion, he looked at her. Then, to her surprise, he did precisely what she'd suggested. She turned to Lee, who smiled and shook his head, obviously amused.

Lee made quick work of the lock. It was a simple tumbler that gave way with the slightest prodding. The door swung open to reveal a silent and empty hallway.

Lee entered first. Bai tapped Robert on the shoulder to get his attention before entering the apartment to stand in a small vestibule. Reluctant to enter, Robert hesitated at the doorway. She reached back to pull him in by the flat of his lapel, then slapped the door shut behind him.

"Just stand there and don't touch anything," she cautioned.

His face pulled into a grimace as he whispered a reply. "Breaking and entering is a felony. I could be disbarred for this."

"Why are you whispering?" she asked.

He stared at her mutely.

"Never mind," she said, running low on patience. "Just stay here while we have a look around."

"I'll check the kitchen in the back," Lee advised her.

A small metal dinette and chairs were visible through the open doorway. Lee walked toward the back of the flat, while she turned right into a small living room. Overstuffed furniture, old and frayed, sat on a threadbare rug. A portable television with a twelve-inch screen rested on a side table. Doilies draped the arms of the furniture, and one sat under the television—obvious attempts to lend an air of hominess. The furnishings were old, but the flat was clean.

"Oh, my!"

Robert's exclamation got her to turn around. He peered through a doorway on the left. She assumed the doorway led to a bedroom or bathroom. He gripped the wood trim and swayed in place.

"I thought I told you to stay put," she cautioned as she walked across the room to stand behind him.

Her reprimand didn't elicit a response. She had to push him aside to gain access to the blocked doorway. When she had a clear view into the gloomy room, she stopped and gasped with surprise.

A nearly naked Park lay across the bed, her only adornment a red silk scarf wrapped tightly around her neck. Her tongue protruded obscenely from blue lips. Eyes stared wide, bulging and red. Folds of fat hung from her flabby limbs and torso—a testament to a sedentary life. A fluffy pink negligee with fake feathers pooled on the floor like a felled bird. A half-empty bottle of bourbon and two glasses sat on the nightstand. The room smelled of urine. Stained sheets beneath her body bore witness to her final humiliation.

Bai's mind registered the details of the scene in a brief instant. Robert stood at her back, his hand over his mouth as he gagged.

"Out, Robert!" she said forcefully, pushing him out the doorway.

"Lee," she called, loudly enough to be heard in the kitchen.

She spun Robert around and pushed him toward the exit. He made it halfway down the hall before stopping.

Her voice must have carried some urgency because Lee came from the kitchen with his gun in his hand.

"What is it?" he asked.

Robert was bent over, heaving.

"It's Park. She's dead."

Bai put her hand over her nose to avoid gagging in reflex to the acrid smell. Until that moment, she hadn't realized she'd been instinctively holding her breath. She looked at Lee and spoke through her cupped hand. "Have you touched anything?"

"I might have left prints on the front door and maybe the handle on the refrigerator. I opened it out of curiosity."

"Find something to wipe down anything you've touched. I'm going to take a quick look around. Then you and I are going to leave while Robert reports her death to the police."

Robert wiped his mouth with the back of his hand. "Why me?"

She turned to him, her frustration and anger hidden behind the hand held to her nose. "Because you're her employer. And when she didn't show up for work, you became concerned and came looking for her. Her door was open, which you found odd, so you entered the apartment calling her name, only to find her dead on her bed. Besides which, you silly ass, you just puked in the middle of a crime scene. Do you think the detectives might miss that little detail?"

He stared at her blankly before his ability to reason kicked in. "I see your point," he said, looking a little green. "I just don't want to be here alone with her."

She could understand his fear of being alone with the dead. It was a fear she shared.

"You can walk downstairs with us and make the call from the street. There's no reason to wait for the police in the apartment."

Her words seemed to mollify him. He looked at her, a pained expression on his face. "I'm pretty sure this is the worst day of my life, Bai. And it seems as if it'll never end."

He had tears in his eyes. She put her hand on his arm to steady him.

"'A day of sorrow is longer than a month of joy,'" she acknowledged.

He looked at her with a pitiable expression on his face. Then he started to cry. She had to stop herself from joining him.

"Why don't you wait downstairs, Robert? We'll be down as soon as we're finished here."

He nodded curtly in reply and walked shakily down the hall to let himself out of the flat. Lee came from the kitchen with his handkerchief in his hand. He'd obviously been wiping his prints.

"I want to take a minute to look around," she said.

"What are we looking for?"

"I don't know. Anything that'll shed some light on what's going on, I suppose."

She walked back into the bedroom. Park's red eyes seemed to follow her as she made her way across the room. Lee shadowed her to lend his handkerchief. She used it to open drawers and rummage through Park's things. He busied himself in a small closet, flipping open shoe boxes with a shoehorn he'd found.

"This is something," Lee said, turning to her.

She walked over to see what he referred to. An open shoe box, sitting on the floor, was filled with neatly stacked gambling markers. The piles were held together with rubber bands.

"Her entire life in a shoe box," Bai observed. "It looks like she had more than one addiction."

She looked around the shabby room and shook her head. "From all appearances, Park lived a sad and lonely life."

He pushed at the bundles of IOUs with the shoehorn. "I wonder if this has anything to do with that." He gestured to the body lying on the bed. "She let someone into her life and into her apartment, someone she trusted. It's dreadfully apparent she wasn't any good at picking a winner."

"Let's finish up. Just being here depresses me."

They hurriedly went through the rest of the apartment but found nothing of consequence.

As they left, Lee opened the entry door and closed it again with his handkerchief. When they returned to the street, they found Robert waiting for them on the sidewalk. He leaned with his back against the car. His face looked pale.

"Are you going to be all right?" Bai asked.

"I guess so," he replied. "Did you find anything?"

"We found gambling markers in a shoe box in the closet. Does she have any family?"

Robert paused and seemed to give thought to his answer. "I don't know." He looked at her sadly. "I should know, but I don't. I feel terrible."

He started to cry again. She put a hand on his shoulder to console him. She felt helpless. She always felt that way when faced with death.

chapter 29

A bit of fragrance clings
to the hand that gives flowers

Tires squealed in protest until the Clubman came bumper to bumper with the same black sedan that had blocked the alley earlier. Bai's heart thumped in her chest as she stared, wide-eyed, through the windshield.

The driver of the black sedan, a triad soldier, stared back. His jaw hung slack in shock. He then scowled while he shook his index finger at her in silent reprimand. She showed him one of her fingers in return. His scowl deepened before he slammed his car into reverse and backed the sedan down the alley to clear the way. She pushed the button on the garage door opener and gunned the engine to slip under the lifting door.

"You'd think that idiot would put his car someplace where I wouldn't run into it."

Her anger was disproportionate to the situation. The sudden hostility she felt didn't make sense, but she couldn't seem to bring her emotions under control. She looked aside at Lee to see if he shared her indignation.

"I don't think a car blocking the alley is the source of your anger," he replied quietly without turning to look at her. "Stress is making you nuts. You're letting fear and anger rule your emotions. I'd shake my finger at you, too, but I've already seen where that leads."

His words made her pause and reflect.

"So you're saying I'm being a jerk?"

The words came out louder and more strident than she'd intended. She bit down on her lip to stop herself from venting further

He turned to study her. "That would be putting it kindly."

She clamped her lips together before letting up on the clutch to steer the car into its parking slot. She set the emergency brake and

197

turned off the engine, her movements slow and calculated. It seemed important to at least appear as if she had everything under control.

She was angry. She was angry with Lee. She was angry with the world. And she was angry with herself for being angry. Her head dropped against the steering wheel as she closed her eyes and felt the cold, hard plastic press into her forehead.

When she spoke, she was close to tears. "I can't believe I pay you to insult me."

Lee took a deep breath. "You don't pay me to insult you. You pay me to run interference for your business and organize your life. The insults are complimentary, as is the witty banter."

He turned in his seat to give her privacy and waited for her to pull herself together.

"If you're in charge of organizing my life, why is it such a mess?" she blurted. "I've started to seriously think about what I want from life. I need to make changes. I'm not getting any younger, you know."

"Time is a greased pig, fast and slippery," he noted. "But if you don't get your head on straight, you won't have to worry about getting old. Need I remind you? Somebody wants you dead."

Her hands held the steering wheel in a death grip as she let Lee's warning sink in. She knew he was right, but knowing he was right didn't really help.

"I'm a mess. I know that. My life has been on hold for a decade. I've never had a plan. And as depressing as it might be to face middle age, I'd like to live to see it. Is that asking too much?"

"I get it, Bai. But if you're serious about changing your life, why don't you start by apologizing to the guard in the alley first. You made him soil his shorts, then you flipped him off." He lifted the latch on the door and stepped out of the car. "Sometimes, it's not all about you."

She got out of the car to stare at him, her jaw tight. He ignored her. She hated apologizing, as Lee was well aware.

"Shit!" she said, as she marched out of the garage and into the alley.

The enforcer in the black sedan visibly winced when he saw her coming. She marched from the garage to the parked car with her arms swinging at her sides, her fists balled, to stand beside the driver's door. She motioned, wind-milling her hand, to get him to roll down the window. He did so reluctantly.

"I'm sorry for being a jerk." The tone of her voice implied she was less apologetic than her words suggested.

Older than she'd first thought, his face lined with age, he sat quietly as if in thought. She realized, belatedly, he was probably a retired soldier, doing a favor for the brotherhood.

He turned to look at her solemnly, his voice soft and graveled. "Your grandfather was a good man. He once said to me, 'A bit of fragrance clings to the hand that gives flowers.' It seems a small gift, but there are no small gifts of the heart."

Her face turned red with shame. The generosity of his words humbled her. She was speechless. Then she bowed low, giving the man the respect he was due.

"Please forgive me. I apologize for my reckless and rude behavior." The words came out meekly.

He nodded slowly. "Your apology is accepted."

Bai turned and quickly retreated toward the garage, her face burning. Lee had been right, as usual. She was being a jerk.

Lee waited for her just inside the garage. He didn't say anything. He fell in beside her as she walked toward the lobby.

"That was appropriately mortifying," she said. "Feel free to be insufferably self-righteous. I deserve it."

He didn't respond. He didn't have to. Words weren't necessary.

She stopped to close the garage door before walking to the lobby to pick up the mail. Her brass mailbox was crammed full. A large manila envelope, folded and crammed into the slot, proved difficult to extract.

When she managed to yank the envelope free, she looked at the return address with surprise. "It's from Benny, posted from Sacramento."

She ripped open the packet to draw out site maps, a copy of a deed, and a handwritten note.

"The note's also from Benny," she said as she tried to decipher the scrawled writing. "It says the enclosed deed is for a partially developed subdivision he purchased at auction. The property was listed as four hundred home sites with additional acreage. Sewers, electrical, gas, and roads are already in place. It says he'll probably already have talked to me before I receive this . . ." her voice trailed off as she thought about the implications of the note, "which means he expected to be back in San Francisco before now."

Her eyes closed, and she took a deep breath.

The sound of Lee's voice forced her to open her eyes.

"Don't jump to conclusions," he warned.

She felt hollow as she tried to ignore the feeling that something really bad had happened to Benny. Lee was probably right. There was no point in assuming the worst. Still, she couldn't manage to shake off a feeling of dread.

"It looks like the development Benny purchased is in a place called Folsom," Lee said, unfolding the site map. "I think that's near Sacramento. Folsom Prison is around there somewhere."

"It's about fifteen miles east of Sacramento," she informed him.

She waved the deed. "I need to look at this property. Let's drive to Folsom first thing tomorrow morning. I want to see this subdivision in daylight."

"Sounds good to me." He was preoccupied. His attention was on the site maps. "How much would you guess a property like this might be worth?"

"In a hot market, a property that size might bring thirty, maybe forty million. In today's market, it's probably worth a fraction of that. We'll have to hold the property until the market turns. It might be years."

"But still a good deal for five million?"

"Sure. It looks like a great deal for five million."

She thought about the process involved in auctioning properties like the one Benny had purchased. "This property would already have gone through foreclosure in order to be auctioned by a bank. That's standard procedure. So, if this purchase is the cause of his disappearance, we're still missing something."

"Maybe I should take these papers over to Robert later and see what he can find out about the property," he suggested.

"That's a good idea. Tell him to make copies of the documents. I want a set to carry with me tomorrow. And have him see what he can find out about the developers as well as the bank that foreclosed on the property. It won't do any harm to get background on the transactions, just in case something interesting turns up."

"I'll let him know." He looked at the watch on his wrist. "I imagine he'll be tied up at Park's place for a while yet."

She handed Lee the handwritten note from Benny. "Give this to him, as well."

"This note won't ease his mind."

"Benny's his partner. He deserves to know."

Lee eyed the note with apprehension before tucking it into a pocket inside his jacket. "Fair enough," he said, obviously reluctant to be the bearer of bad news. "What are you going to do?"

"I'm going to bed. I've had about four hours sleep in the last thirty-six hours. Exhaustion is clouding my judgment. I want to be sharp tomorrow."

"Is there anything you need tonight? Some takeout maybe?" His face showed concern.

She smiled to let him know she was all right. "No. I just want to sleep. I'll knock on your door around eight in the morning."

She turned and pressed the button for the elevator, which opened immediately.

Lee hovered. "Call me if you need anything. I mean it."

The door to the elevator started to close. "If you come across a nice man with a fetish for neurotic Chinese women, send him my way."

chapter 30

Do not employ handsome servants

The elevator doors opened to an uncharacteristically silent apartment. Absent was the noise and commotion of a twelve-year-old and the rattling of pots in preparation for dinner—the sounds a family makes.

Bai often complained about the noise, bemoaning the lack of serenity in the tumultuous house. In retrospect, she'd gladly have traded the oppressive silence to have her family back. Solitude might be chosen. Loneliness was simply endured.

She stepped out of the elevator and made her way to her bedroom in the back of the apartment. She changed into a robe of indigo blue with a golden dragon embroidered on the back. The silk felt cool and slick against her bare skin. Her gun went into the pocket of her robe, where the weight of the Beretta Compact pulled at the material. She wasn't willing to give up the cold comfort of the firearm in the empty house.

Her bare feet led her to the kitchen, where the wine fridge offered up a cold bottle of pinot grigio—compensation for a really rotten day. Grabbing the bottle and a crystal goblet from the cupboard, she headed for the living room. Her glass and bottle found a place on the coffee table within easy reach as she tucked her feet beneath her to settle on the leather sofa. She picked up the bottle and poured a glass, stopping to watch as moisture beaded on the delicate crystal.

The first glass of wine rapidly vanished. She poured another and raised the cool, damp glass to press it against her forehead while trying to mentally reconcile herself to the notion someone wanted her dead. The exercise proved difficult. She was pouring a third glass to encourage the process when the phone rang. It was a blocked number.

"Hello?"

"Bai, it's Martin, downstairs. We got some crazy *seigwailo* down here who says he works for you. He put up a pretty good fight. I'm guessing he's up to no good, but I thought I better check with you before we take care of him."

Seigwailo refers to a male foreigner, a white guy. Her thoughts immediately turned to John Race. She wondered if he'd be foolish enough to track her down in Chinatown. If Martin "took care" of him, he might never be seen again.

"What does he look like?" she asked.

Martin spoke in Cantonese. He asked one of his men to turn over the *gwailo,* the foreigner, so he could see his face. She wondered why the intruder needed someone to roll him over.

"Blond guy, blue eyes, about six foot one or two, good build. A tough sucker. He didn't go down easy. Hang on. Here's his wallet," Martin said, pausing. "Name's Jonathon Milford Race. They don't get much whiter than this guy."

Bai closed her eyes and shook her head in dismay. Robert had been right about it being a bad day that might never end.

"Bring him up, Martin. I'm releasing the elevator. I want to see him."

"You sure, Bai?"

She was already walking toward the elevator to release the lift with her thumbprint. "I'm sure. Bring him up."

She waited in the foyer while the elevator traveled to the ground floor then came back up. When the doors opened, Race was being held up by two of *Sun Yee On's* enforcers. He seemed to be semiconscious. His hands were tied together in front of him with a plastic tie. His eyes tried to focus on Bai while his knees wobbled precariously.

"What did you do to him?" she asked.

He looked as if he'd been caught in a stampede and trampled. His clothes were rumpled and dirty from being rolled on the ground. A red lump was visible on his cheek. She didn't see any blood.

"We hit him a couple of times," admitted Martin, shrugging off the comment. "This guy broke Jimmy Fong's arm, Bai. He's lucky we didn't kill him."

"Protecting you," Race mumbled, seeming to momentarily focus on her.

She smiled in response.

"And how do you think that's going so far?" she asked.

She doubted his lucidity. His eyes rolled and then seemed to stop and gaze at her.

"Not so good," he muttered.

He moved his head around, ostensibly to see what worked and what didn't.

"Cut him loose, Martin, and bring him into the living room."

"You sure that's a good idea?"

Martin worked for Jason. If anything happened to Bai on his watch, Jason would, in all likelihood, kill him. He had good reason to be cautious.

"He works for me. I hired him today. I should have told you, but I didn't think he'd be showing up here tonight. I didn't realize what an eager beaver I had on my hands."

Martin didn't look happy with the situation. His brow furrowed with concern, but he whipped out a flicker knife and cut the plastic bonds restraining Race. He motioned with his hand, and the two enforcers carried Race into the living room where they deposited him on the couch.

"I'll call you if I need you, Martin," Bai said.

He looked at Race and then at Bai. "I don't think this is a good idea. I don't think I should leave you alone with this *gwailo*."

"Don't worry about Jason. I'll let him know what's going on."

"I still don't like it. Anything happens, it's my ass on the line."

She'd known Martin most of her life. She'd gone to school with his younger sister. He was family.

She tapped her pocket. "I have my gun, Martin. You don't have to worry."

Unhappy, he looked at her, then at Race.

"I still don't like it," he stated, before turning to leave, taking his two men with him.

Bai listened to the elevator dropping to the ground floor as she sur-

veyed Race. He gingerly explored the back of his head with his fingertips and seemed to be coming around. His tongue rolled around in his
mouth as he checked his teeth to see if any were missing.

"Ouch!" he said, obviously finding what he was looking for. He
looked up at her. "Could I bother you for some ice?"

"Let me take a look," she said.

She moved to stand over him, so she could see the back of his head.
There was a big lump but no blood. She cupped his chin and turned his
head back and forth to inspect the damage. He had plenty of scrapes
and bruises, but she couldn't see anything that would require stitches.

"Do you want to go to the hospital?"

"You smell really good," he mumbled.

She looked down to see that his eyes were focused on the opening
of her robe.

"I'll take that as a 'no.'" She released his chin to take a step back.

"Don't stop now. I was just beginning to feel better." He winced
with pain as he spoke.

"Serves you right for peeping. I'll get the ice. You stay put."

"If you want to put some whiskey over that ice, I won't complain.
And I wasn't peeping. I was closely guarding your person. I take my job
seriously."

She returned with an ice bag and a tumbler full of whiskey. He put
out one hand to accept the drink. She placed the ice bag in his other
hand, and he pressed it gingerly against the back of his head.

"Who were those guys?" he asked.

"They're triad enforcers. I should have warned you. I'm under their
protection while in Chinatown. I didn't get a chance earlier today to go
over all of the details with you. I'm more than a little surprised to see
you here tonight."

"I got to thinking you might need protection. I should have called,
but I didn't plan on bothering you. I was just going to walk the neigh-
borhood and make sure everything was all right. I saw this guy in the
alley and decided to have a word with him." He looked at her and grimaced. "Things went downhill pretty fast from there."

"You're lucky to be alive," she said, taking a seat across from him.

As she picked up her glass of wine, she studied him. He returned her stare.

"I like the robe." He smiled then winced, the happy expression obviously causing him pain.

"Yes, it's a nice robe. Now that we have that settled, I'd like to know what really brought you here."

He raised his glass slowly and took a long drink before speaking.

"I came because I was worried." He looked uncomfortable, his mouth turning down into a frown. "I can't explain it, and I know it sounds stupid—I was afraid for you." He looked confused. "I really wanted to make sure you were all right tonight, especially after telling me this afternoon that someone was trying to kill you. I'm not generally this impetuous."

She shook her head at him. "Men can be so strange. You came all the way over here to protect poor, defenseless, little me?"

He had the decency to look sheepish. "I have to admit it sounded better in my head than when you said it just now."

"I'm calling you a cab," she said, getting up to find a phone. She arranged for a cab then called Martin to let him know she was sending Race down in the elevator. Martin sounded relieved.

She walked him to the entry and pushed the button for the elevator. When she turned back to face him, he pulled her into him and kissed her, hard, wrapping his arms around her. She was surprised but didn't fight him. His lips felt nice. His arms wrapping her felt comforting. She kissed him back then slowly pushed him away. He let go and took a step back to look at her.

He looked confused, flustered. His face turned red with embarrassment. "I don't know what's gotten into me."

"Are you sure you're all right?" she asked. "You took a pretty good hit on the head."

"I don't know. I'm sorry about the kiss. It just happened. Am I fired?"

"No." Her voice sounded husky. "I think we can safely say we've cemented a good working relationship. Go home and get a good night's rest. We have a busy day tomorrow. We're going to be looking over an unfinished subdivision in the town of Folsom. Lee and I will stop by your place and pick you up sometime after eight tomorrow morning. You're at the address listed on your resume, right?"

"Yes, I'm still on Lombard Street." He stepped reluctantly back into the elevator. "If you need anything, Bai, call me."

She pushed the button on the elevator to shut the door, sending him to the ground floor. She couldn't help but smile at his boyish behavior but then stopped to soberly consider the ramifications of getting involved with him. An old saying returned to niggle at her conscience, "Do not employ handsome servants."

She was acquiring a new appreciation for its meaning.

chapter 31

There is no wisdom like silence

A little after eight the next morning, Bai raised her hand to knock on Lee's door. Before she could drop her arm, the door opened. Dark circles rimmed Lee's eyes. He shuffled out of the doorway to walk beside her as she silently turned to make her way toward the garage.

"Did you sleep?" she asked.

"Not much. How about you?"

"Not much." She looked at him tiredly. "Fear is a powerful stimulant."

She walked into the garage and flicked the switch next to the entry. Bare overhead bulbs snapped on. The lighted space held three cars with room for a fourth.

"I spoke to Elizabeth last night," Bai said. "I asked if we could borrow her Beamer."

The black sedan had been sitting, undisturbed, for more than a year. Elizabeth had stubbornly refused to accept the gift from her son. Jason had stubbornly refused to accept its return. Pigheadedness, apparently, was an inherited trait.

Lee grunted in amusement. "Did she even remember she owned a car?"

"She suggested I keep it. She said she doesn't have any use for a car."

"Or for the son who gave it to her."

He walked around to the trunk of the sedan where he disconnected the tender, a device that kept the battery charged. She opened the driver's door to find the key in the center console. She slipped the fob into the ignition slot and pushed the start button. The car started without hesitation as Lee settled into the passenger seat next to her. A button next to the rearview mirror opened the garage door.

She backed the car into the alley and waited while the garage door closed. The odometer read thirty-one miles. A melding of plastic out-gassing and light machine oil imbued the air with new car smell. Stiff, pristine leather seats cradled them. As she slipped the car into first gear, she turned to smile at Lee, and laid scratch, the wheels spinning as she exited the alley.

Driving past the now-familiar sentries, Lee waved. A black sedan pulled out to tail the Beamer as it headed toward the Russian Hill district where Race lived. As expected, when she turned right on California Street to leave Chinatown, the shadowing car pulled to the curb.

She spoke to Lee, watching in her rearview mirror as the black sedan made a U-turn. "You talked to Robert last night?"

"Yeah, the police didn't keep him long. They don't consider him a suspect in Park's murder. I guess they don't think he has the stomach for it." A small deprecating smile played across his lips. "He's expecting your call this afternoon."

She didn't acknowledge his attempt at humor. She wasn't in the mood for jokes. "Let's hope we have good news for him. His business partner's missing, and his receptionist is dead." She turned to look at Lee. "Don't make life harder for him."

At her not-so-gentle rebuff, he looked aside at her and sighed. "You're right. I shouldn't be so hard on him. I have a hard time liking Robert. He's fussy and he's cheap. He reminds me of my grandmother. I never liked that woman."

"He can be frugal," she admitted, "but he's saved me a lot of money over the years. His penny-pinching is one of the reasons I employ him. That thing about his reminding you of your grandmother, I can't help you with. You'll need therapy for that one."

Lee spoke dismissively. "He's more interested in money than he is in people. You saw how Park lived. It bothers me."

"I don't make it personal, and you shouldn't either. It's business. Besides, I deal mostly with Benny, whom I'm genuinely fond of. My feelings for him give me even more reason to find him." She glanced aside at him to drive her point home. "You need to stop and think about how Robert's feeling. Benny was the rainmaker in their partnership. He brought in the business. Robert did all the number crunching. He probably feels lost without Benny. They were closer than most married couples."

Lee sighed. "You're right. My bad." He changed the subject. "Do you think Park handled the contract on you? Do you suppose that's what got her killed?"

"Maybe. I just don't know." She shook her head, unsure of pretty much everything. "There isn't any evidence Park had anything to do with the contract. And there's no way to question her now. It seems like everywhere we look, we run into a dead end—literally. It's as if whoever's behind these attempts on my life is always one step ahead of us."

"It's time we did some catching up then."

She pulled to the curb at the corner of Lombard and Polk. Dressed casually in tan khaki slacks and a light-green windbreaker, Race stood in the doorway of his apartment building. He wore a baseball cap and sunglasses—Ivy League preppie. A large satchel hung from his shoulder on a strap.

As he walked toward the car, Bai pulled the release on the trunk and heard the soft pop of the lid opening. He stopped to deposit his satchel before firmly closing the trunk and climbing into the backseat.

"What's in the bag?" she asked as she pulled away from the curb.

He caught her eye in the rearview mirror. "Just a few things we might need. I wasn't sure what kind of terrain we'd be reconnoitering, so I came prepared."

Lee took the opportunity to needle him. "'Reconnoitering!' I've never reconnoitered before. Do we need a permit for that?"

She studied Race's face in the rearview mirror. He was clearly annoyed by Lee's banter.

He answered the question tersely. "We're going to look at land. We don't know if the land is flat or hilly. Under certain circumstances, a pistol might prove insufficient in rough terrain. I brought along something with more range than a handgun. My job is to protect Bai. I can't do that without the proper tools, as you so cleverly pointed out yesterday, Lee."

Bai spoke softly as she glanced at Lee. "'There is no wisdom like silence.'"

He had the decency to look contrite. "So, what, exactly, is in the bag?"

"A rifle, set up for sniping and laying down cover fire. It's an army M110 with a suppression unit, if that means anything to you."

"It doesn't," Lee acknowledged, "but I'll take your word it'll do the job. After reading your resume, I suspect you know what you're doing."

"That's what you pay me for."

Race settled into the backseat and pulled his cap down over his eyes, bringing an end to the conversation.

Her passengers remained quiet as she drove through the city. It wasn't until they'd crossed the Bay Bridge that Race broke the silence. "Did you find Park?"

Bai considered her answer carefully. "Yes, we found her in her apartment. It appeared she'd been strangled."

It took a moment for him to reply. "She's dead? Did you report it to the police?"

She glanced at the rearview mirror "Yes. Robert notified the police."

"Do they have any suspects? Is there any evidence Park's death is related to the attempt on your life?"

"I haven't talked to the police. I don't know if they have any suspects. Whether or not Park's death has anything to do with me would be pure speculation. I don't have any evidence to that effect. I have suspicions, but suspicions are useless without a motive or a suspect. And Park certainly won't be providing any answers."

Race stared at her before pulling his cap back over his eyes and settling back into the seat with his arms folded. He mumbled loud enough to be heard. "You certainly are full of surprises."

chapter 32

If you are in a hurry, you will never get there

A freeway exit led to the old town of Folsom. Developments, visible from the road, looked like upscale housing mass-produced for urban professionals—two-story block houses with three-car garages and room for a pool. According to the Google map, the turnoff for Golden Heights wasn't far away.

"I did some research on this area last night," Bai said. "The high-tech industry has invested heavily in Folsom. A couple of research-and-development campuses have poured hundreds of millions into the community. The white-collar jobs make property in this area a promising investment since homeowners would be mostly professionals—engineers and scientists."

Lee pointed off to the right. "This is the road coming up. You're going to want to turn here."

As he suggested, she steered the car onto a two-lane blacktop road. They drove a short way before cresting a rise that blocked the main thoroughfare from view. A half-mile farther down the road, they came across another ridge where brick walls abutted the lane. About eight feet in height, the walls curved around the knoll in both directions. Large metal letters, painted gold, proclaimed the name of the development—"Golden Heights."

She stopped the car to look.

"It certainly looks promising," offered Lee.

"What? The sign?" she asked.

He looked at her and smiled. "I'm just saying the brick walls are impressive and the gold lettering is nice. I have a good feeling about this place."

"Who knows?" she conceded. "Maybe Benny scored the big one."

Race leaned forward from the backseat to look at the sign but didn't offer an opinion.

She placed the car back in gear and drove slowly past the brick walls. The road took a steep turn down a hill into a small vale filled with large oak trees. They followed the road out of the vale to crest a second hill. The road suddenly came to an end. Braking slowly, she nudged the nose of the car to the edge of the asphalt and turned to stare at Lee.

"Where's the development?" asked Race from the backseat.

She turned to look silently through the windshield. The hill sloped down to reveal a wide valley filled with scrub and tall oak trees. Where the asphalt road stopped, a dirt road picked up to disappear into the woods a short distance from the car. She reached forward to turn the engine off and open the door before getting out of the car to view the scenery.

She walked to the front of the car. Lee and Race joined her as she looked over the unspoiled valley. Tranquility blanketed the pastoral landscape. Bai became immersed in the solitude of the countryside. It was quiet, peaceful.

Lee's voice, soft and questioning, interrupted her thoughts. "What's happening here?"

A suspicion had begun to form. She turned to look at him, her mouth skewed in consternation. "It's more like what didn't happen here."

"I don't get it," said Race. "Where's the development?"

Turning aside to look at Race, she barked a humorless laugh. His look of surprise made her laugh again. If both Benny and her money hadn't been missing, the situation would have been a lot funnier.

Race stared at her, obviously questioning her odd behavior.

She reached out to grab his arm. "I'm sorry, John. I'm not laughing at you. It's just the circumstances have me a little rattled. You see," she said, motioning with her arm to take in the valley below, "there is no development. It's a scam."

He stared at her in confusion. "I still don't get it."

She took a second to look out over the valley.

"I have the feeling I'm the spoiler. Or rather, Benny was the spoiler. I'm guessing he got himself involved in an auction he wasn't invited to attend. I believe it's a matter of being in the wrong place at the wrong time and screwing with the wrong people."

Lee gestured at the valley below. "I still don't get it."

She could see from Race's expression he still didn't get it either. The men turned to her for an explanation.

"All right then," she said, taking a deep breath. "Suppose I wanted to make money in a down economy, but nobody was buying what I was selling. In this case, houses. If I owned this land, I could go to a friendly bank, one where I had friends on the board of directors. My friendly bankers might provide a loan to put in sewers and water for this sub-division. But, instead of putting the money into installing sewer and water lines, let's say I put most of the money into my pocket. I then used some of the money to purchase false documentation and bribe key officials to support the fabrication that sewer and water lines were properly installed. The documented improvement would increase the value of the property. I would then be free to take out another loan to put in the electrical and gas improvements, again increasing the value of the holding. This, in turn, would allow me to get another loan for sidewalks and streets, and so on. Every time I increase the value of the land on paper, I have the ability to justify more loans against the property. We're talking about tens of millions of dollars."

"But at some point don't you have to sell houses to get the money back?" asked Race.

"Not if you're a crook," she said with a sense of futility. "I would guess whoever took the loans out on this property was in collusion with an insider at the bank. They let the property go into foreclosure with the assumption they could buy it back at a fraction of its assumed value. A lot of foreclosures are on the market now. Most properties sell for far less than their actual worth, especially with the secret auction system the banks have devised for insiders. In the end, the shareholders of the bank will assume the loss on the defaulted loans. With all of the defaults taking place, it's pretty unlikely anyone would bother to follow up to see if this property had actually been improved as the paperwork claims."

"But Benny stepped in and bought the property out from under them," said Lee, nodding his head in understanding. "They must have come unglued when they realized that their entire scheme was about to unravel."

"But why kill you?" Race asked. "You had nothing to do with this."

She turned to him and took a moment to study his face. He seemed sincere in his concern.

"I suspect they were buying time. If I were to die, this property along with most of my holdings would go into probate. They'd have months—probably years—to cover their tracks. My death would give them time to regain possession of the property."

Lee spoke up. "So to avoid exposure, they kill everybody associated with the purchase of the property? Now we're talking about a conspiracy of bankers and developers, just to start. Who knows how many people are involved?"

She noticed that Race had stopped paying attention. He stared up. Following his gaze, she strained to see a cluster of black birds circling in the gray sky above.

He pointed to where he was looking. "Do you see those birds?"

"Hawks?" she asked.

"You're close." He dropped his gaze to look at her. "They're carrion birds—turkey vultures—sailing on a thermal updraft."

Lee stared at the birds and then at Race. "Are you thinking what I think you're thinking?"

Race took a moment to unravel the question. "It doesn't matter what I think. It's what they think," he replied, while pointing his finger up into the air, "and they think something down there is dead. Or dying." He looked down into the wooded valley. "But they're not down there having lunch. Their caution leads me to believe there's something, or someone, protecting the kill."

He looked around at the surrounding hills, putting his hands on his hips. "These foothills are home to mountain lions. It could be a lion has killed a deer and is sitting on the carcass."

"Or?" She asked, pretty sure she already knew what he was going to say.

He knelt on one knee at the end of the road and pointed at rows of tire tracks grooved into the soil. "Some of these tracks are recent, the last couple of days. You can see how the wind hasn't had time to wear down the edges of the impression; the lines are still strong and clean."

"Do you think Benny might be down there?" she asked.

"Anything's possible," he said, getting to his feet. "If I were Benny and had just spent five million dollars of your money, I'd want to get a good look at this property. It could be that someone was waiting here for him."

"It could be that he's still alive and being held down there as bait to draw us in," she theorized. "What do you think we should do?"

Lee interrupted. "We're here, and we're armed. I say we take a look."

Race looked at him and then at her. His expression was troubled. "The smart thing would be to turn around and call the cops. But I'm guessing you're not going to do that."

Her shoulders lifted in a shrug of acknowledgment. "I think you're beginning to understand me. He's my friend. Leaving him down there isn't an option. We're going to find him and bring him home." She pulled the Beretta out of its holster at her back, racked the slide to chamber a bullet, and flipped off the safety with her thumb. "Besides, I'm tired of being hunted."

He reached out to put his hand on her gun and gently push it down to point at the ground. "All right, Annie Oakley. I understand your feelings. But let's not be stupid about this. If it's a trap, and it certainly has the look of one, let's not run blindly into it. Let me work my way into the valley quietly, on foot, to see what the situation is."

She was anxious and didn't want to wait. "How long will it take you to get down there?"

"Give me time to work my way around the ridge and come back from the other side. I need a chance to familiarize myself with the terrain and to look for anything suspicious. And I need to do it slowly."

"Do as he asks," Lee urged. He leaned against the fender of the car and watched Race with interest. "There's no point in rushing into a trap if we can avoid it. Remember what Ho Chan always told us. 'If you are in a hurry, you will never get there.'"

She looked from Lee to Race, reluctant to sit idly by while Benny might be in trouble. "You've got an hour. Then I'm going down there to see what's what—with or without you."

Race looked at his watch and then at her.

"One hour," he repeated.

chapter 33

Man has a thousand plans, heaven but one

Race pulled his duffle bag from the trunk of the car to extract a rifle and a muzzle suppressor. He attached the silencer to the barrel of the carbine. His hands moved over the weapon with practiced ease. The sniper rifle appeared to be an old friend.

"The suppressor will lessen the noise of the firing gun and hide the muzzle flash," he explained as he donned a camouflage vest carrying enough spare ammo and equipment to fight a war. "So if you see a muzzle flash, it won't be me."

He made eye contact with Bai to make sure she understood the implication of his statement.

She nodded in response. If she saw a muzzle flash, she'd shoot back.

"And watch your back. If I don't run into problems, I'll be in front of you," he added.

Without any further explanation, he turned to lope down the hill and disappear into the nearest copse of trees and brush. She looked but couldn't see any sign of him. He'd disappeared.

Bai and Lee settled in to lean against the front of the Beamer. Her eyes continued to scan the valley below. Tree limbs stirred in an early afternoon breeze. As the breeze grew stronger, the limbs and leaves on the trees grew more animated. Dark, billowing clouds scuttled in from the west to stack up against the foothills like layers of burnt marshmallow.

Lee pulled his phone out of his pocket to check the time before tilting his head up to look at the darkening sky. "I think we're about to get wet."

She glanced at him. "I have a strange feeling today is just going to be one of *those* days."

He looked at her and grinned as he crossed his arms. "Think of this as an adventure. And look on the bright side. We're getting closer to finding out who wants you dead."

She frowned in response. "I'm having a hard time finding solace in that."

He looked out across the valley and took a deep breath. When he spoke again, his tone was more sober. "Is the loss on this property going to hurt you?"

She turned her head to look at his profile. "Not as much as the loss of a friend. I'm not really worried about the money. Grandfather always said, 'Fortune and flowers do not last forever.' But if Benny's come to harm, it will be up to me to make things right."

He reached out to find her hand. "It's up to *us* to make things right."

She was grateful for his offer—and for his friendship. Still, she worried about the danger they would face. Whoever was behind the land swindle had already shown they wouldn't stop at murder.

"It might be better if you stayed clear of this," she said.

He assumed an injured air. "Aw ... do you doubt my abilities, Grasshopper?"

She shook her head. "I just think maybe it's my fate to take responsibility for Benny. If only he'd come to me before buying this property, we might have avoided all this."

He let out a long sigh and stared at her until she turned to meet his gaze. "I imagine Benny wanted to surprise you. He's always been more than a little smitten by you. It's easy to understand his motives."

She considered her long association with Benny. "He's had a crush on me since the first grade," she admitted, kicking at the ground. "The guy's a putz—but a sweet putz. I just want him to be all right."

She looked over the treetops below and wondered if Benny was down there, maybe held hostage or injured. She didn't want to think he might be dead.

"It's time," Lee advised her. "Race has had more than an hour to work his way around the valley. Do you want me to drive?"

The question didn't require much thought. "I'll drive. You're better with a gun. You ride shotgun and keep a sharp lookout."

He started to turn away then hesitated. "What am I looking for?"

"Anything that can shoot back," she replied, walking around the car to the driver's side.

Before getting in, she again pulled the Beretta out of its holster in the small of her back to place it within easy reach on the center console. Lee plopped down in the seat next to her then held his gun up in a two-handed grip in front of his face.

"Fast or slow?" she asked.

He smiled nervously. "Slow, I think, unless somebody shoots at us . . . then fast—very, very fast."

She put the car into gear to pull forward at a hesitant five miles an hour. The car thumped off the paved road and onto the dirt track. She steered with both hands gripped tightly on the steering wheel as the car slowly rolled down the steep dirt incline toward the valley below.

Raindrops plopped intermittently onto the windshield. More rain quickly fell: big drops, plunking against the car like pellets against a tin can. The wind subsided as the rain became a deluge. The road turned to mud, and the shallow grooves in the track became puddles.

She kept the car creeping forward, slowly but steadily. Windshield wipers slapped back and forth on high. The whipping blades allowed only brief glimpses of the surrounding woods.

"If we can't see them," Lee noted, "it's likely they can't see us, which may be to our advantage."

"Like blind mice," she acknowledged. "When I imagined racing down here to rescue Benny, this wasn't how I pictured it. It's hard to be dashing at five miles an hour."

"'Man has a thousand plans, heaven but one.'"

"I'm pretty sure heaven has nothing to do with this mess," she assured him.

About a mile into the valley, the road leveled out. Oak trees and manzanita scrub bordered the road on both sides. The dirt track widened to the width of a fire lane.

The storm slowed to a heavy downpour as large raindrops fell from a gunmetal sky. Bai slowed the car as she spied something blocking the road in the distance. After a few seconds, she braked to bring the car to a complete stop.

"Didn't Benny drive an old Mercedes-Benz?" asked Lee.

"Yeah, a gray one."

"I think that's it up ahead." His voice sounded subdued.

She looked aside at him. "What are you thinking?"

He stared at the surrounding woods with a penetrating gaze. "Do you see how close to the road those trees are, the ones up ahead on the approach to his car?"

She looked to where he pointed. The dense copse of trees bordered both sides of the road.

"What about them?"

"If I had to pick a spot for an ambush, that's the place I'd pick. Driving past those trees we'd be an easy target."

She looked again at the copse of trees next to the road. A ditch, some kind of drainage canal, ran alongside the road on the driver's side. The channel cut through the trees next to the road to disappear from sight in tangled brush. She suggested, "I could walk down that ditch and cover you while you bring the car up slowly."

"I've got a better idea," he said, opening his door. "I'll walk down the ditch, and you drive the car. I'm better at skulking than you. Wait here until I get in place."

He jumped out of the car before she could nix his plan. He ran behind the car and slid into the ditch feet first. Waving to her with his gun, he hunkered down and slogged forward to disappear from sight. She waited with the car idling while she watched for his signal. When she saw a hand in the distance waving above the ditch, she knew he was in position. Her foot came off the brake pedal to let the car slowly roll forward.

She didn't hear the shot that put a hole in the windshield, but she felt the wind as the glass spider-webbed. As she turned her head away, she saw the passenger-side headrest explode. Bits of foam flew in all directions, while cracked glass obscured her view ahead. She reflexively hit the gas. The car swerved to the side then careened wildly on the muddy road as another volley of bullets punched through the roof of the car.

There was no way to tell where the shots were coming from. She yanked the steering wheel to swerve the car in the opposite direction to correct the slide and pushed the gas pedal to the floor. The engine roared in response. Race stepped out from behind a tree on the right side of the road. His rifle was aimed in her direction. She ducked and heard a small explosion. The car pulled to the left, spinning around in a half circle, completely out of control as it drifted, back end first, toward the ditch, where it slid into the trench sideways.

For Bai, everything shifted into slow motion. Adrenaline surged through her body. Loud, wrenching groans erupted from the car as the passenger side plunged into the muck of the ditch. The seat belt cut into her shoulder when the car lurched onto its side then rocked back to cant at a forty-five-degree angle. The engine screamed, wheels spinning in the mud.

Her foot slipped off the pedal. The engine quieted. She lifted her head from where her cheek lay pressed against the passenger seat cushion and tried to get her bearings. A concussive blast from behind threw her violently forward against the seat belt. Sounds of screaming shrapnel and rending metal filled the air. The car shuddered and the engine died.

She thought the gas tank on the Beamer had exploded. Her first instinct was to bail out of the car. The seat belt refused to release; she was trapped. Her second instinct was to scream mindlessly with fright. She managed that admirably.

She stopped screaming abruptly when she realized she was still alive and there weren't any flames. The car was pointed in the direction from which she'd come. She poked her head up hesitantly to look through a hole in the windshield and saw Lee wading frantically though the ditch toward her. He stumbled, one arm dangling limply at his side, his gun gripped tightly in his other hand. Rage and fear contorted his features.

He yelled, "Bai! Bai, are you all right?"

He leaned against the hood of the car to peer through the fractured windshield. She met his eyes and grinned foolishly while objects other than water rained down from above—bits of tree and debris.

Something larger landed with a thump on the hood of the car. She stared through the windshield at the burnt fingers of a hand and saw a school ring. It was Benny's ring.

Lee stared at the hand, obviously mesmerized by its sudden appearance. He shook himself and shoved the hand off the hood of the car with the barrel of his gun. Then he looked through the window to meet her shell-shocked gaze.

"Can you move?" he yelled. The sound of his voice seemed to echo inside the car. "We need to get out of here!"

He looked around frantically, his gun held at the ready.

"I don't think I'm hurt," she muttered as she swung around in her seat and used the palm of her hand to hammer at the release on the safety belt. It snapped open to drop her across the console, head first, up against the passenger door. As she lay there, she could see her gun on the floor below the passenger seat. She grabbed it before squirming upright to wiggle around and stare through the splintered windshield.

Lee stared back across the hood of the car with a concerned look on his face. He yelled, "Kick out the windshield! It's your only way out!"

Bai wasn't sure why he felt the need to yell. She put the soles of her shoes against the glass and gave a trial push with her legs. The window surprised her and popped out effortlessly to screech across the hood of the car. She scrambled after it as fast as she could and joined Lee in the ditch. They stood in water past their ankles.

"What happened?" she gasped.

He stared at her. Rain dripped off the end of his nose "Bang, bang . . . bang, bang . . . BOOM!" He cocked his head and seemed to gather his thoughts. "I couldn't see anything in this ditch. Bullets were flying, and shit was blowing up. The explosion knocked me on my ass. Something plowed into my arm."

She looked at his arm, which hung at his side.

"The last thing I saw was Race stepping out from behind a tree to shoot at me." Her words felt disembodied, as if she were observing someone else speak.

He looked startled and turned to lean against the hood of the car.

"Well, I guess that answers the question as to whether or not we can trust him." He raised the gun in his hand. "I hate killing pretty men. It seems such a waste."

chapter 34

Of all the stratagems,
to know when to quit is the best

Bai's hand reached out toward Lee. "How bad is the arm?"

He shifted around to put the injury out of her reach. "It's broken." He caught himself and turned back to her. "Sorry. I'm a little out of sorts. Intense pain does that to me."

"Maybe I can help," she offered. "Do you want me to strap it to your side?"

He took a step back to look at her warily. "I'd rather you found some other small animal to torture. I'll have it set when we get out of here. Speaking of which, now seems like a good time to leave—before somebody figures out we're still alive and finishes the job."

She shook her head. "I can't leave yet. I need to find Race. I need to find out what's going on." She pointed at the driver's side tire that rested against the side of the ditch. "That looks like a bullet hole. I don't think Race was trying to kill me."

Annoyed by her stubborn refusal, he glared at her. "'Of all the stratagems, to know when to quit is the best.'"

"Yeah, well, you know me. I never know when to quit."

She turned away to look for a way out of the ditch.

"I think sticking around here is a really, really bad idea," he argued. "We have a pretty good idea that Benny's dead. That was his hand, wasn't it?"

She turned around to look at him. "The hand was wearing his class ring. I think we can safely assume Benny is dead."

She realized he was making sense. They were obviously out-gunned and out-maneuvered. Lee was wounded, and Elizabeth's car was history.

"Don't you think maybe we should quit while we're behind?" he said.

"Your objection is noted, but I have to find out if Race is still alive. And I have to find out what the hell happened here. I can't leave without answers. It isn't in my nature."

She regarded the tightness of his jaw and decided to temper her answer. "As soon as I get some answers we'll scurry back down this ditch like the scared, drowned rats we are. I promise. In the meantime, let's find a way out of this slimy hole."

The car was slippery with water and mud. The chassis tilted into the ditch. She managed to scramble up the hood of the car and use the side of the sedan as a platform while hanging on to some scrubby plants that grew along the gully. Using the plants as a screen, she inched up to survey the road. Lee climbed gingerly up beside her to see for himself what the terrain looked like.

The area outside the ditch looked like a war zone. Small fires burned here and there on the wet ground. Rain helped dampen flames that sputtered and sizzled. Tree sap popped like firecrackers. Branches burned brightly in a twenty-foot radius around the spot where Benny's car had been sitting.

The old Mercedes was a charred mass of crumpled metal, a twisted pretzel. Nearby oaks had been stripped naked. Pale trunks stood stark against the backdrop of a gray sky.

The area of devastation extended well past where Bai leaned against the side of the trench. The ditch had protected her from the brunt of the blast. Even so, the back windshield of the Beamer had been blown into the backseat, while the trunk looked as if it had been peppered with shotgun blasts from debris thrown against the thin metal panels.

Her eyes tracked to the last place she'd seen Race. She couldn't find him. Then she saw something stirring. A mound of dirt with branches and leaves shifted to reveal a person.

She pointed to where he was lying next to a large oak. "It's Race, and he's hurt."

Lee turned to stare at her. "What do you want to do?"

They were soaked to the skin and splattered with mud. Lee had only one good arm. She looked back at Race lying on the wet ground and came to a decision. "I'm not leaving him like that."

The look on Lee's face was incredulous. "Are you sure he wasn't trying to kill you?"

"Look around," she insisted, gesturing with her arm. "Where would I be if I'd been caught by the blast when Benny's car exploded?"

He looked around with a conflicted expression on his face.

"He shot my tire out, Lee. If he'd wanted to kill me he would have shot me in the head. But he didn't. He shot my tire. He wanted me in the ditch. He saved my life."

Lee looked at the devastation on the road and the relative safety of the trench. "Shit!" he swore. "I was just getting used to hating the guy."

She nodded her head toward the other side of the road. "Cover me while I see how badly he's hurt."

Lee didn't look happy with her plan but nodded in agreement. "All right, but if somebody starts shooting, you find a tree to hide behind and forget about him. You can't help him if you're dead."

She shoved her gun back into its holster and scrambled up the side of the muddy ditch by grabbing hold of burnt manzanita bushes. Using the blackened scrub for cover, she crawled toward the road on all fours before crouching to sprint across the dirt track and into the trees on the other side.

Nobody shot at her—a good sign. Playing it safe, she scrambled from tree to tree to maintain cover as she worked her way toward Race. When she finally got to him, she slid down into the mud next to him. She stayed low as she brushed branches, dirt, and leaves away.

He lay face-down. His cap was missing, and there was a cut on his temple where something had sliced him. The gash looked deep. Blood ran from the wound. She rolled him over slowly to look for other injuries. He moaned. His eyes blinked open to look at her.

"Shooter . . . on the ridge," he said haltingly. "Think I got him . . . not sure." He blinked some more. His eyes were dilated. She feared he had a concussion or possibly something worse.

She got on her knees to unsnap his vest. She pulled open his shirt to examine his chest and felt his back for injuries. There wasn't any blood. When she checked his legs she found more reason for concern. He had a laceration on his inner thigh that bled profusely.

"You're bleeding," she said to him as she pulled off her belt to use as a tourniquet. A snapping branch startled her. She jerked around reflexively. Lee stood over her with his gun in his good hand as he watched the surrounding woods.

"I got tired of waiting for you," he said, as if she were somehow to blame. "How bad is he?"

"I can't tell." She pulled the belt tight around Race's thigh. "Do you have any signal here with that super phone you carry?"

He put his gun in his waistband and pulled the phone out of his pocket to look at it. "We'll never know." His voice was dismal. "It seems this particular model isn't waterproof. It must have drowned in the ditch when the explosion flattened me."

Race raised a hand, and then seemed to forget what he was going to say. Bai looked down at him. He smiled.

"You're so pretty," he said, his eyes closing.

"Head wound must have caused brain damage," Lee observed dryly.

"Men pick the strangest times to get romantic," she observed as she fished her phone out of her pocket.

The phone was dry but had no signal. She started looking through Race's vest, hoping he had a phone that worked. She found pain medication in a first-aid kit—codeine and an ampule of morphine.

She handed the codeine to Lee. "For the arm."

He looked at the drugs, nodded in appreciation, and downed the pills without water.

"I like him better already," he said grudgingly.

She finally found a phone tucked into a pocket on the inside of Race's vest. It was an odd-looking phone—old-fashioned and bigger than the one she carried. She opened it up to look at it.

"Can I see that?"

Lee took possession of the phone. He looked at it for several seconds. His face scrunched up as he looked down at Race then back at the phone.

"Does it have a signal?" she asked.

"Yes, I have no doubt it has a signal. It's a government-issue satellite phone. The only problem with this phone is that once you push this button, this place will be crawling with cops. It's your call, both literally and figuratively."

He handed the phone back to her with a look of disappointment. It took her a moment to register what he was saying. Race had lied to her. He was a federal agent. She didn't know whether to hit him for lying to her or kiss him for saving her life. At the moment, she wanted to do both.

She momentarily debated whether or not to make the call. In the end, she didn't really see any choice in the matter. Race needed medical attention. He might die if she procrastinated.

She took a deep breath and pushed the first speed-dial button.

The answering voice was male and spoke in a clipped tone. "Special Agent Jim McKay."

She hesitated. As a triad affiliate, she had ample experience with being questioned by federal agents. She'd made a habit of avoiding them whenever possible. Old habits were hard to break.

"Who is this? Identify yourself."

"You don't know me," she said haltingly. "You have a man down with serious injuries. Send help."

"Who is this?" the agent repeated.

"My name is Bai Jiang. I'm about three miles south of the town of Folsom on a dirt track that's supposed to be the Golden Heights subdivision, but strangely enough isn't. The man with the injuries is known to me as John Race. I'm not sure whether or not that's his real name."

She looked down at Race. He was still unconscious. There was a long silence on the other end of the line.

"Hello, is anybody still there?" she asked, fearing the connection might have been lost.

Agent McKay came back on the line. "Just hold on. Keep the line open and don't hang up. I'm sending help. How bad are his injuries?"

"I'm not a doctor," she said sharply, losing patience, "but his wounds look serious to me. He got caught in a blast from a car bomb. I have a tourniquet on his leg, and he has another wound to his scalp."

"It's all right. Don't panic. We have help on the way. Just stay put until we get there, and please keep this line open. We're using it to GPS your location to the medevac helicopter. We also have ground units in transit to your location. What else can you tell me?"

"I'm not panicking," she replied in a surly voice. "This is me being angry. Somebody was shooting at us. Then they tried to blow us up with a car bomb. It's been a really bad day."

She was dangerously close to telling Special Agent Jim McKay to stuff it.

"Are you under fire?" he asked, his voice harried.

"Nobody's shooting at us at the moment. Maybe the explosion scared them off, or maybe your agent took care of them. He said a shooter was on the ridge."

There wasn't any response, so she guessed Agent McKay was tired of talking to her. She lowered the phone but kept it gripped in her hand. A few minutes later, she could hear sirens in the distance. It was another ten minutes before a fire truck came lumbering down the muddy road with a half dozen police cars trailing behind.

While she watched the procession slowly make its way toward her, she became distracted by the sound of beating helicopter blades. Dropping down from the rain-drenched sky was a red and white Life Flight copter. It hovered as the pilot looked for the best place to land before setting down in the middle of the road about a hundred feet away. Three people jumped from the cockpit of the medevac unit to run toward them.

The fire engine came alongside and stopped. Firemen were the first to reach Race, but they stood back when they saw the medical personnel from the helicopter approaching. Everyone was asking questions at once. She ignored them as she watched the medical team working on Race.

The medics strapped him on a board, then lifted him onto a gurney before racing him toward the waiting helicopter. Within moments, he was airborne.

Lee and Bai were left surrounded by curious police officers and solicitous firemen. The police asked for identification and demanded an explanation as to exactly what had taken place while arguing among themselves as to who had jurisdiction. Firemen wrapped them in blankets and offered hot coffee.

She had forgotten she still held Race's phone until she heard it squawking. She put the phone to her ear. "Is anybody there? What's happening?"

"I'm still here." She suddenly felt very tired. "Your man has been airlifted."

She looked at one of the nearby firemen who smiled at her. She seemed to be a hit with the firemen, at least.

"Thank you. Ms. Jiang, is it?" Agent McKay asked for clarification.

"Yes."

"We have an incident team on the way to pick you up. Just stay put, and we'll be there in a few minutes. And, Miss Jiang . . . ?"

"Yes?"

"Don't talk to local law enforcement. Simply tell them we're on the way and stay put."

"Who are 'we'?"

"We're the Federal Bureau of Investigation," replied the man who called himself Special Agent Jim McKay.

"Swell." She handed the phone to a sheriff's deputy who seemed intent on arresting her for something, though he wasn't entirely sure what. "It's the FBI," she said to the persistent deputy. "He wants to talk to you."

She turned away to see Lee chatting up a brawny fireman, his broken arm obviously forgotten for the moment. He looked so happy. She didn't have the heart to tell him the Feds were on their way.

chapter 35

A rat that gnaws at a cat's tail invites destruction

The FBI arrived in force. Four black SUVs rolled single-file toward them, oversized wheels throwing mud and debris onto the following car. Windshield wipers slapped back and forth on high to scrape the mess off in clumps. The locals—highway patrolmen and sheriff's deputies—turned around to watch as the caravan braked to a halt and eight agents disembarked from the splattered vehicles. A parade of Feds in bright-yellow slickers headed their way. Each wore a fluorescent jacket with "FBI" emblazoned in big letters on its back.

"Do you think the big letters are a reminder in case they forget who they are?" asked Lee.

"I don't think so," she replied, watching the approaching agents with interest. "The letter jackets are for when they get lost—kind of like self-addressed envelopes."

"That makes sense."

An authoritative-looking agent, who seemed to be in charge, gave directions. His arm pointed first to the wreckage of Benny's car and then to the BMW in the ditch. He watched as agents carrying large metal cases descended on the damaged cars to gather forensic evidence before he turned to march over and stand in front of Bai. He seemed annoyed. The corners of his mouth pulled down into a frown as he placed his hands on his hips to glare at her. A female agent—young, blonde, and pretty-without-makeup—came to stand deferentially at his side.

"Ms. Jiang?" the man inquired. "I'm Agent Rivers, and this is Agent Carrey."

Bai nodded. She couldn't think of anything to say. Now that the adrenaline was wearing off she felt cold, wet, and tired. She was sore from being tossed around in the car, and her mood wasn't improved by his officious attitude. Dry clothes, a warm fire, and a big tumbler of scotch would have been her choice at the moment. A wistful smile started to form on her lips at the thought.

Agent Rivers waited for her response, then abruptly stated, "You'll come with us."

His voice was harsh and challenging. He managed to drop Bai out of her happy place.

"Am I under arrest?" she asked, her voice calm but resentful.

Lee moved closer to her. He still had his gun in his waistband. After viewing their concealed carry permits, the local cops hadn't bothered to disarm either of them. She thought they might have been warned off by McKay, which left Bai to conclude that either his word carried some authority or confusion had triumphed once again. The locals looked unhappy with the situation and stood a few feet away—too curious to leave the scene despite having nothing to do.

Agent Rivers noticed Lee's gun and hesitated a moment before responding to her question. "Not at this time, but we have some questions for you."

"What if we don't want to go with you?" asked Lee.

"That's not an option. You're both material witnesses to an assault on a federal officer. You'll have the opportunity to retain counsel if you feel it's necessary. I'm hoping you choose to cooperate." His tone changed when he saw his suggestion wasn't being met with even polite acceptance. "I would ask you to please accompany us. It's in everybody's best interests if we clear up this incident as soon as possible."

She somehow doubted Rivers had her best interests at heart but appreciated his need to get statements. Race probably wouldn't be doing much talking for a while. His condition left only her and Lee as witnesses. Stalling would only prolong the inevitable.

She looked at Lee, who shrugged his shoulders in capitulation. He knew the drill as well as she did. Turning back to Rivers, she said, "My friend, Mr. Li, has a broken arm. He needs medical attention."

Rivers turned to the young woman standing next to him. "Agent Carrey, will you ask Agents Little and Branner to escort this gentleman to the emergency room and have his injuries seen to? Once he's been cared for, he can join us in our offices downtown."

The young woman nodded in understanding. "Mr. Li, your gun?"

Her outstretched hand waited patiently. He reluctantly handed his weapon to her.

"If you'll come this way?" the female agent said as she gestured for Lee to precede her toward the waiting vehicles.

He balked and looked at Bai with a questioning gaze.

"I'll be all right," she said softly, reaching out to touch his shoulder. "See to your arm and we'll meet up later."

He nodded once in acceptance then turned to accompany Agent Carrey.

Bai knew it wouldn't have made any difference if Lee had decided not to be compliant. The authorities would have separated them anyway. Their stories would need to be compared and corroborated to see if there were discrepancies.

She'd been having little chats with law enforcement officers since early adolescence. It was a consequence of being a triad associate. The routine might have slight variations but never really changed much. Government agencies were big on standard procedures.

Rivers addressed her again, his tone formal. "Miss Jiang, are you armed?"

She turned around and raised the back of her jacket to expose her holstered gun. Rivers removed the Beretta from its holster. When she felt the weight of the gun being lifted, she turned back to face him.

He looked speculatively at her gun before speaking. "What do you say we get out of the rain and find someplace dry to have this conversation?"

He gestured toward the line of waiting SUVs then walked by her side as they made their way toward the cars. He opened the back door of a vehicle and waited while she climbed into the seat before shutting it. She watched as he walked around to the driver's seat.

Agent Carrey opened the door opposite her and slid into the backseat, smiling a greeting. Bai couldn't muster a smile in return. Benny was dead. The investment property was a bust, and Elizabeth's car was toast. Lee's arm was broken, and John Race, or whatever his name was, was an FBI agent. She didn't have a smile left in her.

She was trying to remember if she'd ever had a worse day when Carrey interrupted her thoughts. "I think we're about the same size. When we get to the office, I'll try to find you something dry to wear."

Bai looked at her blankly. She had a hard time forming a response. "Thank you."

From the front seat, she could hear Rivers on the phone telling someone he was returning to FBI headquarters and about Lee's injury. She didn't try to follow the rest of the conversation. It seemed pointless. She leaned her head back against the seat and closed her eyes.

Carrey leaned over to direct a question at her. "Do you know what this is all about?"

Bai thought about Benny and the ballsy move he'd made to acquire the housing development. Poor guy hadn't a clue as to what he was getting himself into. She doubted he'd even understood why he'd been killed. The sad turn of events had bad karma written all over it.

She opened her eyes to stare at the young woman. "It's about a rat that bit a cat's tail."

The agent looked at her in confusion. "I don't understand."

"My people have a saying, 'A rat that gnaws at a cat's tail invites destruction.'" She could see the agent couldn't comprehend what she was saying. "I fear that's exactly what has happened. And now I have to exact revenge on a very large, very mean cat because that's what friends do."

Bai put her head back against the seat again and closed her eyes, willing herself not to cry. It wouldn't do to show weakness to the enemy. And that, unfortunately, was exactly how she viewed the FBI.

chapter 36

Dogs have so many friends because they wag their tails, not their tongues

Agent Rivers turned the SUV around and headed back to the main road. The four-wheel-drive vehicle sloshed through deeply rutted mud while rain continued to beat a steady tempo on the roof. When the vehicle approached the brick walls announcing "Golden Heights," a line of men in dark fatigues with rifles braced across their chests jogged past in the opposite direction.

"Somebody called in a SWAT team," Agent Carrey remarked.

"This is turning into a photo op," Rivers replied, his disgust showing. "The crime scene will turn into a three-ring circus if we don't shut it down. Make the calls. Get this road sealed off until we can clear the scene."

The SWAT command vehicle sat outside the brick-walled entrance. A behemoth, it would have become mired in mud on the unpaved road. Pulling up next to the SWAT motor coach was a smaller vehicle, a white van with a satellite dish on top. It wouldn't be long before talking heads would be standing in the rain to inform the public they didn't have a clue as to what had happened. Reporting live—*nothing*—for as long as someone—anyone—was willing to watch.

When they reached the freeway, Bai leaned back in the seat to relax. The warmth of the car provided a welcome relief from the wet and cold. It didn't take long, however, before the heat and confined space intensified the smell of her ditch-slimed jeans. She reeked. Agent Carrey, her nose twitching, slowly edged away.

She looked aside at the agent and scowled. "It feels even worse than it smells."

Her trainers squished and she could imagine the skin on her toes pruning inside her socks. Her underwear was binding and chafing. She shifted uncomfortably in the seat. Carrey stared inquisitively.

"Shorts are in a twist," Bai explained blandly.

The black SUV eventually pulled off the freeway and into Sacramento's business district to arrive at a large gray building located on the Capitol Mall. The mall was composed of several blocks of government buildings anchored on the east end by the domed capitol. The one-way streets were divided by a grass strip. The mall was considerably less grand than the name implied.

Wheeling into a basement garage, the vehicle came to a halt next to a bank of elevators.

"We're here," Rivers announced.

Carrey motioned for her to get out of the car. Both agents joined her in front of the elevators, where Rivers used his identification badge to gain access to a lift. Bai looked around while waiting for the elevator. She spied two closed-circuit cameras trained on them. Security was tight.

They boarded the elevator and rose to the seventh floor, where she and her escorts stepped out of the lift and into a secured lobby. A manned guard station, just outside the elevator doors, required both agents to show identification. Rivers took the opportunity to turn Bai's gun over to the guard for safekeeping. She thought about keeping her sheath knife but recognized a metal detector leading into the inner offices. She decided to relinquish the blade before it was taken from her.

Rivers took the knife and immediately turned it over to the guard. He held out his hand again. "And your phone, please, Ms. Jiang."

She hesitated, reluctant to give it up. The cell was her lifeline to her family and the outside world. She wasn't a trusting soul.

"It will be returned to you when you leave, along with your knife and your gun," he said, gesturing with his hand.

"I hope someone is taking notes on how cooperative I'm being," she remarked as she handed him her phone.

He smirked, leading her to conclude the Feds weren't giving out points for good behavior.

The guard buzzed them into the inner offices, where Rivers led her straight to a glass-walled enclosure. An agent, male, sitting behind a desk, stood up to greet her. He offered her his hand while beaming a smile in her direction. "Miss Jiang, I'm Special Agent McKay. We spoke on the phone earlier."

She studied him as she took his hand, her eyes eventually meeting his gaze. Special Agent McKay was tall with hair clipped short to hide the fact he was balding. Black plastic-rimmed glasses made him look scholarly. The white shirt and dark tie with an American flag pin made him look like a Fed. He didn't look especially special to her.

His eyes studied her, in turn, with the same guarded intensity.

Not stupid, she decided. They stood with hands locked, warily sizing each other up.

"Would you like a cup of coffee?" he finally asked, releasing her hand and edging back to give her space.

"And some dry clothes, please," she replied, "unless, of course, this interview is going to be a short one. In which case, I'll just answer your questions and be on my way. I don't want to smell up your office."

He hesitated, his eyes taking in her soggy attire.

"Agent Carrey," he said, not bothering to look at his subordinate, "why don't you go with Miss Jiang and find her some official FBI sweats while I arrange for coffee? Agent Rivers, thank you for escorting Miss Jiang. I'm sure you're anxious to get back to your team in the field. I won't keep you waiting."

Not a short interview, Bai mused.

Agent Carrey touched her elbow, and Bai did an about-face to follow her out of the office. Rivers followed to walk off in the opposite direction. McKay had issued marching orders. Everyone shuffled to do his bidding, which suggested that McKay was, in fact, special, and Bai just couldn't see his special-ness.

Carrey escorted her down a hallway to a ladies room that also served as a locker room for female agents. Bai gladly exchanged her wet clothes and soggy trainers for a pair of clean sweats, adorned with the FBI logo, and a pair of heavy cotton socks. Forsaking underwear, she decided to go commando rather than sit around in soggy briefs. She stuffed her identification and credit cards into her baggy pockets. Carrey provided a plastic garbage bag for the cast-offs, which Bai carried with her back to McKay's office.

Carrey ushered her into a seat directly across from McKay. He hadn't bothered to rise when they'd entered and seemed absorbed in paperwork. A large ledger sat on his desk. Carrey handed Bai a paper cup containing coffee, while McKay continued to ignore them both. He appeared to be deep in thought.

"You seem to have made some enemies, Ms. Jiang," he observed. He lifted his eyes from the ledger to pick up a stained coffee mug. His elbows rested on his desk. While sipping, he regarded her with interest. "Just exactly what were you and Agent Ranse doing in Folsom this morning?"

"Ranse? So that's his name." She mulled the name over. "Is his first name John?"

She'd avoided the question with a question. She could see from the exasperated look on his face McKay wasn't fooled by the evasion.

"John Ranse is the man you know as John Race. But getting back to my question, what were you doing out there?"

She took a sip of coffee and leaned back in her chair. "You make a good cup of coffee here. It reminds me of Starbucks. The Bureau isn't working with them, are they? I've had my suspicions for some time now that, contrary to popular opinion, Starbucks harbors a subversive agenda."

He smiled tightly but played along. "Although their prices may seem exorbitant, I don't believe they could be considered un-American. But you haven't answered my question about Golden Heights."

"That's another thing," Bai shook her head with concern. "Why would someone name a land development in what is, essentially, a valley, 'Golden Heights'? That's like buying a strawberry surprise only to find out the surprise is there aren't any strawberries."

Special Agent McKay didn't appear to be amused. "This interview can go on for as long as you'd like, Ms. Jiang," he said wearily. "How much time do you feel like spending here?"

She stopped to think. "I would assume the reason for our trip to Sacramento would be in Agent Ranse's report."

She stalled, trying to determine how much to tell him. She didn't want to divulge any more than she had to, but she didn't want to piss him off either. He could tie her up for a long time if he wanted.

Smiling, he nodded his head. "I need to hear it in your own words, if you'd be kind enough to indulge me." The tenor of his voice said she wasn't going anywhere until she told him what he wanted to hear.

"Perhaps an exchange of information is called for?" she asked.

He frowned. "You're hardly in a position to barter."

"And you have no reason to hold me. Your own agent will clear me of any wrongdoing. You're on a fishing expedition and we both know it. Have you ever heard it said, 'Dogs have so many friends because they wag their tails, not their tongues'?"

His face clouded over. "I can hold you indefinitely on suspicion of terrorist acts. That was a car bomb that went off in Folsom this morning, and it was loaded with enough explosives to take down a building. Do you have an explanation for that?"

He was bluffing. There was no way he could pin the bomb on her.

"You'll find the bomb was aimed at me. The car, in all likelihood, had my good friend and attorney inside. I don't make a habit of killing my friends. And if you have any illusions about holding me here, let me give you some advice. I can turn this incident into a case of racial profiling, and sue both you and this agency for false imprisonment. I really don't think you want to go there."

He sat back in his chair to stare at her, a sigh escaping from between his lips. He dismissed her threat with a flick of his hand. "I think we've gotten off on the wrong foot. We're on the same side here. Is it asking too much for a little cooperation?"

She looked at him, unmoved by his appeal. "Have you read my file?"

He looked ill at ease. "I have."

"Did you bother to count the number of interviews I've had with the FBI over the past fifteen years?"

He shifted awkwardly in his chair. "You're a known associate of criminals."

"My only offense was being born, Agent McKay. I've been persecuted by this organization you happen to work for my entire life because of who my parents were. I don't owe you anything."

"Just let me ask, then, who's behind this attempt on your life, if that's what it is?"

She threw up her hands. "If I knew that, would I be sitting here?"

"Then let me ask again. What were you doing in Folsom today?"

She gave him what was already public record. "We were looking at property my lawyer had recently purchased on my behalf."

"And that would be the same lawyer in the car that exploded this morning?"

"That's correct."

"And his name?"

"Benny, Benjamin Chin."

"Do you have any idea why someone would want to kill your lawyer, Miss Jiang?"

"No." She looked up defiantly. "Benjamin Chin was a nice man, a sweet man. There was no reason to kill him."

When she spoke the words, she meant them. There'd been no reason to kill Benny. It'd been a spiteful and malicious act.

He studied her from across the desk, his mood softening a little. "Is there anything else you can tell us?"

She looked at him and shook her head. "I really don't know what's going on. My lawyer purchased some real estate. As a result, he's dead. I'm assuming his death has something to do with the property, but I don't have any firsthand knowledge to back that up. Right now, your guess is as good as mine. Did you find a shooter on the ridge? Race, er, Ranse said he'd seen someone on the ridge."

He stared at her mutely a moment. "We found a body. It hasn't been identified yet."

"I see."

It was pretty obvious he wasn't giving away information, or maybe he just didn't have anything to give. The FBI had a dead shooter, and sooner or later they'd identify him. It seemed unlikely they'd share that information with her.

He interrupted her thoughts. "What you've told me pretty much substantiates what Agent Ranse put in his reports. I can't make you confide in me, but I'd caution you about looking into this on your own."

"Why?" she asked while staring at him coldly.

"I'd hate to see you come to any harm."

The look he gave her might have been construed as a threat. Then again, maybe he was just trying to talk sense. It didn't matter. Her friend was dead, and she was going to find out who killed him.

"Is there anything more you'd like to tell me?" she asked.

"I believe that's my line, Ms. Jiang," McKay said affably.

She shrugged off his clumsy attempt at chumminess. "Am I done here?"

"That's all we need for the time being. Agent Carrey will see that you're comfortable until your associate is ready to join you. Have a good day, Miss Jiang."

She blinked. The dismissal came as a surprise. She'd expected endless hours of grilling. She stood, and Agent Carrey showed her out of the room and down the hall to an interview room where she was left with her coffee cup and her garbage bag for company. When she tried the door, it was locked.

chapter 37

Do not insult the crocodile
until you've crossed the river

Two hours later, the door opened and Lee came into the room wearing FBI sweats and a plastic cast on his arm. He carried his clothes in a plastic bag identical to Bai's. His smile said he was happy. Behind him came Agent Carrey. She looked considerably less happy.

Bai nodded a curt greeting at the female agent then turned her attention to Lee.

"How bad is it?" she asked while gesturing at his arm.

"I feel great. I can't remember the last time I felt this good."

She looked at his eyes. They were dilated. He was stoned.

Carrey interrupted. "You're both free to leave. I'll escort you out."

The offer was delivered tersely, her expression sour. Obviously, questioning Lee had proved futile. From the look of him, Bai was pretty sure it had been entertaining.

The agent walked with them to the security desk where their weapons and phones were returned. She stuffed her gun back into its holster then tucked it into the waistband of her sweatpants. Her knife went into the plastic bag, wrapped up in her wet jeans. She flipped her phone open to find she didn't have a signal inside the building.

"You'll have cell access in the lobby," Carrey informed her as she gestured toward the elevator, a pointed indication it was time for them to leave.

The agent followed them into the elevator.

"We can see ourselves out," Bai suggested.

"My orders are to escort you to the lobby."

They rode in silence to the ground floor. Agent Carrey waited until they'd stepped out of the elevator to punch the button for her return trip. She stared at them wordlessly as the doors slowly closed.

"Nice woman," Lee remarked. "I think she might have a thing for me."

"That 'thing' is probably an arrest warrant."

She flipped open her phone and was grateful to see it had a signal. She called a cab, providing their location to the dispatcher as she walked toward the glass doors in the front of the lobby. While they waited for the cab to arrive, she dug her muddy leather jacket out of her bag and used her tee-shirt to clean it off.

She slipped the jacket on and transferred her identification and credit cards into pockets, surreptitiously sliding her knife back into the sleeve sheath.

"What's the stuff in ditches that makes them smell?" she asked, sniffing diffidently at the sleeve of her jacket.

He looked at her and grinned.

"They gave you more meds in the emergency room, didn't they?" she guessed, looking at his happy face.

"Yes, they did," he replied triumphantly. "But to answer your question, the technical term for the stinky stuff is *muck*. Muck, muck, muck, muck . . . muck. I really like the sound of that word."

"So what's in muck?"

"You really don't want to know the specifics. Suffice it to say, everything on God's green earth poops, even slimy things that live in mud."

"That's a little disturbing. And you're right. I really didn't want to know."

A cab pulled to the curb in front of the building. She took off her heavy socks and ran barefoot out the door to clamber into the backseat of the taxi. Lee piled in on top of her, laughing as he tossed his bag of dirty clothes on the floor and sat with his legs crossed, Indian-style, on the seat.

The cabbie's grizzled face turned around at the commotion with a surprised look. In a strong Southern accent he asked, "Y'all FBI?"

She lied. "Yes, we are. We're special agents on assignment. Take us to the nearest BMW dealership. We need to requisition a car. And step on it. We're in a hurry."

She dismissed the man with an imperious wave of her hand. It seemed like the kind of thing a Fed would do.

"Why?" Lee's query caused the cabbie to turn around again, a witness to their conversation.

"Two reasons," she replied, looking back to glare at the cabbie. He ignored her as she slipped her socks back on her cold feet. "One, we need a car, and two, I don't want to have to explain to Elizabeth what happened to her BMW. Would you like to be the one to tell her how it got blown up while I was inside the car?"

The cabbie's face continued to show surprise. "Y'all's car got blown up?"

Lee lost focus and looked at the cabbie. "Who are you?"

She looked at the cabbie in exasperation. "If you don't turn around and drive I'm going to run you for warrants. What do you want to bet I don't get a hit?"

The cabbie turned around and hit the gas. The momentum jerked her back into the seat as he accelerated around the corner. She could see his eyes nervously checking the rearview mirror and decided it was kind of fun being a special agent.

When she turned back to Lee, he was sound asleep, his head pillowed against the glass of the side window.

"That can't be comfortable." She grabbed him by the shoulder of his sweatshirt to pull him toward her and let his head settle in her lap.

It took fifteen minutes to reach the dealership. They stopped under a large portico where customers dropped off cars for service. She paid the cabbie and woke a reluctant Lee, who seemed disoriented by the drugs. She pushed him out of the car and grabbed their garbage bags before following him. It was cold outside as evening approached. The rain had subsided, but the wind had picked up to bite at exposed flesh. She herded Lee through the service door entrance to get out of the wind.

She stopped to stand just inside the doorway of the dealership to get her bearings. They stood, wearing soiled socks and blue sweats with their plastic bags full of smelly clothes. She looked at Lee and laughed. He laughed too, though she suspected he didn't know why he was laughing, an assumption that made her laugh even more.

No one approached. Several people stared. They continued to wait while minutes passed. Bai's merriment eventually turned to anger. She folded her arms across her chest and tightened her jaw. Lee rocked in place, fighting sleep.

A young woman wearing a tailored suit and stilettos minced across the showroom with a look of obvious disdain.

"Are you lost?" she asked.

Bai took a fast step toward the woman, who correctly read the anger on her face and immediately retreated. The young woman took three quicksteps back, high heels clacking noisily against the tiled floor as she fought for balance. Nearly complete silence blanketed the large vaulted room as everyone watched—some with interest, some with shock, and one with amusement.

"I'm here to buy a car!" Bai made the declaration loud enough for everyone in the showroom to hear. She turned away from the frightened saleswoman to the man who smiled at her from across the room. "I think I'll buy it from him."

She grabbed Lee's arm and walked swiftly across the room. He waved his index finger in the saleswoman's face to mock her as he was dragged away.

The smiling man, a middle-aged gentleman with graying hair, stood at their approach. He wore a gray suit, worn open to show a sizable paunch. He put out his hand and smiled. "I see you've met Charlotte. My name's Doug Hathaway. How may I be of service?"

She took his hand, her fury melting away as quickly as it had taken shape. "My name's Bai," she said, "and this is my friend Lee." She steered Lee into a seat in front of Doug's desk. "He broke his arm today, but he doesn't care because he's full of codeine and I don't know what else. The story is, Doug, we need a fully loaded five-series four-door, in black with a black interior. Do you have one on the lot? We're in a hurry."

He seemed a little taken aback by her request but recovered quickly. "Let me take a look in inventory. I'm sure we have something to suit you."

He sat and turned to his computer console while motioning her to take a seat next to Lee. He punched some numbers and looked up. "We have eight black sedans in stock in the five series—a 528i, 535i, and a 550i. Which are you interested in?"

She looked at Lee. He stared back, but she could see his eyes didn't focus.

She turned back to Doug. "Could you bring one of each up front for me to see? I'm sure I'll know it when I see it."

He looked at her, chewing his lower lip while he studied her. "I know it's terribly rude, but before I start pulling cars from inventory, I need to know that you have the means to pay for a seventy-thousand-dollar luxury automobile."

"I understand," she replied. She took her American Express Black Card out of her pocket along with her identification and handed it over the desk.

He studied the card, his eyebrows raised in appreciation, before looking at her picture ID. "We don't see many of these," he said, handing her back her card and identification. "Now let's get those cars up here for you to look over."

He picked up his phone and started ordering cars to be brought to the front. In less than ten minutes, three cars were lined up under the portico for inspection.

To Bai, they all looked pretty much the same. She finally decided the most likely candidate was the 535i. "I'll take this one, Doug. Have them fill the tank while we're doing the paperwork."

"You don't want to barter on the price?"

"I'm in a hurry. I want to be back in San Francisco as quickly as possible. How fast can you get us out of here?"

He thought about it for a moment. "I'll do everything I can to get you out of here in thirty minutes, Bai." He was starting to get into the spirit of things. "And I'll knock five thousand off the sticker as a sign of good faith. I'd like your return business."

She walked inside to sit at his desk while he ran her card and the people in finance worked on registering and licensing the car. Charlotte brought coffee and cookies. The treats brought a smile to Lee's face. Bai glanced at Doug; she was surprised that a saleswoman would be drafted to serve refreshments.

Hurrying to finish up the paperwork on the new car, Doug responded to her unasked question without looking up. "Charlotte's doing penance." A smile appeared on his face. "I saw how she treated you when you came in the door. Besides selling cars, I also manage this store." He looked up and met Bai's gaze. "She's learning it pays to be nice to everybody."

Suppressing the smile that would have been unkind, Bai sipped her coffee. "'Do not insult the crocodile until you've crossed the river.'"

"What's that?"

"It's an old proverb, like saying 'Don't burn your bridges.'"

He smiled warmly. "I'll have to remember that. As a matter of fact, I might suggest Charlotte put it on her business card as a reminder."

By the time Bai's coffee cup was empty, Doug had the papers ready for her to sign. She walked with him to the portico. He assisted Lee into the passenger seat then shook her hand. She dumped the garbage bags into the backseat of the car and drove away. As luck would have it, just in time for rush hour traffic.

"Are you hungry?" asked Lee. The car sat in stand-still traffic on a main thoroughfare that the GPS system insisted was a direct route back to the freeway.

"I hadn't thought about it." She suddenly realized she was famished.

He pointed across the street. "There's an IHOP. I like pancakes. I don't know why. I just do."

His confession sounded heartfelt.

"I didn't know you liked pancakes."

"I didn't either." He sounded surprised.

"Well, pancakes sound good to me. And we're certainly dressed for IHOP." She turned to him with a grin. "Maybe we can get them to make whipped-cream faces on our pancakes."

"Now you're talking," asserted Lee, his face beaming with pleasure.

chapter 38

When the tree falls, the monkeys scatter

Lee slept. He appeared to be happily adrift on a cloud of pancakes and painkillers. Bai returned calls to Elizabeth and Dan as she sailed down the freeway. The evening traffic was light; the weather clear.

"Jia's doing much better," Elizabeth assured her. "The doctors say she'll be released sometime around the end of the week."

Bai realized that was only four days away. She worried that her current state of affairs might not be resolved before Elizabeth insisted on returning. With a target on her back, she didn't want her family anywhere near her.

"That's good news," she responded, keeping her voice light.

"Are you in trouble, Bai?" Elizabeth's question was blunt and to the point, as usual.

"Of course not." Which was true, if one discounted the loss of a small fortune and multiple attempts on her life. "I've just been busy clearing up some real estate deals. I didn't have the chance to mention it, but I've traded the Hong Kong estate for the Businessmen's Association Building here in Chinatown. A lot of details require my input."

Her lie had enough truth to it to be bulletproof. Tommy's corroboration of the real estate trade would serve to alleviate any misgivings Elizabeth might have.

Bai ended the call after saying a loving good-night to her daughter.

"Four days," she said quietly to herself. It wasn't much time to bring closure to the mess she'd unearthed. But time enough, she hoped, to take the fight to the enemy. She was tired of being a target.

"It's time to dance," she uttered cryptically.

Lee roused himself. "Good," he mumbled. "I love to dance. Let's boogie."

She looked at him and smiled. "Are you back?"

"I think so. My arm hurts, and I ache all over."

"Getting blown up will do that to you."

"Who were you talking to?" he asked, sitting up straight and rubbing his face with his good hand.

"Myself."

"How sad," he observed, turning to smile at her.

Her voice became serious as she changed the subject. "We took a beating today, Lee."

"We certainly did," he admitted, "but things have changed. We'll know who 'they' are as soon as we find out who owned 'Golden Heights.' I think a little payback is owed us."

He nodded his head in satisfaction.

"I get the feeling the FBI knows exactly what's going on but won't intervene," she replied. "If that's true, we're up against a person or an organization big enough to give the FBI pause."

"It's always questionable what the FBI knows, if anything. But I will give Race credit. He probably saved your life."

"'Ranse,'" she said, correcting him. "His name is John Ranse."

He looked at her, his face serious for a change. "John Ranse is infatuated with you."

Her reply was testy. "He doesn't even know me."

"That's why he's smitten with you," he teased.

She smiled, remembering Ranse's semiconscious flirtation. "If I brought a Fed home to meet the family, there'd be total chaos," she said mockingly. "What would the neighbors think?"

"I'd be more concerned with what Jason might think," insisted Lee. "I'm not sure Ranse would survive his introduction to Jason. He left a message last night to call him, by the way. Jason, that is."

"I know. I'm not ready to talk to him. I don't want to have to lie to him. He'll interrogate me worse than the FBI. You know how he is."

"Yeah, it's probably wise to avoid him for the time being. I don't think he'll find out about Benny and the exploding car for a while—unless, of course, he's tapped somebody inside the FBI."

He looked at her speculatively. She felt uncomfortable with the thought of Jason's finding out about the day's events. She pushed the thought aside.

"Do me a favor. Dial Robert for me?"

Lee brought up the Bluetooth display and tapped in the number. Robert picked up the call.

"Robert, it's Bai. Are you available to meet at my place at nine tonight?" She didn't want to break the news of Benny's apparent demise over the phone.

"Sure, Bai." He sounded reluctant. "Also, I have some research on the property you asked for. The bank loaned the development company nearly fifty million for improvements. It should provide a good return on your investment if you want to flip the property quickly and get your money back."

"We can discuss that tonight when I see you. Be sure to bring all of the paperwork with you," she replied. She didn't want to have to tell him the land was raw, the improvements a bank scam. She ended the call before he could ask any more questions.

Lee looked aside at her. "I could tell him about Benny if you don't feel up to it."

"Thanks." She shook her head in refusal. "It's nice of you to offer, but Benny is my responsibility, not yours. He died while in my employ. Honoring those who serve is something my grandfather taught me. I owe Benny."

He nodded in acceptance and grew silent. Having to tell someone a friend or loved one is dead isn't a job you'd wish on a friend. News of a death is a blow that can't be softened. It strikes at the most vulnerable part of the body, the heart.

Pulling into the alley behind her house, they passed the now-familiar black sedan guarding the rear of her home. Bai found the triad presence oddly comforting. Chinatown, and her building in particular, was the only place she still felt safe. *Sun Yee On* had made a mess of her life, but she was indebted to them for protecting her. It was a debt that Tommy would in time, no doubt, collect.

Parting company in the lobby, Lee retreated to his own apartment while she went to the third floor to get cleaned up. He would rejoin her upstairs when Robert arrived. But first, she needed a hot bath and a drink. She smelled like frog poop, and there was grit in places she didn't even want to think about.

She walked into her apartment and headed straight for the kitchen to get a highball glass out of the cupboard and fill it with ice before topping it off with Glenlivet. She adjourned to the bathroom to draw a hot bath. She put her phone and her drink on the edge of the tub and dropped her FBI sweats to the floor before slipping into the hot, steaming water. She closed her eyes to luxuriate in the heat.

When she opened her eyes, Jason sat on the edge of the tub staring down at her, the highball glass in his hand.

She bolted upright, her heart beating in her chest. Water sloshed over the side of the tub, but not before he stood to avoid the chopping water.

He looked her over appreciatively as he berated her in a soft voice. "Don't you ever return calls? And, if you're trying to think up a good story to tell me, I already know about the exploding car. I like your FBI sweats, by the way." He toed the blue sweats on the bathroom floor with his shiny black shoes. "And you bought the wrong model BMW," he added, "not that my mother would ever know."

"What are you doing here?" She was too shocked to be angry.

"Tommy doesn't need me in Vancouver right now. He's trying to patch things up with some of our dissident brothers and thought my presence would only add to their rancor. He's acting very conciliatory these days. Did you have a talk with him? Peacemaking seems out of character for him though I have to admit his tactics seem to be working. His detractors have been caught completely off-guard by his appeasing attitude. They're wary and nervous but are back at the bargaining table. It seems odd, but a nice Tommy is more frightening than a menacing one."

"I might have said something to him about how to cook a small fish," she replied vaguely. She eased back down into the tub. "But that doesn't answer my question. I didn't mean, what are you doing in San Francisco? I meant, what are you doing in my bathroom?"

"I'm admiring your outfit."

She shook her head in exasperation. "I'm not wearing anything."

"Which just happens to be my favorite outfit." He wore a sly smile on his face. "And since you've decided you're moving on, I find the sight even more arousing. There's a saying about forbidden fruit, but it escapes me at the moment. It's hard to think while being distracted by such lovely melons."

She laughed. She should have been furious with him for invading the privacy of her home, but she couldn't work up the effort. "You're a shit for sneaking into my bathroom and scaring me."

She tried to look annoyed. He didn't appear to be fooled. He dangled his fingers in the water. "I could join you. We could play submarine."

"I don't have the time. And besides, we're through. Remember?"

"I seem to forget that every time I see you naked." He looked at her and smiled. "What's on your schedule that you're in such a hurry?"

"Robert and Lee are meeting me here at nine. I have to tell Robert that Benny is likely dead. It's a conversation I'm not looking forward to."

"*Likely* dead?" he asked, an amused look on his face.

"All I saw was a singed hand with his class ring."

He gave the remark a moment's thought. "I'd go with *very* likely dead."

"You're probably right. I'm pretty sure the car was Benny's. It seems anybody connected to the purchase of Golden Heights is marked for death, including me."

He let out a long breath. "'When the tree falls, the monkeys scatter.'"

"What are you trying to tell me?"

"They're scrambling to cover their asses. Their haste has made them careless. Tell me about the property." He took a sip of her drink.

"Any chance you might share my drink with me?"

He handed her the highball glass. She took a gulp and let the cold scotch swirl in her mouth and warm up before swallowing. "I don't have all the facts yet," she confided. "Robert's bringing over the particulars tonight. Loans were secured for improvements, but the land is still raw and untouched."

He tilted his head back in thought. "So somebody pocketed the money and doesn't want it made public. Seems like sufficient motivation for murder."

"That's the theory I've been working on. But so far, it's only a theory."

"Maybe I'll stick around for your meeting."

He studied her for a reaction.

"I wish you wouldn't," she replied. "You'll make Robert nervous, and the news I'm delivering will already place enough stress on him. It would be better if you let me handle this."

He thought a moment, closing his eyes and tilting his head to the side. When he opened his eyes, he smiled. "Perhaps you're right. But I'll want to know the particulars on the financing of the property. You'll call me after you've met with him?"

She knew the only way to get rid of him was to agree to his conditions. "Fine," she said, capitulating without a fight. "I'll call you tonight and let you know what I've learned."

He stood. She could tell he was reluctant to leave, but she was serious about moving on with her life. Her determination must have shown on her face because he smiled and shrugged before turning to walk away.

She watched him go and felt a twinge of longing. Not enough to call him back but enough to make her want to.

chapter 39

Crows everywhere are equally black

At five minutes past nine, the elevator door opened. Robert stepped out of the lift with Lee at his side. The past few days had taken a toll on the normally stodgy lawyer. Rumpled clothes and dark circles under his eyes testified to his distress. His head jerked up to nod at her as he stepped into the foyer.

She tried to set him at ease by greeting him warmly. "Welcome, Robert. I'm sorry to take you away from home at this late hour."

"I don't mind, really," he quickly replied. "Did you know men are watching your house?"

"Yes, they're friends. Why don't we have a seat in the living room where we can talk?"

She escorted both men into the living room where Robert took a seat on the sofa and Lee settled into a comfortable side chair. Robert set a manila folder carefully down on the glass coffee table and perched on the edge of the leather cushions, as if he might bolt at the first sign of danger. He pulled papers out of the folder to arrange them neatly in piles on the table. His hands trembled.

Bai took a seat across from him in an overstuffed chair to watch with interest as he sorted the papers—straightening and rearranging them until he had them precisely the way he wanted. When he'd finished, he looked up expectantly.

She glanced at Lee, who nodded his head in encouragement.

She turned back to face Robert with her face composed. "There's no easy way to say this, Robert," she said reluctantly, "so I'll just come out with it. Benjamin is very likely dead. I'm sorry."

He sat very still. His head shook and he looked confused. "What do you mean by 'very likely'? He's either dead or he isn't. I wasn't aware there was a middle ground."

She looked at Lee, who shrugged to let her know she was on her own.

She took a deep breath before replying. "Let me start at the beginning." She ran a hand through her bristly hair as she gathered her thoughts. "Benny somehow got wind of a secret bank auction—I'm assuming an invitation-only auction. When he purchased property at this auction, he became a threat to people who'd embezzled money in an elaborate money scheme. The fifty million dollars in loans for Golden Heights was never used for improvements. The property is still raw land. The money was siphoned off."

"That doesn't explain what happened to him." Robert looked nervously from Bai to Lee then back again.

She continued. "I think he went to look at the land the day of the auction. When Lee and I went to see the property today, a car, which appeared to be Benny's Mercedes, exploded. It isn't confirmed yet that he was in the car, but there was a hand with his class ring in the debris. I think it's safe to say Benny was in the car."

His face caved in. He looked crestfallen. "So there's no subdivision, no roads, no sewers, no utilities, and no Benny?"

Lee intervened gently, his voice soft. "They haven't done anything to the property. He stepped into the middle of a swindle. The people who killed him thought they could recover the property if they killed Bai as well."

Robert was silent a moment. "Who are these people?" He sounded incredulous. "What kind of person commits murder over real estate?"

"That's what you're about to tell us," she said, pointing to the table covered with papers. "Who owned the property? Who made the loans? There had to be collusion to carry off the theft of millions of dollars. Banks have safeguards, so whoever's involved had to have been someone high enough in management to subvert the rules."

Robert reached for the papers on the coffee table. His hands trembled so badly he pulled them back to clasp them together.

"Could I trouble you for a drink, Bai?" He stared up at her, a distracted look on his face as tears started to roll down his cheeks. He seemed to be suffering from shock. "I don't normally drink," he said automatically, then seemed to reconsider. "But I think I could use a drink right now."

She retrieved a brandy. When she handed him the snifter, he hesitated, looking at the glass before downing the contents in a single swallow. He took a deep breath, exhaled, wiped the tears from his face with the sleeve of his jacket and shook his head. Then he carefully put the glass down and continued sifting through the papers while he cried silent tears.

When he was ready, he took a deep breath. "Here is what you're looking for, I believe."

He handed her two sheets of paper.

While she read, Robert spoke. "The first sheet lists the directors of the bank. All large loans would have gone before them for approval. A loan officer wouldn't have had the authority to handle such a large expenditure. One or more of them had to have been involved."

Looking over the list, she wasn't too surprised to see a familiar name. "John Romano is serving as president of the board," she said aloud for Lee's benefit.

He got out of his chair to stand behind her and read over her shoulder. His broken arm dangled in a sling made from a silk scarf with a pink flamingo emblazoned on it.

Robert continued. "The other sheet is a list of the principals in the development firm. You'll notice Ray Martinez Junior and Oscar Martinez are the primaries in this firm. Ray, or rather, Raimundo Martinez, the old man, is not listed. Ray Senior is a major player in the real estate market and very much a political insider. His sons are reputed to act as his proxies. They're all set to inherit his empire, or, at least, that's the story. There hasn't been any official announcement as such."

"It's all starting to tie together," remarked Lee. "The Martinez family buys the land and applies for loans to the bank controlled by Romano. They pillage the bank then file for bankruptcy. They then buy the land back to cover their tracks and let the shareholders of the bank eat the fifty million. Nobody's the wiser."

"Unless, that is, some little schmuck comes along and horns in on their game. They must have gone ballistic when Benny outbid them," Bai said. She was dismayed he could have been so naive. "He had no idea what he was getting into. They might've been inclined to buy the property back, but he went straight out to look at the development."

She looked over the table at Robert. "Somebody probably panicked when Benny confronted them. I suspect they killed him on impulse then decided there was no turning back."

Robert looked confused. "But old man Martinez is worth more than a billion dollars. Why would he risk everything for a quick fifty million?"

"Maybe it wasn't the old man," Lee suggested. "Maybe he's protecting his sons."

Bai looked at Robert. "Or maybe he found himself squeezed for capital. With real estate prices plummeting, he may have needed the cash to shore up his holdings. The reason doesn't really matter anymore, at least not to Benny. Now that we know who, why doesn't really matter."

"So what do we do now?" asked Lee.

A plan was forming in her mind, but she wanted more time to think about the repercussions of what she considered. "I'd like to sleep on it." She looked from Lee to Robert. "In the meantime, Robert, do you have someplace other than home where you can stay?"

"I don't know." Robert looked flustered. "Do you think I'm in danger?"

"At this point, I'm not sure. I think it's better to be safe than sorry."

"I don't really have anyone, now that Benny's gone," he said, sounding a little lost.

"How about staying with Lee?" she said. "A few days will be all I'll need. By then, this mess should be cleared up. You'll be safer here, in this building, than anywhere else I can think of."

Lee looked at her as if she'd lost her mind. She ignored him.

Robert didn't look reassured, but he nodded reluctantly. "If you feel that's best."

"Lee will take you downstairs and get you settled into his guest room. If you need anything else, let me know."

"Thank you," he replied, getting to his feet tiredly.

Lee accepted the inevitable with his usual graciousness. He smiled encouragingly at Robert and led the way toward the entry hall with the dazed and slightly drunk lawyer in tow.

She went to the kitchen to make drinks and wait for Lee to return. When he came back, the two settled on the couch to talk.

He speculated as he sipped iced vodka. "Do we kill them all?"

"That's a lot of killing," she observed dryly.

"They deserve it. They killed Benny and Park. Jia was nearly beaten to death. They definitely deserve it—an eye for an eye."

"That's very Catholic of you."

"They're evil men."

"'Crows everywhere are equally black.'"

"Your point being?"

"If I put a bullet in every greedy and selfish person I come across, I'll run out of bullets long before I run out of jerks."

Lee let his exasperation show. "So how do you want to handle it?"

"I'm not sure yet. That's why I'm thinking."

She placed her index finger against her temple and tapped.

"I thought I smelled something burning." Standing, he waved his glass in her direction. "I need a refill. Do you want another?"

Bai shook her head to let him know she'd had enough. She continued to dwell on the problem while she listened to the icemaker grinding out fresh cubes. By the time he returned, she had a rough idea about how she wanted to proceed. There was only one problem.

"Jason's back in town," she stated.

He looked surprised to hear of Jason's return. "When did that happen?"

"When I opened my eyes two hours ago and found him sitting on the edge of my tub."

He looked alarmed. "Does he know about today? I mean . . . you know, the bomb, Benny, the FBI?"

"He let me know we'd bought the wrong car. I wouldn't be surprised to find out he knows what color underwear we have on."

"That's somehow disturbing and at the same time scintillating." He appeared worried. "But I understand exactly what you're saying. If he knows everything we know, what we think doesn't really matter. He'll take matters into his own hands regardless of what we decide."

She drew in a deep breath. "Unless I can convince him otherwise."

"And how do you plan on doing that?"

She stared at Lee blankly as her mind went over the different tactics she might use on Jason. One by one, she mentally discarded them. He wasn't like most men. She couldn't lie to him. And using sex was no longer an option unless she was willing to swallow her pride and whore herself, which she wasn't.

"There's really only one possible way to sway him."

"And what's that?"

"I'm going to have to beg," Bai replied sadly, acknowledging her fate, "like a dog."

chapter 40

Just as tall trees are known
by their shadows,
so are good men known by their enemies

Jason picked up on the first ring.

"I have the information you want," Bai informed him.

He got straight to the point. "What did you find out?"

"I'd rather we didn't have this conversation over the phone. Why don't you come over, and I'll show you everything I have?"

"That sounds deliciously promising," he replied. "Even though I've already seen everything you have, it's always good to get a refresher."

"Don't get too excited. The only thing you'll see tonight is paperwork."

She waited for him to respond.

When he spoke, his voice sounded distrustful. "Two hours ago, you threw me out of your house. Now you're inviting me back. You're up to something."

"I can't believe you'd say something like that to the mother of your child," she said and hung up the phone.

She was playing a delicate game. Guilt, as a weapon, has a sharp edge. Used too often, it will dull. She got up from the couch and went into the bathroom to run water over her face. She looked into the mirror at her reflection. Her own steely gaze stared back at her; she had a hard glint in her eyes that hadn't been there before. The woman in the mirror, she realized, could kill when angered.

"Congratulations. You're a killer." Her voice echoed her disgust.

She wandered to the back of the flat and found herself sitting in Dan's room. Her daughter's stuffed animals littered the canopied bed. She picked up Dan's favorite teddy bear and hugged it. Her eyes filled, but she fought back the tears. Her daughter would be home soon. The nightmare was coming to an end.

When she walked back to the living room, Jason was sitting on the couch reading the documents left on the coffee table.

"Don't you ever knock?"

"I didn't want to disturb you."

He continued to examine the documents.

"Would you like a drink?"

He held up a glass. It was nearly empty. She took a seat across from him to watch as he read. His eyes flashed across the pages.

She leaned forward to get his attention. "I want you to do me a favor."

His face remained inscrutable. He stopped reading and looked up. "Is that why you guilted me?" His expression was wary. "It seemed out of character for you. You must be desperate."

She leaned back in her chair. Her attempt to manipulate him appeared to be a total failure. She was going to be forced to resort to honesty. Framing her answer carefully, she replied, "I want you to give me two days to settle things with the Martinez brothers and Romano. Let me do things my way."

He smirked. "I hope your way includes killing them."

"I haven't come to a decision yet. If I can remove the threat, maybe there doesn't have to be any more killing."

He didn't look convinced. He brushed away her request with a flick of his hand. When he spoke, his voice was brittle. "These men threatened my daughter. They tried to kill you. They need to die."

"They threatened *our* daughter," she leveled at him. "And I want them to pay for the crimes they've committed just as much as you do. They need to atone for the deaths of Benny and Park. I'm just asking you to give me the chance to settle this score my way. I'm the injured party here. I'm the one they're trying to kill. Don't I deserve the first shot at these creeps?"

He shook his head and looked at her, his jaw so tight the muscles in his cheeks rippled. Finally, he responded. "Two days . . . then they're mine."

She swallowed a victory cheer and spoke, instead, in a measured voice. "Deal!"

Tossing off the last of his drink, he stood to leave. "Whatever you're up to, be careful."

She nodded. "Thanks." She was afraid to say more, fearing he would change his mind.

He turned to walk out of the room and disappeared with the same ease he'd demonstrated in gaining access to her home.

"I need to upgrade the security system," she muttered to herself. The idea of his coming and going as he pleased left her more than a little disconcerted.

She leaned back in her chair and put her feet up on the coffee table. The first part of her plan had succeeded. Jason had given her two days. Now she had to bring all of the actors together to play their parts. The timing would have to be perfect. Her plan left no room for error and her only leverage was the real estate; Golden Heights was going to be her golden ticket.

If Romano and the Martinez brothers wanted to hide their bank fraud, they needed to recover possession of Golden Heights. She'd sell them back the property—and her silence—for a price. But she wasn't gullible enough to hand over the property without guarantees. She fully realized nothing ensured a person's continued silence like death. The difficulty she faced was in making sure that killing her was not an option.

She picked up her phone to make some calls. A host of things needed to be put in place to make the plan work. It took a couple of hours to acquire everything she needed. The last item on her list was to get the private number of John Romano. That took a little longer than expected. An hour and a thousand-dollar bribe later, the phone number she'd asked for got e-mailed to her via a temporary Hotmail account.

Bai used her home phone, the one without a blocked ID, to dial. When Romano picked up, his voice was groggy with sleep. "Hello. Who's this?"

She spoke softly but confidently." We haven't met, but you know who I am. Look at the caller ID."

Silence on the other end of the line. She waited.

His voice was tense. "You must have me confused with someone else. This is an unlisted number. How did you get it?"

She ignored his question. "I have something you want, and I'm willing to return it to you and the Martinez brothers—for a price. You can buy back your property and my silence. It's as simple as that. I'd suggest you call your associates and come to a decision about how you'd like to proceed. You have until tomorrow morning. If I haven't heard from you by eight a.m., I'll go public. I don't think I can be any plainer than that. I didn't block this call, so you have my return phone number. Don't be late."

She ended the call before he had a chance to reply.

Bai made coffee and sat down on the couch to wait. She knew they would eventually come to the same conclusion she had—they had no choice in the matter. They could either silence her with money, or they could spend several years fighting felony fraud charges in court. Regardless, with their wealth and their political connections, she doubted they'd ever spend a day in jail. But the proceedings would ruin their reputations and probably taint any business dealings they might hope to have in the future. They really couldn't afford not to pay her off.

An hour later her phone rang. The number was blocked.

She answered, keeping her voice pleasant. "Hello."

"Miss Jiang?" It was a deep voice on the other end of the line, a voice she didn't recognize.

"Speaking."

"I'd like to take this opportunity to apologize to you." The voice sounded sincere. "My name is Ray Martinez, and it's my understanding my sons have caused you some inconvenience."

The voice was raspy, that of an older man's. She was surprised the senior Martinez would involve himself in the matter. He would have been smarter to distance himself from the banking scheme. Perhaps things had gotten so far out of hand he now felt compelled to intervene. Whatever the reason, she was a little stunned to find him on the other end of the call.

"I think inconvenience is a massive understatement," she stated emphatically. "But I appreciate your apology, Mr. Martinez."

"Please, call me Ray."

"As I was saying, Mr. Martinez, the death of close associates is more than a mere inconvenience."

He didn't respond immediately.

When he did speak, his voice was just as congenial. "Yes, well, the young are sometimes overly exuberant in their attempts to succeed. I'm just glad you didn't suffer any personal long-term ill effects from their enthusiasm."

She smiled, recognizing the opening gambit of a negotiation. "I wouldn't be so quick to say there are no long-term consequences. I've been permanently deprived of several resources I'd grown very fond of. It's true you can't put a price on some things. But, I believe, Mr. Martinez, you can put a price on most things. Wouldn't you agree?"

There was another silence on the other end of the line. Bai suspected others were in the room with the old man, very likely his sons.

When he spoke again, he got to the heart of the matter. "What, Miss Jiang, do you feel is an appropriate number?"

Smiling again, she wished she could be in the room with them when they heard her reply. "I want twenty, in cash, nonsequential hundreds. I also want apologies, in person, from Mr. Romano and your two sons. And, Mr. Martinez, none of these terms is negotiable."

She could hear muttering in the background. It was obvious her demands didn't sit well with everyone. But the fact was, even if she were to be eliminated, her demise wouldn't stop the information on their swindle from going public. She'd already seen to that.

His voice no longer attempted to appease. He spoke gruffly. "Do you know who you're dealing with? Are you aware of the consequences of making an enemy of a man of my stature?"

Bai could hear the bluff in his voice. Her reply held a note of disdain. "'Just as tall trees are known by their shadows, so are good men known by their enemies.'"

Confident they would come around, she waited.

"All right, Miss Jiang. I really don't see that we have any choice. We need some time to put the finances together. Perhaps a week."

A week would give them too much time. There was no telling what kind of pressure they could bring to bear given a week. She didn't want to find out what they were capable of.

"You have until the day after tomorrow at three o'clock in the afternoon." She spoke forcefully into the phone. "We'll make the exchange at the old Alameda Naval Air Station. It's been closed for years. I'll meet you where the runway ends at the Bay. There's nothing but open ground for about a mile in all directions. You can bring as many men as you like. I'll be well-protected. Are you clear as to what I'm saying?"

Blustering, he tried to stall. "I'm not sure I can raise the money that fast."

"I'm not stupid, Mr. Martinez. You control a bank. Make use of it. You have until three o'clock the day after tomorrow. Don't be late." She hung up and exhaled.

After she put the phone down, Bai wondered if she'd made the right decision. Her resolve nearly cracked when she considered what she was trying to do. The men she was attempting to extort were dangerous, killers. In two days, she'd confront them. Then she'd find out who had the biggest balls.

chapter 41

One can't refuse to eat just because there's a chance of choking

Bai called Lee to wake him and get him out of bed. She had a job for him. When it came to electronics or anything mechanical, he was brilliant. More importantly, she trusted him with her life.

"Are you alone?" she asked.

"Yes," he replied tartly. "Alone and sleeping soundly. Until rudely awakened, that is."

She ignored the sarcasm. "Come upstairs. We need to talk. It's important."

His voice was muffled. "I'm in bed."

"I'm making coffee. Hurry, I have lots to tell you."

Five minutes later, he came stumbling up the back stairs in his pajamas. She handed him a cup of coffee, and he staggered into the living room to fall down on the couch. His eyes were only half open as he sipped the strong brew.

"I want you to build me a suicide vest."

He looked over his cup at her with a frown on his face. "Things aren't that bad, Bai," he said consolingly. "There will be other men. Take my word for it."

Appalled, she looked at him. "No! . . . don't be silly. I'm not going to kill myself. I need the vest for insurance."

"Now who's being silly?" He dismissed her argument with a wave of his broken arm like a flailing chicken wing. "The only thing explosives ensure against is living to an old age."

She looked at him in exasperation and took a seat across from him. "I've arranged a meet with Romano and the Martinez brothers. I don't trust them."

Now more alert, he sipped his coffee but looked interested. "I'm following you so far. Keep going."

"When I make the exchange, I'd like them to be convinced my death would have catastrophic results for everyone concerned, not just me."

He sat silently in contemplation. When he spoke, his voice was thoughtful. "Your plan sounds crazy, but I have to admit I'm of the same mind when it comes to Romano and the Martinez boys. If they can kill you without reprisal, they will. At the same time, what you're proposing is very risky."

"That's why I need the vest. These men will only behave themselves as long as they believe killing me is detrimental to their health. I really don't think anyone will be stupid enough, or crazy enough, to commit suicide along with me. At least, I hope not."

Lee didn't immediately commit to building the vest, but Bai could tell he was already thinking about it. She explained in detail what she wanted and why. He nodded and smiled in response. He loved the challenge of putting together clever gadgets. Assembling the vest would test his skills, especially with an injured arm.

"All right," he said reluctantly. "I'll do it. But only because I know that if I don't do it, you'll find someone less competent who will. I might have a couple of ideas to make the vest even more intimidating." He looked thoughtful. "How do you feel about ball bearings as a fashion statement?"

The question caught her off guard. "As long as you don't make the vest too heavy," she cautioned. "If worse comes to worse, I need to be able to run while wearing the vest."

"Then maybe I'll go with aluminum instead. The jacket will still have the same visual effect, but it'll be much lighter."

"I'll leave the details to you. While you're doing that, I need to get my hands on an armored truck, the kind banks use to transport money. Also, Robert will need to prepare the paperwork for the exchange."

"He may not like the idea of trading Benny's life for money, Bai."

Lee had a valid point. It would be up to her to convince Robert she was handling the situation in the best possible way. She would need his help with the exchange.

Her cell phone rang, interrupting the conversation. She looked at the display and was surprised by the caller ID. "Hello, John. How are you?"

"Alive," he replied.

"I'm glad to hear that."

"Are you angry with me?"

"You mean for saving my life and getting blown up in the process? Yeah, I'm furious. Who do you think you are, anyway?"

Ranse didn't respond. Bai wondered if the call had been disconnected.

"Sorry," he said, "the nurse was checking my vitals. It seems just talking to you makes my blood pressure go up."

"Are you sure it's me and not your nurse causing your blood pressure to rise?"

"My nurse's name is Bill." There was another prolonged silence. "What I'm trying to say, Bai, is that I'm sorry I lied to you. I wanted to tell you I was a federal agent, but . . ."

"I understand you were working under cover, but why me? What did the FBI hope to achieve by having me followed?"

"It wasn't you we were interested in, Bai. When you came to Dan's school with Jason Lum, my superiors saw a chance to get someone close to organized crime in Chinatown. We've been trying to get inside information on *Sun Yee On* for years. As it turned out, we didn't find exactly what we'd hoped to."

"I've been telling federal agents for years that I don't have anything to do with *Sun Yee On's* business."

There was a protracted silence on the other end of the conversation. "I believe you, Bai. I'm sorry."

"You saved my life. I owe you one."

He jumped at the opening. "Really? Then I want to collect."

She smiled and wondered where the conversation was headed. "What do you have in mind?"

"I want you to go out with me."

"I don't think you're going anywhere for a while." She tried not to laugh. "What does your doctor say?"

"My doc says I'll be out of here tomorrow. My leg will take a week or two to heal. My head was grazed by a piece of shrapnel, but the wound is only superficial. Mostly, I'm just bruised by the blast."

She couldn't afford any distractions until the exchange had taken place. She needed to keep focused until then. "Why don't you call me later this week, and we'll make a date?"

"You won't be sorry. I promise. No more lies."

"Don't make promises you can't keep," she cautioned him.

"I always keep my promises."

The thought of dating an FBI agent made her head swim. Two people coming from such different worlds would make having a relationship difficult. She didn't think Ranse had a clue what he was asking of her.

"Are you still there, Bai?"

His words brought her back from her musings. "Yes, I'm still here, John. Remind me to kiss you the next time I see you."

He chuckled. "That's a promise. I'll call you Friday."

"Be well," she said, ending the call.

Lee scrutinized her.

"What?"

"Nothing," he replied, a glib look on his face. "Is falling for an FBI agent a good idea?"

"'One can't refuse to eat just because there's a chance of choking.'"

"I think I hear the sound of sirens in the distance," he chided.

"I've already decided to change the way I live. Maybe he's just what I need."

"Jason may not see it that way."

She wasn't as concerned about Jason as Lee was. She knew he was seeing other women—Dr. Shannon Brian, for one. "Don't worry. He has other interests."

"What makes you so sure?"

"I met one of them, a long-legged redhead in Vancouver by the name of Shannon."

He shook his head. "You shouldn't jump to hasty conclusions. You make a habit of doing that."

She eyed him suspiciously. "Just what do you know about his love life?"

Lee avoided eye contact. "He loves you. He's loved you since we were kids. He protects you by staying away."

She stared at him, her suspicions aroused "You've been talking to him, haven't you?"

It was Lee's turn to be silent.

Her voice was chilled as she leaned over the coffee table to get into his face. "At least I now know how he's getting access to my security system."

Her remark hit home. He was decent enough to look contrite. "He's my friend, Bai."

She looked at him and shook her head in denial. "If he's your friend, he's not a very good one. Friends aren't ashamed to be seen with each other."

His head jerked up. She could tell her words stung by the hurt expression on his face. Words flew out of his mouth. "Did you ever stop to think what it was like for him to grow up in your home as the son of a governess? Look around you, Bai. You've always had wealth and privilege. Tommy and your grandfather showed him what he needed to become to be a part of that life. How could you expect him to walk away from the only family he knew, the only life he knew?"

His words shook her. What he said was true but didn't alter the fact that Jason could have turned away from the money and power. He'd chosen not to.

"He made his decision," she stated without rancor. She waited for Lee to meet her gaze. "I'm not saying the choices were easy for him. And it isn't easy for me to make a life without him."

He nodded his head, but she didn't think she'd changed his mind. She was reminded that everyone has secrets and everyone has weaknesses. Jason had a weakness for money and power. She and Lee, apparently, shared a weakness in Jason.

chapter 42

Before you beat a dog,
find out who its master is

Bai stood at the edge of the old Alameda Naval Air Base to look out over the gray, choppy waters of San Francisco Bay. A cold, wet wind swept across broken asphalt to set water-filled potholes shimmering in the late-afternoon breeze. Weeds thrust green spears through the cracked runway as nature reclaimed the abandoned airstrip while a grizzly sky overhead threatened rain.

Lee turned to her. "Do you think they'll show?"

"They'll be here. They have too much to lose by not showing up." Her cell phone read ten minutes to three. "They still have time."

Tommy's bulletproof limousine rested on the tarmac directly in front of them to serve as a shield. Negotiating the use of the vehicle had taken some hard bartering. Behind Bai idled an armored truck bristling with manned gun ports along its armored sides. Two black SUVs bracketed the armored truck. Four men stood outside each vehicle wearing flak jackets and carrying semiautomatic weapons.

She'd hired private security for the meeting. Tommy had provided contact information for reliable men. They hadn't come cheap.

Chilled to the bone, Robert and Lee stood on either side of her. Robert held the papers for the property exchange. Lee carried a pump-action shotgun cradled in his good arm. The pink flamingo sling cradled his other arm. Neither of them looked particularly happy to be there.

Robert hadn't been pleased when she'd explained her plan to him. He'd wanted retribution for Benny and Park. His desire for revenge had surprised her. It revealed a bloodthirsty side she hadn't imagined him to have.

She turned to glance at him. He wore a deep frown. "Are you sure you want to be here, Robert? It isn't too late to step into the armored truck where you'll be safe.

He turned to look at her and attempted a smile. "This is where I need to be. I know I'm not a brave man, but I owe Benny and Park at least this much. I need to confront the people who killed my friends."

Lee grinned at her when she turned to look at him. The suicide vest fit snugly over her leather jacket where everyone could see it. Rows of pockets had been sewn around the garment. Wires ran from pocket to pocket, each of them leading to a battery pack mounted on her back. True to his word, he'd fashioned the vest to be light enough to run in.

Another fifteen minutes passed before a line of cars advanced along the road leading to the airstrip. The cavalcade swung around in a curve to travel in Bai's direction. She counted ten large SUVs. Romano and the Martinez brothers were bringing a small army with them.

When the line of SUVs approached to within forty feet, the vehicles swung around in an arc to face the limo. The doors on the vehicles opened. Forty men wearing fatigues and carrying assault weapons disembarked with military precision. Twenty of the men advanced to within twenty feet of the limo and stopped. They dropped to one knee and trained their weapons on her and her entourage.

"I'm having a WTF moment here," Lee said cleverly, looking aside at her with a smile. "You really know how to stir up shit, don't you?"

She shrugged in response and turned back to survey the enemy troops. The pointed weapons were an attempt to intimidate. Their show of force just made her angry.

The doors of the idling SUVs remained open. The rear guard positioned themselves behind the doors that formed a metal barricade. There was no sign of Romano or the Martinez brothers. She was beginning to get really annoyed when a black sedan approached.

"They're not taking any chances, are they?" she said, glancing at Robert and then at Lee.

"I am so nervous," Robert replied. "I'm sweating and freezing at the same time. Why are they pointing their rifles at us?"

"They're just trying to scare us."

"It's working," Robert informed her.

The sedan drew her attention as it swung in behind the line of SUVs. Three men got out of the car to walk around and stand in front of the vehicles. All three wore flak jackets over business suits. Two men in fatigues carrying large duffle bags joined them. When a sixth man in battle dress joined the group, they started to slowly walk forward.

She'd done Internet searches to better know her enemy and studied the men as they approached. Romano looked nervous, fidgety. The man she recognized as Ray Martinez Jr. walked toward her, his face set in an angry scowl. The other Martinez brother, Oscar, smiled when he saw her looking at him. He was handsome and knew it. The man in camouflage showed no emotion. His head turned from side to side as he walked, his eyes constantly assessing the situation.

When the small delegation reached the front line, they stopped. Ray Jr. and the man in battle dress exchanged words. She couldn't hear their conversation, but the discussion became heated. Finally, the man in fatigues broke off the dialogue by dropping his hand in a curt motion. Whatever Junior had wanted, the man had denied. Anger reddened Ray Jr.'s face.

"Things might get a little tense during this exchange, Robert." She glanced aside to see if he was listening. "No matter what anybody says or does, just remember to stay at my side. I'll see you don't come to any harm."

"If you turn and run," Lee added. "I'll shoot you myself." He pointed two forked fingers at his eyes and then pointed them at Robert to get the message across.

Robert turned to confront him. "I wouldn't run away and leave Bai." He took offense at Lee's dig. "I'm not brave, but I'm not a coward either."

"Settle, boys," she ordered, as the contingent with the money separated from the line of soldiers. "It's showtime."

The six men walked to within five feet of the limousine and stopped. The two duffel bags dropped to the tarmac. The soldiers who'd carried the bags took one step back and placed their hands behind their backs to stand at parade rest. Romano and the Martinez boys looked at her expectantly.

She nodded in the direction of the waiting money, then led Robert and Lee around the limousine toward the exchange. She smiled as she walked to show the enemy she wasn't afraid. The swap had to take place on her terms for the plan to work. She needed to be in control of the situation.

The man in fatigues smiled as she came to stand before him. Widening her smile in response, she was mindful that some cultures consider a grin to be a predatory gesture. She bared her teeth. The symbolism didn't seem to be lost on the uniformed man. His eyebrows raised in silent appraisal.

"Gentlemen," she said, gesturing at the bags lying on the tarmac. "I assume the duffle bags contain the money."

The man in military garb replied, "They do. You're welcome to inspect the currency."

She looked at him, curious. "And you are?"

"You may call me 'The Major.' Let's leave it at that. There's really no reason for introductions."

She looked at The Major a long moment before turning to nod at Lee, who handed his shotgun to Robert and knelt down next to the bags. He opened the first one and rummaged to the bottom, pulling out stacks of bills at random for inspection.

While Lee inspected the money, she spoke to The Major. "I believe we have a mutual acquaintance."

"And who would that be?"

"I didn't get her name, but she carried a garrote—a chunky woman with blonde hair."

His face tightened and his lips drew into a thin line, but he didn't reply.

When Lee was satisfied the money in the first bag was genuine, he checked the second bag before standing.

"Satisfied?" Ray Jr. asked, anger written across his features.

Lee nodded his head to let her know the money was acceptable.

"Yes," she replied.

"Then I want to check your vest," The Major said. "As an act of good faith, I'd like to see that it's real."

The request didn't come as a surprise. She carefully opened a pocket on her vest to pull out a square of Semtex, a high-grade explosive. It was embedded with solid aluminum balls the size of marbles. She pulled the detonator cap out of the clay-like substance and tossed the explosive to The Major for inspection. "You can keep that. I have lots more."

The Major inspected the Semtex and pulled out one of the aluminum balls.

He tossed the ball bearing in his hand and seemed surprised at how light it was. "Very ingenious." He looked at her and nodded. "It would appear we're ready to finalize this deal."

"Not quite," she said forcefully. "I want to hear the apologies."

Martinez Jr. blurted out, "What are we apologizing for?"

"To start with, which one of you killed Benjamin Chin?" she asked. "I want an apology from the man who killed my friend."

He answered angrily, "You want me to say I'm sorry for killing that jerk? It's his fault he's dead. He put his nose where it didn't belong."

"Just do it," said his brother Oscar, looking uncomfortable. "You knew it was part of the deal coming out here, Ray. We all did."

Ray Jr. stared at her, petulant and hateful. Without wavering, she patiently met his gaze.

"Fine!" He shouted the word while turning to give his brother a dirty look. "I'm sorry I killed the guy. When he saw the property, he threatened to go to the authorities. I couldn't let that happen." He turned back to look at her. "Are you happy now?"

She looked aside at Robert, who nodded his head subtly. He'd been determined to hear the truth about what happened. Now he had it.

She turned back to the men confronting her. "To answer your question, no, I'm not happy. But then, I'm not nearly as unhappy as Benny Chin's mother, who'll never see her son again. And what about Benny's secretary, Park?"

The men looked at one another a moment in confusion before The Major answered. "We had nothing to do with the death of Park," he said, shrugging his shoulders. "The woman performed a task on our behalf and was paid handsomely but didn't know who we were. We had no reason to kill her."

She stared at the men. They seemed sincere, which didn't really mean much. It had occurred to Bai that Sammy Tu might have killed Park to silence her. Then again, Park was an alcoholic gambling addict who'd come into a windfall. They might never find out who killed the woman.

"And the attempts on my life?" she asked.

"I'm sorry we tried to have you killed," Oscar Martinez said lamely. "But what's done is done. You've got your money." He put his hand out for the papers.

"There's one more thing," she said, looking at Romano. "I want to know why John Romano's son assaulted my daughter at her school."

She watched as the men exchanged glances with one another. Apparently, no one, other than Romano, knew what she was talking about.

"It was all a big misunderstanding," he blurted. "I had no idea my son was listening in on my conversations. He took matters into his own hands. I don't know what he was thinking. He's a kid, fer chrissake."

The Major raised an eyebrow at her. "Don't take it personally."

She ignored the suggestion and turned to nod at Robert. He handed the folder to Oscar Martinez, who opened the envelope to look carefully at the papers.

When he was satisfied, he nodded to The Major. "We have what we came for."

Lee and Robert each picked up a duffel bag and walked toward the armored truck. As soon as they reached the truck, they heard the whupping sound of an approaching helicopter.

The Major looked at her with a question in his eyes.

"Transport," she said. "No reason to be alarmed."

Ray Jr. turned to The Major angrily. The Major shook his head and shrugged his shoulders at the change of circumstances. When he looked back at her, he smiled again with a crocodile's grin. She recognized a threat when she saw one. The Major was just biding his time.

"I assumed there would be transponders in the money," Bai explained.

"The Bell helicopter circling in for the pickup has a three-hundred-mile range. It will drop the money at a half dozen locations where the currency will be scanned for electronics, rebundled, and placed in new cases for transport. Don't waste your efforts looking for it. The money's gone."

Arcing around swiftly from the Port of Oakland, the copter swooped in low over the water coming in fast and hot. The chopper dropped to hover behind the armored vehicle. Robert and Lee wrestled the heavy duffle bags full of money into the back of the copter. Then it immediately drifted out over the water to head toward San Francisco. The entire operation took less than a minute.

The Major spoke. "Miss Jiang, I can't say it's been a pleasure doing business with you, but it has been interesting." He turned to the men at his side. "Gentlemen, I believe our business here is concluded."

"You're not going to let her get away with this, are you?" Ray Jr. asked. His face was fused with anger.

The Major was about to answer when his earbud squawked. He listened intently before raising his arm straight into the air and opening his fist to show an open palm.

He turned back to stare at her. "We have company."

"Do tell," Bai said blandly.

He spoke into a microphone attached to his collar. In the event someone had missed his hand signal, he repeated his order to stand down. His men responded by laying their rifles gently on the tarmac before forming up to stand at parade rest.

Vehicles poured out of abandoned hangars at the other end of the runway. Dozens of cars and SUVs sped toward the meet. FBI logos clearly identified them as official government property. Bai stood quietly to wait as they approached.

Ray Jr. stared at her. "Is this your doing?!" His eyes bulged as he furtively looked for a way out. Unless he was prepared to swim, he had nowhere to go. "If this is your doing, you're wasting your time."

"Just shut up," said Oscar, putting a hand on his brother's arm in an attempt to rein him in.

Ray Jr. brushed off his brother's hand and moved toward Bai. His arm swung back to strike her. She pulled her knife from the sheath on her sleeve and met his hand as it came toward her. She drove the blade into his fist.

A hand grabbed Ray Jr. by the back of his flak jacket and jerked him to the ground on his back. The Major stood over the injured man and put up both hands, trying to defuse the situation.

"Everyone should remain calm!" he commanded, staring at Bai's vest.

Ray Jr. tried to get up while holding his bleeding hand.

The Major placed a foot on his chest and shoved him back to the tarmac. "Your father paid me to protect you, Ray. You're not making it easy."

Federal agents surrounded the meet as dozens of agents poured out of their vehicles and brought assault rifles to bear before moving in to collect weapons.

The Major looked at her and smiled in amusement. "You're going to have a tough time explaining that suicide vest. Making bombs is a federal offense."

She looked at the Semtex he still carried in his hand and smiled back. "That's my understanding as well."

Agent McKay was the first to reach her. "Are you all right, Bai?"

"I am, Jim." They were officially on a first-name basis. "And I think you'll find everything you need in the recordings inside the vest." She unstrapped the vest and handed it to him. "There are confessions to murder and other assorted crimes on the recording. You shouldn't have any problem putting these scumbags behind bars forever."

She turned to smile at the men being cuffed. "And don't forget The Major." She pointed to the hand holding the Semtex. "He's carrying explosives. I think he might be a terrorist."

The smile disappeared from The Major's face.

She walked over to face him and spoke softly. "'Before you beat a dog, find out who its master is.' But don't take it personally." She left him with the thought and walked away, not entirely comfortable with being an FBI informant.

epilogue

Love is blind, but friendship closes its eyes

The newly remodeled Far East Café boasted red leather booths and blue marble tabletops in a retro-deco style. The old Formica soda counter had been replaced with a horseshoe-shaped wine bar with brass fittings. Floors of dark polished wood gleamed. A wine refrigerator took up an entire wall.

Bai marveled at the opulent interior. "Do you think you might have gone a little overboard on the remodel?"

Lee smiled and ducked the question. "You should try the roasted crab soup. It's made with fresh Dungeness. The crab butter is blended with roasted garlic and goes great with a full-bodied Chardonnay."

He obviously had no intention of discussing money. His deflection was a gentle reminder that the topic was none of her business. For the time being, he had money to burn. His portion of the twenty million would keep him entertained for quite some time. And the Yan children didn't have to worry either. Funds had been put into a trust for their benefit. Bai had placed Robert in charge of managing the account. She knew he could be trusted.

A million dollars had gone to Benny's mother. It wouldn't lessen the pain of losing her only child, but the money would see to it that she never wanted for anything material. Bai had recouped her initial investment and, after paying *Sun Yee On* for their assistance, had placed the rest of the money into a trust account under Benny Chin's name, destined for local charities.

Ling approached the table. She wore a black chef's outfit and looked happy.

"What do you think?" she asked, looking around at the new furnishings.

"It's beautiful," Bai admitted. "How is business?"

"Surprisingly, it's been really good. We've been open less than a month, and we're already turning a profit. It's still slow for lunch, but we're booked solid for dinner. I talked to Robert, and we're looking into buying the place next door to maybe expand. There isn't another place like this in Chinatown. We seem to have filled a niche."

Bai reached out to put a hand on Ling's arm. "That's great. I'm happy for you. How are the kids?"

"They're great. Robert has them at the dentist this afternoon. He's been a life saver. I don't know what I'd do without him." She hesitated a moment before continuing. "Jia stopped by yesterday. She says she likes living with you. She feels safe there. It made me a little sad she doesn't want to come home, but I understand."

"She needs time, Ling," Bai explained. "We're all family now. It'll all work out."

Jia's physical injuries were healing quickly. The emotional damage would take longer, but Bai was optimistic. She was a fighter.

"So you think maybe Robert's a keeper?" she asked. She smiled when she saw the question embarrassed Ling.

Ling smiled back shyly. "We'll see."

Theirs wouldn't be the first romance to bloom between an older man and a younger woman. He was a nice man even though he was her senior by almost fifteen years. For him, Ling and the children seemed to fill an emotional vacuum left by Benny. Robert had opened his heart and his wallet to show that people really were more important to him than money.

"I have to get back to the kitchen. We're doing prep work for dinner. Ma, your waitress, will take good care of you. Come back soon, Bai."

"I will."

Ling turned her attention to Lee. "Let's meet tomorrow and go over expansion costs with Robert."

He nodded in agreement. "I'll be here at three tomorrow."

She dipped her head once and was gone. Ma, who looked like a courtesan, stood against the far wall out of earshot. She was a beautiful girl dressed in a traditional red Chinese cheongsam, a sheath dress made of silk. The woman was as much a part of the ambiance as the marble and wood.

Bai complimented Lee. "You have an eye for beauty. Have you thought about designing for a living?"

He smiled at the compliment. "Are you trying to get rid of me?"

"You know better than that." She reached across the table to put her hand on his. "We're a team, remember?"

"I haven't forgotten." His features took on a more serious demeanor. "How are things going between you and Ranse?"

She took a deep breath. "He's being transferred to Boston. His superiors felt he was becoming too attached to an asset."

"Since when did you become an asset?"

"Beats me," she replied. "One day, I'm the enemy; the next, I'm Special Agent Jim McKay's best buddy; and then, I'm an asset."

"Do you think there was fallout over the twenty million?"

"McKay signed off on the deal. I don't think that's the problem," she said, a hint of sadness in her voice. "I think McKay is looking out for Ranse. If he gets serious with me, his career as a federal agent is pretty much over. Transferring him to Boston solves the problem."

"What did John say?"

"He made some noises about quitting, but he wasn't serious. I wouldn't want him to stay under those circumstances, anyway. Being an FBI agent is his dream."

"That's very mature of you."

"Yeah, it surprised me too."

He didn't say anything. He looked thoughtful. "What was John doing at Dan's school?"

Bai frowned. "Collecting information. The high-tech surveillance system at Hopkins wasn't just to protect the children. It was designed to spy on them."

"Why?"

"Because they're the children of diplomats and politicians and the wealthy. Kids are unfiltered mimes who repeat whatever they hear."

"Still, spying on kids really sucks."

She decided it was time to change the subject. "Elizabeth is speaking to me again, though my credibility has taken a nose dive."

"I could have predicted that," Lee said, chuckling. "She loves you. She'll always forgive you. How about Dan?"

"She's fine. She loves having Jia around, and school is back to normal. The Romano boy has transferred. His mother took the children back East to shield them from the press."

Lee looked at her and hesitated, his expression anxious. "There are a couple of things I need to talk to you about."

"Why the long face?"

He brushed aside the question. "By tomorrow it'll be on the news. I wanted you to hear it from me first."

Stalling, he looked around the café at nothing in particular.

"What have you done?" she asked as a feeling of apprehension started to build.

"The Major's real name is Thomas Bennett," Lee stated. He still wouldn't look at her. "He was attached to special operations for the Central Intelligence Agency before freelancing. Anyway, I thought you should know. He's been found dead in Brussels."

She looked at him in disbelief. "How could he be in Brussels? He's under detention in a federal lockup."

Lee grimaced. "His CIA friends got him released two days ago. They managed to get him out of the country before anybody even realized he was gone. Then sometime last night, he was found in his hotel room. He'd been garroted. His head had been removed and posed in his lap. Someone had literally handed him his head."

Her mind whirled. Then something occurred to her. "How did you find out about it if it isn't even on the news yet?"

He looked away again, unwilling to meet her gaze. "A friend told me."

"A friend like Jason, you mean?"

He dipped his head.

"He had no right to take matters into his own hands," she said, anger bleeding into her voice.

Lee became defensive. "This wasn't just about you, Bai. We needed to send a message. Otherwise, The Major would have sent assassins after you until one of them finally succeeded. It was the only way to put an end to it."

"This isn't the end of it." She shook her head in frustration. "Martinez isn't going to get over the fact I put his boys away. He'll just hire another Thomas Bennett to do his dirty work, and we're right back where we started. You haven't solved anything."

"Well, that's the other thing I wanted to talk to you about." He seemed ambivalent about what he had to say, drawing circles on the marble with his finger while staring at the table top. "This morning, old man Martinez died from a coronary seizure. It seems his pacemaker inexplicably failed and threw him into cardiac arrest. They rushed him to the hospital, but it was too late. Poor man."

He looked up to meet her eyes. She flashed back to a lecture he'd given her a couple of months ago about an electromagnetic gun he was fooling around with. It would drain a car battery from forty feet away. She could well imagine its effect on a pacemaker.

"'Poor man'?" She looked at him and shook her head. "'Poor man'? . . . that's all you've got to say for yourself?"

"We did it for you, Bai, and for Dan. We did it to protect our family."

Staring at him, she wondered what was next. "If I'd wanted them dead, I'd have killed them myself. I can't believe you and Jason would do this after all the effort spent to avoid killing. I'm a Buddhist, Lee. I don't get to absolve my sins by twisting some beads and saying 'I'm sorry.' At this rate, I'll be reincarnated as a cockroach."

"Look on the bright side. In case of a nuclear holocaust, cockroaches will rule the world."

She was numb, at a loss for words.

"I know you're angry, Bai, but I also know you'll forgive me."

"Why is that, Lee? You knew how I felt about killing those men, and yet you and Jason took it upon yourselves to kill them anyway. Why do I have to forgive you?"

"Because I'm your friend, Bai, and 'Love is blind, but friendship closes its eyes.'"

acknowledgments

I'd like to thank the following people for their help in bringing this work to press. First and foremost, my agent, Kimberley Cameron, and my publisher, Dan Mayer, were invaluable. It couldn't have happened without them. Ellen Torgerson, Kiersten Robinson, Dennis Mangers, Valerie Fioravanti, and the late Joe Sheehan provided invaluable feedback during the creative process. To Donald, Jeani, Auntie, Shao, Wei, Sam, Gale, Ivory, Lu, Don, Jan, Sandy, Miyuki, Robert, Dave, and Carol, I really appreciate the moral support and the wine.

about the author

Thatcher Robinson lives and writes in Northern California with his wife and two cats, all of whom boss him around. If you'd like to learn more about his indentured servitude, visit his website at thatcherrobinson.com.